GIVE ME LIBERTY

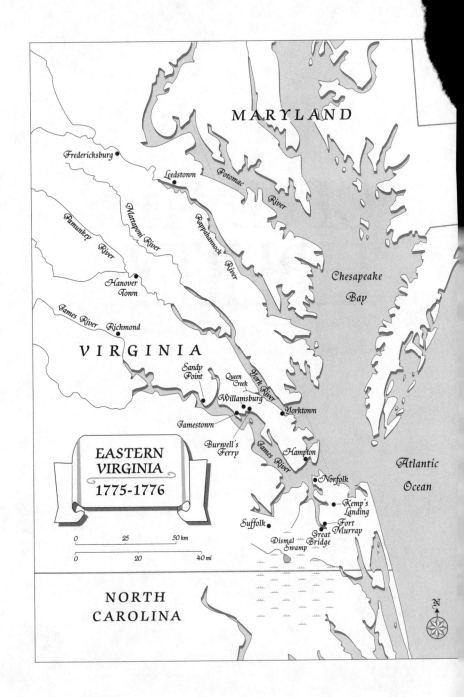

MARYLAND

Fredericksburg

Leedstown

Potomac River

Rappahannock River

Pamunkey River

Mattaponi River

Hanover Town

James River

Richmond

VIRGINIA

Sandy Point

Queen Creek

Willamsburg

York River

Jamestown

Burwell's Ferry

Yorktown

James River

Hampton

Chesapeake Bay

Atlantic Ocean

Norfolk

Kemp's Landing

Fort Murray

Suffolk

Great Bridge

Dismal Swamp

EASTERN
VIRGINIA
1775–1776

0   25   50 km

0   20   40 mi

NORTH
CAROLINA

N

GIVE ME LIBERTY

L. M. Elliott

Katherine Tegen Books
An Imprint of HarperCollinsPublishers

To the memory of Diane Granat Yalowitz,
extraordinary writer, friend, mother, and humanitarian

Epigraph from *Books I Read When I Was Young: The Favorite Books of Famous People*, edited by M. Jerry Weiss and Bernice E. Cullinan, National Council of Teachers of English, 1980. Reprinted with permission.

Library of Congress Cataloging-in-Publication Data is available.
ISBN-10: 0-06-074421-9 (trade bdg.)—ISBN-13: 978-0-06-074421-2 (trade bdg.)
ISBN-10: 0-06-074422-7 (lib. bdg.)—ISBN-13: 978-0-06-074422-9 (lib. bdg.)

Typography by Joel Tippie
1 2 3 4 5 6 7 8 9 10

First Edition

All the changes in the world, for good or evil,
were first brought about by words.
—Jacqueline Kennedy Onassis

PART ONE

May 1774

Oh, that I was where I would be,
Then I would be where I am not,
Here I am where I must be,
Go where I would, I can not,
Oh, diddle, lully day,
Oh, de little lioday.

—"Katy Cruel," eighteenth-century ballad

~ Chapter One ~

NATHANIEL PRESSED HIS nose against the coarse linsey-woolsey of his sleeve. He breathed in deeply. It was the first time in almost a year that it hadn't stunk of horsehair, dirt, straw, and leftover grease from wiping dinner off his lips. He kept his face buried in the fabric. It smelled instead of lye soap, of clean, of the warm sun that had dried it. The smell was wonderful.

Nathaniel dropped his arm to look across the York River, swollen and muddy from May rains. His mother had made him the shirt two years ago, right before they left England for the New World. Now it was barely long enough to protect his backside from the scratch of his breeches. It was well made, though, twenty tiny stitches to an inch in the seams. And it was clean. Silly, he knew, but somehow the feeling of clean gave Nathaniel a sense of rebirth.

Standing atop a bluff overlooking the Virginia river,

Nathaniel watched gulls drop out of the sky into the slow-moving waters. He assessed the horizon for a good omen. Blue skies would promise fortune, surely. But the heavens were coy about their thoughts. Wispy clouds fogged the sky, coloring it a shy white-blue. It was, in fact, just the color of Nathaniel's eyes—a veiled, barely-there blue.

His father had hated the paleness of Nathaniel's eyes. When irritated, he'd curse them as bewitched and lily-livered. Nathaniel could judge the souls of strangers by their reaction to his eyes. Those with meanness inside smirked. Those afraid of devils looked away. Kindness smiled.

His mother had said, "They're the color of sky and mist mixed together, as the world's waking up to the day, my son. Those be your eyes—the promise of a new day."

She was like that, his mother. Her own eyes had been the brilliant hue of bluebells, abloom with springlike hope, always believing in possibilities. Even during their six-week voyage across the Atlantic Ocean to Virginia—while they and seventy other passengers clung to the below-deck posts of the merchant ship lurching through storm after storm during the winter of 1772—she held fast to his father's promise of the faraway colonies being a place of dreams to be had for the taking. She believed even as she lay dying of ship fever.

"'Love *hopes* all things,'" she quoted Corinthians from the Bible, the one book Nathaniel's family possessed.

A breeze brushed Nathaniel's face and ruffled his blond hair, lifting it to dance in the air—another unfamiliar feeling of clean. He'd been startled after scrubbing himself with the lye to look down into the barrel of water and to see the reflection of such fair skin and hair, bleached by the Virginia sun. Grimy for so long, he'd forgotten what he really looked like.

Nathaniel took another deep breath, this time pulling in the sweet smells of new bloom, of greening grasses. There had been a wild hailstorm earlier in the month that destroyed all the peach blossoms and sent the plantation's owner into a fit about the loss of peach brandy for the year. But now the earth was in full blossom, joyfully shaking itself awake, spewing out millions of flowers in field and trees. Nathaniel looked back up to the gulls. He wondered if they rejoiced in the festival of color beneath them.

When the breeze rustled his hair and shirt again, Nathaniel felt a hesitant happiness creep through him. He closed his eyes and held his arms out, imagining, just as he had when he was a small boy. The wind picked up a bit, flapping his billowy sleeves. He willed his feet to lift up off the ground, his arms to sprout feathers. He could almost feel himself float on the pale blue air of soft breezes, delicious new-life smells, and fledgling possibilities.

Today was a day that would change his circumstances. Perhaps today, he could brave hoping for his own spring.

"All right, sir, let's see what you have to offer," spoke a voice behind Nathaniel.

Nathaniel dropped his gaze to his bare feet, waiting. Two long shadows slid across the clover toward him. A well-polished set of boots came into view alongside a set of fat, cracked shoes with tarnished buckles.

"What? This? This here? This be nothing but a runt of a lad."

Nathaniel lost the scent of new bloom in the stench of rum, garlic, and sweat the men carried. His heart began to pound.

One of them rattled papers as he spoke: "He's thirteen years of age, Mr. Owen. He'll grow into your needs. Remember he has eight years more on his indenture until he turns twenty-one. If you purchase a grown man's time, you only have him four years. Price is eleven pounds, his cost of passage from London. If you want a strong slave, like that one, it'll cost you upwards of sixty pounds." The man pointed to Nathaniel's friend, Moses, who stood nearby amongst a group of slaves. He was sixteen but tall and strong, and could handle a hogshead of tobacco on his own.

"Hmmm . . ." Owen growled. He grabbed Nathaniel's arms and squeezed, looking for muscle. "Blacksmithing is hard work, boy. I need someone to stoke my fires, carry water, sort scraps of iron. You've no meat on you." He began testing Nathaniel's legs.

Nathaniel tried to keep from recoiling from the bruising, sausage-thick fingers. It'd been like this at Leedstown, when their ship had finally docked in the Rappahannock River—people checking him over as they might an ox, assessing strength and the amount of feed the animal required to pull a plow for as many seasons as possible. He'd been purchased then by the plantation owner, who'd seemed kind enough. But the planter turned out to be a gambler. He lost most of his tobacco fortune on horse races held in Fredericksburg. The rest evaporated when an unusually large tobacco crop in Virginia caused the prices England would pay for it to plummet.

As the planter became poorer, he'd starved his servants—twenty-some slaves and a dozen indentured servants. Since winter, Nathaniel hadn't eaten anything much but corn and hoecakes. The only kindness done them had been the recent laundering to make them presentable, because all of them, along with everything in the estate—the house, the acres, the hogs, plows, featherbeds, pots, pans, and hoes—were up for sale to pay off the master's debts.

"Any pestilence about him?"

"No. He's fit. They say he is exceedingly good with horses. Useful for a blacksmith, I thought." The man holding the papers was clearly an auctioneer, assigned to market the plantation's human merchandise.

Owen grunted. He seized Nathaniel's jaw and twisted it around so that sunlight fell full on his face. Prying Nathaniel's mouth open, Owen stuck a filthy finger in and counted his teeth, lingering over the one in the back that had just finished growing in.

"Well, they look sound." He shoved Nathaniel aside and wiped his hand on his jacket. "If nothing else, if I work him to death, I can sell those teeth. There's a surgeon in Norfolk giving forty shillings a tooth. I'd make a profit." Owen jabbed the auctioneer with an elbow and guffawed.

The auctioneer straightened his waistcoat and asked coldly, "Do you want him?"

"Aye, he'll do for something. But I'll only pay seven pound for him."

Nathaniel's heart sank. This man seemed worse than the planter. *No! Say it's not enough coin. Make him go away.*

The auctioneer thought a moment. "Nine."

"Eight and ten shilling."

"Agreed." The auctioneer made a note in his papers. Nathaniel fought off fainting.

"Right then," said Owen. "Let me see what horse-flesh you have. Come, boy." He shoved Nathaniel to walk abreast of him.

Hopes all things?

Only fools hoped. Hope made life's disappointments hurt the more. Hope is what had brought him to bondage.

Owen hadn't even asked Nathaniel's name. And he certainly hadn't looked him in the eye. That was the other kind of reaction to Nathaniel's eyes—none—born of such indifference to his existence as a human being that a person never saw them because they never bothered to look Nathaniel in the face.

❧ Chapter Two ❧

MISERABLE, NATHANIEL TRUDGED toward the stable, listening to the heavy, grunting breathing of his new master. From sideways glances, he saw that Owen was a massive man, with a lot of weight to pull along on gout-inflamed legs. He dared a backward look toward Moses. His friend was being questioned by a man in a fine frock coat with silver braiding and lace sleeves dangling beneath the cuffs. Moses would be all right, then. Such a richly dressed gentleman had to be a merchant or such. It was sure to be better than the circumstances to which he was headed.

Nathaniel swallowed hard. It'd been Moses who'd convinced him to eat, to breathe when he'd nearly died of grief at first coming to the plantation. Moses had a large goodness about him. The smaller slave boys used to skip along behind him, like devoted puppies. Remarkably tall, Moses had a long, odd scar like a crescent moon across his forehead. It came from his mother having to work the fields with him on her back when he was a baby. One day her hands were full with tobacco leaves, and he'd fallen. But Moses liked the moon shape of it. He claimed it was an omen, a mark showing that he was destined to travel. He loved to hear Nathaniel's stories of England and the sea. Nathaniel had just started to teach Moses the alphabet, scratching letters in the sand down by the river after their chores were completed. Nathaniel would miss him sorely.

The two of them had discussed the possibility of being separated this day. Moses seemed resigned to it. Many years before, he had been sold away from his family. All Moses remembered of his father—who'd been a "saltwater slave," stolen directly from West Africa—were his gold earrings and face tattoos.

"It's the way of it," Moses had said. "But it won't be forever, Nathaniel. We hear about good men talking on liberty, breaking with the king. If they be arguing against their master, they see it wrong to use us the way they do."

Nathaniel, Owen, and the auctioneer passed the manor house, a rectangular, brick building of two stories and long windows, with a commander's view of the river.

In front of the door was a crowd of people as if it were a market day. A man waddled down the stone steps, bracing a huge basket filled with china against his legs. In the drive, a wagon was being filled with delicately made chairs. Several slaves balanced rolled-up Persian carpets atop their heads, following a gentleman whose arms gleamed with a mass of silver candlesticks.

An older, gawky man struggled to toss a sack stuffed with leather-bound books up into a two-wheel, bright green riding chair. Nathaniel noticed that the carriage horse fretted and shied away from the man, who foolishly flapped his arms and grabbed at the harness, further flustering the horse.

That one would be fortunate to make it home in one piece, thought Nathaniel. *He knows naught about horses.*

In the past year, Nathaniel had come to know almost everything about horses. He'd fed them, brushed them, soothed them when the farrier hammered in their shoes, soaked their sore spots after races, walked them to health when their guts twisted up in colic. He'd happily slept in the hayloft of the finely built stables. Even in the winter, it wasn't so bad. He'd burrow into the straw like a field mouse and sleep just fine, listening to the comforting sounds of the horses munching their hay. Sometimes he crept into the stalls and curled up against mares that had just had their foals taken from them for training. He seemed to calm their anxiety at losing their offspring, as if they regarded him as just another colt in need of care.

The head groom often commented on Nathaniel's way with the animals. Nathaniel didn't know from where the instinct came. He never had had a horse of his own. That was far too much of a blessing for his poor family. But back in England, his father had worked for a saddler and harness maker. Nathaniel steadied the horses being fitted, even when he was so young his head had barely reached the horse's chest.

That'd been his father's dream—to serve his indentureship with a saddler and then set up his own shop.

But it hadn't worked out that way at Leedstown. A planter who had depleted his rich, Tidewater soil with years of tobacco crops had bought new land on the frontier, past Richmond, toward the wild Indian country of the Blue Ridge Mountains. He came looking for strong men to clear fields. He'd taken Nathaniel's father and several other skilled tradesmen, who'd cried out against the change in their hopes. But Thomas Hodge, the Leedstown merchant in charge of selling their time, hadn't listened, didn't care. Money was money. Unlike most planters who used tobacco as currency, this one had actual coin to pay.

Nathaniel's father hadn't bargained to include

Nathaniel in the deal as other fathers did their sons. He'd said nothing when Nathaniel was taken from him. He'd said next to nothing, in fact, since the horrible night halfway across the Atlantic Ocean when they had wrapped Nathaniel's mother in a hammock and buried her at sea, a victim of the fever coursing through the servants crowded in the putrid cargo hull. It was as if he had died too, along with his wife. She had been the heart and soul, the light and joy of their small family. All his father had done before walking away to the West and out of Nathaniel's life was to hand Nathaniel a German flute. "That be your grandfather's," he said, and turned away.

"You know the horses well, lad, do you not?" the auctioneer asked, startling Nathaniel from his thoughts.

"Aye," he answered, barely above a whisper.

"Speak up, boy," Owen barked, and cuffed Nathaniel's ear. "Know you the horses?"

"Aye, sir, I know them," Nathaniel spoke, keeping his head bowed. He figured the smaller and meeker he appeared, the less trouble would come to him.

Owen shoved him again. "Be off with you, then. Bring back a good mare. One that will pull a cart and breed. No lameness. Hear? If you bring me a horse that goes lame next month, your hide will pay for it."

"Aye, sir." Nathaniel shuffled off. It wasn't until he

was many yards away that he raised a hand to rub his throbbing ear.

No lameness next month? There was no way to guarantee that! Canter on a stone the wrong way, trip over a tree root in the road, and a horse could limp for days. The demand would just turn into an excuse to beat him. Nathaniel could tell that Owen struck out in foul temper as readily as he breathed.

The coolness of the stable greeted Nathaniel. So did the horses. One after another they raised their heads to whinny, hoping for dinner. At least the bankrupted planter hadn't starved them in the last months. Nathaniel gently touched them as he passed, letting them know he carried no treats. Snorting their disappointment, they turned back to their hay.

Nathaniel lingered at the end stall, that of Warrior. He was a tall, muscular, dappled gray, a son of the legendary Dotterell, an English blooded horse that had been imported by the Lee family. Warrior had won many a fifty-pound purse for Nathaniel's master. But Warrior's days of glory were over. Greedy for money, the planter had over-raced him. Finally one of Warrior's tendons had bowed, leaving his right front leg swollen and slow. What would happen to the magnificent horse now? Once he might have commanded five hundred pounds in price, now more like fifty. Still a fortune to Nathaniel, but not a price that would guarantee he be treated as the treasure he was. Nathaniel rubbed his hand down Warrior's neck and scratched along his mane, a trick he'd learned by watching the horses affectionately nibble on one another in greeting.

A rage began to boil up in him. God forbid that someone like Owen get a hold of Warrior. How was it that he, Moses, and this beautiful horse were subject to such unknowns? Nathaniel's hands balled into fists. His feet begin to trot, then run toward the mares' stable.

He knew exactly which horse he was going to present to Owen to consider. And if she were in her usual temper, Owen would receive a thrashing he deserved. Nathaniel knew he'd be beaten for it. But he didn't care. It'd be worth the price to just once hand back what he was given.

∾ Chapter Three ∾

HER NAME WAS River Fox, because of her reddish coloring, but everyone about the stable called her Vixen. They didn't mean it kindly. She'd kicked every last one of them at least once. Even with gentle currying and handfuls of tender clover, she didn't tame. The plantation master kept her because she birthed beautiful foals.

Nathaniel figured she acted the way she did out of anger. Vixen was a gorgeous, rounded animal, but she didn't hold up in Virginia's subscription races that required a horse to win two out of three heats. After running and losing and being whipped for the failure, Vixen was given to the plantation mistress as a pleasure horse. But she threw the lady off onto hard ground. So Vixen was hitched to a lightweight chaise like a common farm mare. Nathaniel just knew the noble-blooded mare felt her new job was humiliating.

Nathaniel crept along the wall of the stall to avoid a

bolt from those brutal back hoofs. "Here, girl," he crooned, and ran his hand along her chestnut coat before attaching her halter to a line. He led her out into the lukewarm sunshine. Dancing along behind him, her eyes wide and her nostrils flared, she snapped her head to and fro, alarmed by the crowd. Nathaniel felt her quiver with agitation.

Good, he thought to himself. *She's in fine fettle, ready to throw a fit.*

He couldn't believe what he was planning. He was so careful to hang in corners, to remain unremarkable. This was asking for trouble. But Nathaniel didn't care. He was so unhappy about the day's twist in fate, he wouldn't care if Owen beat him senseless. He'd almost prefer death to yet another unknown. Maybe that's what he was really after. He kept his head low, his grip tight on the line, and walked on, like a condemned man happy for the gallows.

"What's this, boy?" Owen snapped. "I cannot afford the likes of her. And she'd be worthless hauling iron."

"She pulls a two-wheel chair, master. She can pull a cart." Nathaniel didn't add that she'd nearly kicked the small carriage apart. He was counting on a vanity that he could sense in Owen—a desire to climb up in social class. A fine-looking mare could help. Virginians set a store on their horses.

"What's her price?"

The auctioneer began to sift through his list. "What's her name, lad?"

"River Fox," murmured Nathaniel, hoping she was recorded as Vixen, buying him time as the auctioneer looked for her information.

He positioned Vixen so that Owen was several strides away from her backside. Nathaniel knew that horses hated being approached from their hindquarters, where their vision was blocked and from where predators such as wolves attacked. Stupidly, Owen walked straight toward her rump. *That's it*, Nathaniel thought, watching Owen approach for his inspection. Vixen began to flinch aside and crane her neck to see what was coming.

"Hold her steady, fool," Owen grumbled. He was looking at her silky, flowing tail that cascaded to the ground. How many times had Nathaniel been knocked over trying to comb it out to keep it so attractive?

"I'd have to dock this," Owen said, referring to the practice of bobbing horses' tails. It was a cruel doing in Nathaniel's mind—for fashion's sake, denying a horse his ability to switch away biting flies. "Docking's the macaroni in Williamsburg. No horse has a long tail. A pity, though. Fullest tail I've ever seen. Maybe I can sell that horsehair for surgeon's thread."

Yes, pleaded Nathaniel silently. *Take hold her tail. That'll do it, sure.*

Owen lifted his meaty hand and grabbed up Vixen's tail. He might as well have slapped her with a thorn-studded crop.

Vixen's eyes rolled back. Whinnying in alarm, she pawed the earth with her front hooves, threw her head down, and kicked back with a force that catapulted Owen and all his bulk several feet. He landed with a thud and a curse, in mud.

Nathaniel felt a small, sly smile of triumph slide across his face. It felt good to embarrass someone who'd cuffed his ears. A strange, hot vengeance overcame him. Nathaniel knew that given the chance, Vixen wasn't done with Owen. Oh no. He should have held on to her, as she thrashed and kicked, to prevent her doing further mischief. But Nathaniel didn't. He let go of the line.

Vixen wheeled around, snorting like a dragon, high tailed, murder in her look. Owen had been lying and shouting curses. Seeing Vixen turn, he stopped mid-blasphemy and struggled to get up. But he couldn't right his heft. Instead, he rolled onto his hands and knees and crawled.

Vixen reared onto her back legs, pumped her front legs in the air, screamed shrilly, and then came down, hard, missing Owen's body by inches as he rolled to the side.

She reared again, landed again, missing only because Owen rolled the opposite direction. It was the way horses killed snakes—Nathaniel had seen it—rearing and pounding until the serpent was sliced apart.

"Help, ho!" Owen cried out in despair.

Vixen was in more of a rage than Nathaniel had planned. She really might kill Owen. This is not what Nathaniel had meant to happen. He just wanted Owen humiliated, as he'd been over and over again since setting foot on this accursed shore.

Nathaniel waved his arms. "Hey, hey, Vixen! Off with you now! Hey!" Once more, she reared up. Owen seemed rooted to the ground.

Nathaniel scooted between them. For a moment Vixen balanced herself on her hind legs, as if considering. If she came down straight now, she'd hit Nathaniel. But he held his ground. Her eyes seemed to meet Nathaniel's. She twisted, landed to the side and took off, running the fastest race she'd ever given, straight for the big house.

Feeling like he might throw up, Nathaniel doubled over, all his anger spent. But in the distance came the sound of cries and crashes. Now he'd be responsible for the price of Vixen if she escaped.

Nathaniel straightened. He'd have to try to catch her. Nathaniel struck off as Owen crawled toward him like a crocodile and just missed latching on to him by the ankle.

✑ Chapter Four ✑

IT WASN'T HARD to track Vixen. Nathaniel simply
followed the trail of dropped baskets, scattered
papers, and startled people, all staring in the same
direction. He heard a whinny, a terrified "Great
God!", a clattering and crashing, and the sound of
dozens of items hitting the road—*plop . . . plop . . .
plop, plop, plop, plop. . . .* "Oh my! They'll all be ruined.
Ruined! Someone shoot it. Shoot it!"

Nathaniel sprinted. He didn't care that the crushed
oyster shells in the house's pristine lane were cutting
open his bare feet. If someone shot Vixen, Nathaniel
would be indentured for the rest of his life for sure.

More people scattered, parting the crowd. Now
Nathaniel could see that Vixen's victim was the old
man with the book-filled carriage. Vixen was nipping
and driving the carriage's horse, in play more than anything else, to assert her dominance. But by Vixen's

herding the poor weaker mare, the riding chair was going round and round like a whirligig, spewing out books as it spun. The old man had dropped the harness reins and was clinging to a long, ornate box, crying, "The spinet! Not the spinet!"

None dressed in finery were willing to approach the wild Vixen, churning up clods of mud as she danced the carriage horse around. The scene, in fact, was so ridiculous, the spindly man so silly looking, that a few of the merchants standing about were laughing. But Nathaniel was not amused. The reins were slithering along the ground, beginning to wrap about the carriage horse's hoofs. A few more loops around her front legs and the horse would go down, overturning the riding chair and perhaps crushing the man underneath.

Nathaniel inched his way toward Vixen and the other horse with his arms outstretched. "Whoa, now, girl. Easy, Vixen, easy." The reins, more than Nathaniel, saved them. With the leather wrapped around her, the carriage horse finally refused to move, and Vixen, satisfied that the mare was completely under her control, stopped too. Nose to nose, the horses snorted into each other's nostrils, completing the negotiation between them.

Carefully, Nathaniel took hold of Vixen's halter. He held the carriage horse's as well. Vixen even nudged

Nathaniel in a friendly manner, as if to say the chaos she'd caused had been a fine joke between them.

With a hearty laugh, a man approached Nathaniel. Head bent, Nathaniel got his usual chest-down view of a person. The man's tall boots were polished but well worn, and his plain breeches had rub marks along the thighs from the saddle, telling Nathaniel the man spent many hours riding horses. "Quite a horse, lad," he said in a young, friendly voice. "Is this her usual behavior?"

Nathaniel hesitated. Not exactly, but close enough. "Aye," he mumbled.

"What say you, lad? Would she be good for the steeplechase in Williamsburg? A rare fast mover, she seems."

The man actually laid a gentle hand upon Nathaniel's shoulders. Nathaniel almost gasped in surprise. For the kindness, Nathaniel spoke up honestly. "She does not finish well, sir. But she does have beautiful foals."

"Yes? Hmmm." The man stroked Vixen's neck. She seemed pleased with the touch. "Know you her price?"

"No, sir. But she's caused enough trouble, she'd deserve being bought for shillings."

The man laughed. "That will be useful information when I bargain for her." He called to his servant, "Abel, take this horse, please. Let us see what we can have her for." He patted Nathaniel on the shoulder and turned to walk away.

Oh, why should a devilish-maker horse be treated to such a fine owner, when a hero like Warrior was left? Nathaniel braved to speak. "Sir," he called out.

The man stopped. "Yes, lad?"

Nathaniel was afraid to step forward, afraid to let go the carriage horse, afraid to speak loudly enough for others to hear. The man came back to him with light and athletic strides. He leaned over to be nearer Nathaniel's head. "Yes, lad. Have you a secret to tell me?"

"There is a fine stallion in the stable, my lord," Nathaniel fell back to using Yorkshire's titles for noblemen. "His name is Warrior. He's a gray. You may not recognize him from the track. My master sometimes had us paint him a horse of a different color to get larger odds on him. He oft won disguised as a dark horse. He hasn't run, my lord, for almost a year, because they bowed his tendon. But he'd make a proud riding horse, my lord, and would father fine racers. He and Vix—River Fox"—Nathaniel nodded toward Vixen—"would have comely foals."

"Indeed?"

"One other thing, my lord. Don't put her under carriage. She doesn't like it," he finished in a whisper.

The young man laughed once more. It was a good, deep laugh, no checks, no hesitation about it, the laugh of a free man. "I wager not, lad! Thank you. And you needn't call me 'my lord.' There are no lords here in Virginia, just citizens, with all the rights afforded Englishmen that God granted us. Here in Virginia, lad, a man can accomplish anything when guided by reason and self-reliance. So my father and his friends claim at least." He reached into his pocket, pulled out a coin, and placed it into Nathaniel's hand. "Godspeed, lad."

The young man walked away as others called to him, "John! John Henry! Here's the jolly fellow! Come tell us about the latest trouble your father is causing! Think you Virginians will stop drinking tea and merchants will cast aside their fortunes to forego British imports? On the oratory of that obstinate firebrand Patrick Henry? And does he really think that will convince Britain and the king to change their ways? Is he mad?"

"Indeed, friends, he is. But to listen to him is to embrace what he says. He has the preacher's way about him. He's certainly convinced me of things, when I full planned to disagree with him! I believe if he could have an audience with His Majesty, he could convince King George to pay *us* taxes!"

The men walked out of earshot.

Nathaniel looked into his hand. A shilling! A whole shilling! He furtively bit the coin to test its strength— real, all right—before thrusting it into his pocket. As an indentured servant, he had to carry a pass, a legal permission slip, to run errands for the master off the plantation. He didn't know if he were allowed to have coin of his own. Nathaniel glanced about to make sure that no one saw him pocket the precious money, afraid they might take it away. It was only then that he realized that the old fellow remained frozen to the carriage seat, still clutching the wooden box to his chest, breathing heavily, as if dazed.

Threading the reins back through the harness rigging along the horse's rump, Nathaniel attached them to the front of the carriage. He stooped to pick up the books, dusting them off. *Gu-ll-i-ver's Tra-tra-vels*, he sounded out in his mind. *Ro-bi-bin-son Cru-soe, The Whole Du-ty of Man, The Art of Th-thi-thin-king.*

He gathered up a dozen leather-bound volumes and packed them into the carriage. Still more littered the ground. He paused a moment, worried that the old man was ill, since he remained silent and completely still. Nathaniel came around to touch his shoe, about to ask if he could help him out of the riding chair.

But before Nathaniel could speak, he felt himself lifted and twisted around to confront Owen's bloodred face, snarling in anger.

"You! You saucy whelp! You'll learn to trick me so!"

ಲ Chapter Five ೧

OWEN'S FIRST BLOW caught Nathaniel full in the right eye, sending a concussion of pain through his skull. The second split his lip. By the third, Nathaniel had managed to hold his hands up to protect his face. Owen switched to pounding Nathaniel's back. It felt as if he were being stoned.

"That's enough, man. Hold!" Through hits, Nathaniel heard the alarmed voice of the old man in the carriage chair. "Stop, I say!"

"He's my property," shouted Owen. "I'm going to beat the trouble out of him."

Another blow and Nathaniel crumpled to the ground. Owen gave him a kick. "There, brat. Now get up and find me another horse."

The world was rocking, the feet in front of his eyes spinning around and around. Nathaniel couldn't move.

"Get up!" Owen hauled Nathaniel to his feet. Nathaniel hung limp.

"I insist! Let go the lad!" came the same reedy voice. The riding chair lurched a bit, and delicate but determined hands managed to pry Nathaniel loose and prop him up against its huge wheel. Nathaniel noticed the hands were stained heavily with ink before he slowly slid down the wheel to the ground.

Now came the clatter of running feet. Shoes seemed to dance around him. Nathaniel blinked to clear his blurred vision.

"What's the matter, man?"

"He nearly killed the boy."

"No need to beat him so, blacksmith; you'll lose your investment."

"He's mine to do with as I want," Owen roared.

Another set of feet walked up, boots Nathaniel had seen before. They belonged to the auctioneer. "We haven't signed the indentureship papers yet, Mr. Owen. Seems to me the lad might not be what you need after all. Perhaps you'd like to consider one of the stronger slaves."

"This one will do, I tell you. He just needs forging, like a piece of iron that must be beaten into shape."

"How much is the boy's price?" asked the old man's thin voice.

"Eleven pounds, sir, his cost of passage. Mr. Owen offered eight and ten for him."

There was a momentary silence.

"I'll pay ten for him."

"What?" shouted Owen. "I'll not be outbid for a cur like this."

"The bidding stands at ten pounds, Mr. Owen. Would you care to top it?" asked the auctioneer.

There was another silence. Nathaniel fought to remain conscious.

"Fine," Owen spluttered. "Take the devil child. He'll rob you in your sleep for your pains, mark my word."

One after another, the feet began to move off. After watching the fat, cracked shoes of Owen stomp away, Nathaniel let the world go black.

He awoke in the shade, propped up against a tree. Pulling a wet rag from his eyes, Nathaniel saw the carriage horse tethered beside him, still attached to the riding chair but calm and eating grass. He heard the same voice that had saved him from Owen: "Tsk, tsk, tsk, such a pity. I suppose I have to give up this book on surveying. I won't really use that. And I don't need the *Poor Planters' Physician*. I have Ainsworth's dictionary already, so I suppose I don't need Samuel Johnson's, although I did so covet it for its wit. Truly I did."

Nathaniel watched the old man, sitting in the riding chair, sorting through his books. He could tell his right eye was badly swollen from the beating, as each blink stung horribly.

The fellow continued talking to himself. "That brings the tally to four pounds, ten shillings. What other books should I give back to make up the rest of the boy's cost?" He sighed plaintively and crossed his arms. "A pity it is. But it can't be helped. After all, Aesop said that no act of kindness, no matter how small, is ever wasted. The lad may become the mouse that saves this poor old lion one day. Yes, perhaps."

He eyed the pile of books on the seat next to him. "I will not give up Pope's *Essay on Man*. I have wanted that too long. Hmmm . . . I'll just have to forego Ovid's *Metamorphoses*. That makes six pounds. Four more pounds to make up. Three more books to choose. I'll even get back ten shillings—there's a happy thing."

He was an angular, older man, all elbows and knees it seemed, like a grasshopper. He wore his own gray hair, tied back with black ribbon, bow akimbo. His face was lean, with pronounced cheekbones, and his eyebrows were hairy and a bit wild, sticking almost straight up. He needed a shave. Nathaniel tried to puzzle out the man's circumstances. His English frock coat was simple, dark, with wooden buttons, no shine about him. He was no merchant, clearly, or he was one who had fallen on hard times. A tradesman didn't usually wear a coat like that. A middling planter, perhaps? Why so consumed with books, then? He wouldn't have time from his fields to read that many.

While Nathaniel was looking him over, the old man glanced his way. Instantly Nathaniel dropped his gaze.

"There, boy, feeling better?" The riding chair squeaked as the man climbed out of it. "Let me see that eye."

Nathaniel turned his head away.

"You needn't fear me, child." He knelt and reached out to gently lift Nathaniel's chin. Their eyes met. The man's were hazel, a mixture of green with golden brown, surrounded by laugh lines. There was merriment in them. Nathaniel held his breath. The old fellow smiled. "That's better. It looks as if that swelling will not completely close up your eye. It'd be a tragedy to shut off that, ah . . . unique blue." He let go Nathaniel's chin and extended his hand. "We should introduce ourselves in proper fashion. I am Basil Wilkinson, schoolmaster and music teacher, sometime clerk. And you?"

In disbelief that the man had asked his name, he took Basil's hand. "Nathaniel Dunn, servant, sir," he mumbled.

"What ship brought you here, Nathaniel?"

"The Planter."

"Ah. I came over on the *Justitia*. Was schoolmaster for the children of this household for four years before the sons went off to Harvard and the girls were sent to England to find husbands. It was a happier era for this family then. My time was much easier than I warrant yours has been. Now I make my way as best I can in Williamsburg. When I read in the *Virginia Gazette* this estate was for sale, I came back to purchase the books I used to teach these children. I'm sentimental. Cannot help myself. Besides, I can well use the books to tutor others." He stood. "Can you walk?"

"Aye, sir." Nathaniel lifted himself, head throbbing.

"Good. We'll leave in a moment. I wish to make it across the York River before dark. I just have to settle accounts first. The auctioneer said I could turn in seven books to make up your price." Absorbed in the thought, Basil turned. "Oh yes . . . a slave brought a sack he said belonged to you. He's the one who carried you to this tree."

Nathaniel knew that must have been Moses. "Did . . . did . . ." Nathaniel choked on the words. Was he not to have the chance, then, to say farewell?

Basil waited.

Nathaniel tried again. "Did . . . did he say where he was to go?"

35

"No, lad. He left with a number of slaves. The man taking them spoke kindly to them. That's all I can tell you."

Just like that. Gone. With no knowledge of where Moses had been taken. *That's the way of it.* Nathaniel took a deep breath and squelched his sorrow. Well, if that were the way of it, 'twas better to feel nothing at all. Nathaniel vowed to lock his heart closed.

Basil turned back to sorting. "Perhaps I can keep this book of botany and sell it to Mr. Wythe. A fine man of learning, Nathaniel, who lives next door to the house in which I lodge. Interested in natural sciences as well as the law he teaches. An enlightened man, to be sure. He even has a reverse kind of telescope that allows a man to see tiny things like ants up close and larger."

Basil stopped a moment and stared off into space, then shook his head. "Amazing, truly amazing, what man can invent. We are in such an age, my friend, such an age of discovery and new thought. . . . Well . . . If I sell this volume to him, perhaps he'll let me borrow it. That's a plan. We'll keep the botany, then. But what to sacrifice? I need Wise's *Arithmetic* and Salmon's *Geography and Grammar*. Here: Mercer's *Abridgement of Law*. This one can be left behind. Oh, I've forgotten the count. That would bring me to . . . to . . ."

Nathaniel knew. The way Basil had been tallying

before, each book was priced at thirty shillings. Twenty shillings made up a pound. That meant Basil had now accounted for seven pounds, ten shillings of Nathaniel's price. "That leaves you two and one half pounds to make up, master." Nathaniel spoke with shame. He felt horrible that this man was giving up things he clearly wanted to save Nathaniel from Owen.

Basil looked at him in surprise. "Can you cipher, lad?"

"Aye, sir. A little."

"Read?"

Nathaniel nodded again. "Poorly, sir, but I can."

"This is excellent good news, Nathaniel! I had no idea what I was to do with you in Williamsburg. I have no need of a servant. I barely feed myself by teaching grammar and Latin, violin and flute. But I rent an upstairs room from Mrs. Maguire, and her husband, Edan, runs a profitable carriage-making shop. He just advertised for apprentices. He wants them, let's see how he put it—'genteelly brought up and tolerably educated.' If you can read, well . . . Now, normally, he would expect a boy's family to pay an apprentice fee. Then Edan would keep the boy seven years, teaching him the trade in exchange for his labor. But Edan has little patience for teaching. I came to know him by teaching one of his apprentices to write."

Basil rubbed his face, his beard stubble bristling. "Perhaps we can bargain this way: The spinet is for Mrs. Maguire. She wishes me to teach her to play like ladies of fashion. When she heard that the daughter of Silversmith Geddy, across Palace Green, was being taught harpsichord, she was determined to learn herself. Mr. Maguire lent me this riding chair to bring home that spinet. He bade me promise to tell everyone I met that he had made it. It's a fine one, don't you think? Oh dear, I do hope I have hawked it enough for him. . . . Mmmm . . . Edan sees the value of creative arrangements, yes, yes."

Basil reflected a moment. "He can be harsh with his help, though." He squinted his eyes as if trying to see a memory. "But truth be told, I have never seen him lay more than a slap on his servants. It's more Mrs. Maguire whom he constantly berates. . . . Perhaps in exchange for lessons . . . that way you'd stay under my care mostly. . . . Hmmm . . . I think it would be all right."

It was hard for Nathaniel to follow Basil's meandering thoughts, but it sounded as if he would stay with Basil and be hired out to work for this carriage maker—a common enough arrangement with servants.

Certainly the riding chair was well made. It was a good trade to learn. Still an unknown, but it was a far more promising one than going with Owen. When he saw Basil pick up a transverse German flute and hold it, weighing its value, Nathaniel knew what he should do. He opened his sack as Basil prattled on to himself. "I have an English flute already. It's just that these transverse flutes seem to handle livelier music better than my recorder can. They have a brighter, fuller tone. But its cost is three pound. . . . If I give it up, that would finish Nathaniel's price and give me coin for the ferry crossing as well. Ohhhhh . . ." He sighed deeply.

"Here, master." Nathaniel held up the flute his father had given him. "You may have this." He didn't know how to play it. His father had deserted him. The only thing Nathaniel felt truly precious was his mother's Bible. That and the other pair of breeches and shirt she had made him would remain as treasure in his otherwise empty sack.

Basil took the long, thin instrument and placed it to his lips to test it. A sweet, melancholy tune came out. "Lovely," murmured Basil. "Do you play, Nathaniel?"

"No, sir."

"How did you come by it, then?"

"My father gave it me."

"Where is he now?"

Nathaniel shrugged and looked to his feet.

There was a long pause before Basil played the plaintive melody again. When done, he asked, "Know you the words, Nathaniel?"

Shaking his head, Nathaniel kept looking to the ground.

"It was one of the first songs I learned in this land. A fellow indentured servant taught me. These are some of the words to it." In a quavery voice he sang:

> *"Five years served I, under Master Guy,*
> *In the land of Virgin-ny-o,*
> *Which made me for to know sorrow, grief, and woe,*
> *When that I was weary, weary, weary-o. . . .*

> *"I have played my part, both at plow and cart,*
> *In the land of Virgin-ny-o,*
> *Billets from the wood upon my back they load,*
> *When that I was weary, weary, weary-o."*

Nathaniel fought off tears. Did this man understand what the last two years had been like? The terror and pain of becoming a piece of property, of being left among strangers who cared nothing about him? A beloved parent dead, the other essentially so. He could feel Basil watching him closely, and he could barely stand it.

When Basil finally spoke, it was in a solemn, pact-making voice. "Let us do this, Nathaniel Dunn. I will borrow this flute from you. And I will teach you to play it as well, so that we may entertain ourselves and the Maguires with music. Will that suit?"

Nathaniel was being asked? *"Hopes all things?"* Nathaniel pushed aside the hope that bubbled up within him. *Careful. There's no telling what might happen in Williamsburg and who's to say this old man will keep his promises.*

"Aye, master, it suits," Nathaniel muttered, keeping his voice clean of emotion.

"Let us be on our way, then."

PART TWO

June 1774

You gentlemen of England,
Who live at home at ease,
How little do you think upon
The dangers of the seas.
Give ear unto the mariners,
And they will plainly show,
All the cares, and the fears,
When the stormy winds do blow.

—"You Gentlemen of England,"
eighteenth-century mariner song

❧ Chapter Six ❧

"I HATE RIVER crossings," moaned Basil.

They stood beside a small dock, watching a single-masted sloop bob its way across the York, the boat's sails full in winds that brushed up occasional white-caps.

"A music master drowned on one of these ferries, Nathaniel. He rode from plantation to plantation, staying several days at each. With all the rivers and marshes cutting up this region, he had to use a ferry at least once a week. When he died, I gave up traveling to teach. Too many risks with rivers, so unpredictable. And with horses. Beastly, temperamental animals, really."

Nathaniel could almost feel a smile inside himself. The day had been a quick and full education into Mr. Basil Wilkinson. He was, indeed, no horseman. Basil had so worried the horse with jerking the reins that

Nathaniel had walked alongside the poor creature to steady it. Now it rested its head against Nathaniel's shoulder, almost as if trying to hide.

Nathaniel had never before met such a talkative person. He felt sure he already knew all his new master's history. A Scotsman, Basil was trained in religion and music, but was unable to find work. Times were bad in Scotland—that Nathaniel knew—ever since the British had defeated Bonnie Prince Charlie. In the Highland clearances that followed, British landlords evicted Scottish farmers and placed sheep on their lands. Many had fled to the cities, only to starve or fall into debtors' prison. Basil supported himself by teaching children to read and write, bookkeeping, chimney sweeping, and occasional music lessons. Eventually, Basil boarded a ship for America, looking for a better life. He paid for the trip by selling himself into temporary bondage as a schoolmaster.

Since leaving the plantation, he'd been a field school instructor, a private tutor, a music teacher riding a circuit, a clerk in one of Williamsburg's many shops. Sometimes he played flute for the visiting opera companies. He adapted himself to people's changeable needs for "the gentleman's arts," as learning was considered. "Williamsburg is a very nice town, Nathaniel, but it is not a city like Philadelphia or Charlestown, where music and education are in high demand. Virginia has no major port cities because these cursed rivers are so wide and deep. Merchant ships come straight from England to a planter's private wharf, making little need for town trade."

Basil interrupted himself: "Oh, I would hate to drown. How deep do you suppose this is?"

Nathaniel had already learned that Basil often did not really want an answer to a question. It was more a pause in his monologue.

"I don't mind working so hard," continued Basil. "He that will eat the fruit must climb the tree, after all. Here in Virginia, musicians must be jacks-of-all-trades. Even Peter Pelham, the organist for Bruton Parish, doesn't make enough money to feed his huge brood of children. He also runs the jail."

As crew members lowered the sails to slide the sloop safely into dock, Nathaniel heard waves splashing along its board, the wind rattling the riggings. It was a pretty sound. Nathaniel looked forward to the crossing.

Two gentlemen with horses and another three on foot got off. The boat dipped wildly as each stepped out onto the dock. "That's not sturdy," muttered Basil. "Let us go another way." He jiggled the reins. The horse remained glued to Nathaniel.

A squat, sunburned man called from the deck:

"Passage to Capahosick side, four shilling for you, seven for the chair and horse."

"I . . . I think perhaps we best ride around," Basil answered.

"Where are you going?" asked the boatman.

"To Williamsburg."

"I take you within eight miles of the capital, sir. My ferry saves eighteen riding miles. That's four hours' time."

Still Basil hesitated. "Such a small boat."

Nathaniel had seen smaller, more weather-beaten vessels load tobacco and head out to open sea. Basil's timidity confused Nathaniel. Basil had been so brave in stopping Owen from beating Nathaniel. How could he be so fearful of water? And why now? They had already dallied two hours, waiting for the ferry to show up.

The boatman jumped lightly off the sloop. "This boat is as good as any in the colony," he said. "It will carry nine horses to the other side. With your small weight, we'll fair skip along the water. Once over, you will find our public house. My wife made pigeon pies today. Stay the night. The way to Williamsburg is swampy. Best take it in full light when you can see the bogs. Nice carriage chair like that might snap an axle if the wheels sank in the mud."

Pigeon pie? The last time Nathaniel had tasted pigeon pie was in England. He longed to beg Basil to take the ferry to the pie, yet he knew he could not ask for more charity. Besides, he chided himself, what made him think he'd be allowed to sit at table?

In the end, the thought of harming the chair persuaded Basil. During the twenty-minute crossing, he was silent, hunkered down to withstand the boat's rocking.

Nathaniel delighted in the smell of brine in the wind, the taste of salt when water sprayed into his face, even though it made his split lip burn. He tracked the flight of a huge blue-gray heron, its long legs held straight out behind its wide wings, making the bird look like a crossbow. Black waterfowl dove into the waters to emerge yards away with thrashing fish in their red beaks. The sky still clouded, the water was a dark emerald. No matter how far over the side Nathaniel leaned, he could not see into its depths, but he knew crabs and oysters aplenty were below.

When they landed on the opposite shore, near a vast swath of salt marshes, Nathaniel was disappointed for the voyage to end.

Basil harumphed: "There. What folly. Foolish of you to be fearful, Nathaniel."

"Me, sir?"

Basil hurriedly changed the subject. "Look there, boy." He pointed to a large black-and-white woodpecker darting among the sycamores. "Isn't it beautiful? The

Indians use their ivory bills for necklaces. Magnificent beings, the Algonquians, the Iroquois, the Cherokee. We used to see their canoes on the rivers all the time when I first came. A rare few come into Williamsburg still to trade. Mostly they stay to Kentucky and Ohio now, since Parliament denies our settling there."

Nathaniel had never seen an Indian. He imagined them to be gigantic and painted with blood. The plantation slaves had told him terrible stories about scalpings and demon doings in the night by the tribes. And recently a half-French Mingo had led raids against settlements along the Appalachian Mountains, saying Virginians had murdered his family. Shawnee were attacking there too—right in the area Nathaniel figured his father to be.

Unnerved thinking about Indians, Nathaniel noted how long the shadows were across the marsh path, how eerily the grapevines twisted up the trees in the thinning light. The peepers and bullfrogs were almost deafening in their chant, their song to greet twilight, as insistent as birds at sunrise. Night was coming fast.

"Two hours at a goodly pace to Williamsburg," Basil answered Nathaniel's thoughts. He stretched. "Let us rest. I must admit that pigeon pie sounded fine. Shall we have some, Nathaniel?"

⨀ Chapter Seven ⨀

BASIL HAD CONSUMED his pie before Nathaniel even took his first bite. Nathaniel had crept away from the table, holding his precious slice against his chest. At the large fireplace in the one-room tavern, he sat upon the hobnob metal on its edge, warming his back and savoring the anticipation of biting into the flaky crust. He caught the scent of roasted onion and clove as he bit into the sweet, buttery meat inside the crisp pastry. He closed his eyes and rolled the delicious morsel around and around in his mouth. Finally, he swallowed. The pie was as good as his mother's had been. He took twenty wondrous mouthfuls to consume the four-inch slice, remembering.

Nathaniel sat back to watch the scene before him. The tavern was loud, filled with smoke from the men's long clay pipes. They all seemed slightly drunk and dangerous. Men bet on dice, argued about cards, knocked over their mugs of ale and jumped up to yell at one another. Two men holding caged roosters planned a cockfight, calling each other scurrilous names.

A pasty-faced man in frilly clothes rose unsteadily. His powdered wig was sliding back off his head. Waving a huge handkerchief, he raised a glass, and shouted, "To the glory of his Majesty, King George of England, may his reign be long."

It was as if he had fired a musket. Abruptly, the entire tavern silenced. A few chairs scraped along the floorboards as several well-dressed men rose shakily to their slippered feet and raised their glasses. "Indeed, sir," one of them added, "and to all his loyal subjects, here and in our good mother country, England."

"Hear, hear." The men smiled at one another in a late-night, ale-drenched stupor, a swaying circle of silks and lace and brocade. They didn't seem to notice that most of the inn's revelers stayed seated, either glaring at them or looking down into their cups, studiously ignoring the prompt to praise the king.

But an elegant man who'd been quietly reading would have none of the crowd's silence. He rose, held up a glass of garnet-red wine, and with a high-court English accent, said, "Come, gentlemen all. Raise your glass. 'Tis treason not to toast our sovereign."

Up shot a man with scars thick across his sun-roasted face. He wore buckskin breeches, a leather shirt, and a raccoon tail sticking out of his round hat. "Treason to ye, but not to me and me friends," he barked. He held up his own wooden cup and turned a circle speaking to the crowd: "I give you the people of Boston. Here's to their steeping the king's tea where it belongs—in the harbor. May we all have such backbone when it comes to it."

"Aye!" A dozen men stood and downed the remains of their drinks, slamming the empty mugs onto the table.

The rest of the inn's patrons seemed to slide down into their chairs even further, refusing to look up.

"In Boston, men who speak thus are to be arrested and sent back to England for trial on charges of sedition." The elegant man put his hand atop the hilt of a sword that hung at his side.

"We aren't in Boston." The rough-clad man pulled a thick hunting knife from his belt. "This here is Virginia."

The two swaggered toward each other.

Seeing the trouble he had caused, the man in frills sat down with a gasp, mopping his brow with his lace handkerchief. One of his friends pointed a huge flintlock pistol. The others cowered behind him.

A knot of brawny farmers and woodsmen, grabbing up their table knives, gathered behind the frontiersman. Others scattered to the walls to be out of trouble. The caged roosters crowed as if delighted that their scrap was to be postponed by a human one.

The tavern keeper looked as if he would cry. "Sirs, please, mine's a respectable establishment."

Just as the two antagonists reached one another, toe to toe—the elegant man calm and disdainful, the buckskin ruffian snarling like a hound—a familiar voice cried out, "Stop! Hold, sirs."

All eyes turned. Basil stood atop a table with a glass in one hand and his pocket fiddle in another. His gray hair floated about his head, and his face was flushed. "Let us use a toast I have heard the learned Mr. Wythe bespeak: Here's to the king—may His Majesty long and gloriously reign—"

"Fie, old fool, get down off the table with ye, or I'll be knocking ye down meself," growled the frontiersman.

"Peace," the refined gentleman held up his hand. "We must respect age. Continue, old sir, and then we will proceed with our argument!" He bowed to his opponent and smiled, bringing on a ripple of relieved laughter.

Basil nodded, ". . . may His Majesty reign in the hearts of his *free* American subjects, and to our friends in Boston *and* London, and to a speedy, honorable, and happy reconciliation between Great Britain and America, which will preserve the liberties of all mankind." He took a deep breath. Before the inebriated crowd could think through his long sentence, he sung out, "And let us seal the peace between us with a song. Gentlemen, I give you the *Devil's Dream* to chase the devil out of us!"

Basil gulped his wine, put down his glass, and began playing.

It was a fast, whirling jig, up and down from high to low. Basil's fingers flew along the fiddle's neck. His bow sawed the strings. He almost looked like a flapping chicken. But there was nothing funny about the effect Basil had on them all. First there was simply a pause in the growing trouble, then silence, then one by one people sat back down. As they began clapping to the merry tune, the frontiersman disappeared out into the night and the swordsman took up his book again.

The sigh the tavern keeper breathed was large enough for Nathaniel to feel across the room.

For an hour Basil played, finding melodies to please and to pull out singing. Some were sad, some about heroes, some celebrated poor men's pranks on the mighty. Finally he came to a song from the comic opera *High Life Below Stairs*. The words made fun of the rich and what they were slave to. The tavern crowd needed little prompting to sing along with gusto after the night's earlier clash:

> *"Come here, fellow Servant, and listen to me,*
> *I'll show you how those of superior degree*
> *Are only dependents, no better than we.*
> *Both high and low in this do agree. . . .*
>
> *"See yonder fine spark, in embroidery dress'd*
> *Who bows to the great, and, if they smile, is blest;*
> *Who is he? i'faith, but a servant at best."*

∽ Chapter Eight ∾

THE NEXT MORNING Basil climbed into the riding chair with a wide smile that lit his thin face with a sunburst of wrinkles. He held up several coins before putting them into his waistcoat pocket. "Never underestimate the power of music to soothe or pay the rent, Nathaniel," he chirped. "That innkeeper was very grateful for the help of my fiddle last night. He gave me back the cost of our passage and our board in thanks. Ho ho!"

Basil picked up the reins and slapped the poor horse, causing her to prance nervously along the path. Nathaniel jogged along behind. He admired Basil's self-motivated cleverness. He himself never thought quickly enough to bring on good fortune. And bravery, or defiance—as he found out yesterday—only brought on trouble. He could still barely see out of his swollen and bruised eye. He knew he'd carry the embarrassing mark of being beaten for days.

Nathaniel did long to ask what the tavern brawl had been about. How did men dare to speak ill of the king, and why would such rich men care a wit about what commoners had to say? And what was "sedition"?

When they entered the edges of Williamsburg, a little past ten o'clock, Nathaniel received his answers.

He was already agog at the multistoried brick buildings at the edge of town. Basil had explained they were part of the College of William and Mary, a place dozens of scholars came to study together—philosophy, history, ancient languages.

Fancy that, Nathaniel had thought. He hadn't before realized that there was much to learn beyond adding sums or reading words.

Then he spotted two long rows of elegant gentlemen. Gravely, silently, they followed a man in purple robes, who carried a silver mace. Hundreds of people—some in silk and wigs, some in workmen's frocks and leather aprons—lined the street. No matter their dress, none made a sound. Only a tolling church bell accompanied their march.

Instinctively, Nathaniel lowered his voice to a church-service whisper. "What is this, master?"

Basil watched a moment, before answering in a somber voice, "These men are members of the House of Burgesses. Know you what that is, Nathaniel?"

Nathaniel shook his head, not taking his eyes off the strange and silent parade.

"It is like Parliament in England. They are elected by Virginia freeholders to represent our needs. The royal governor, Lord Dunmore, represents the king. The House of Burgesses passes laws about roads, the militia, fees the ferries can charge, even taxes. The burgesses have been meeting since 1619, starting in Jamestown.

"This procession is in support of the people of Boston. Know you what has happened in Boston?"

Again Nathaniel shook his head. All he knew of Boston was what the frontiersman had shouted the previous night. Little news of the outside world had traveled to the plantation other than word there was new trouble with Britain.

Basil took a deep breath before beginning, as if to give a speech: "For more than a hundred years, colonial legislators, like our burgesses, governed without Parliament's meddling. The burgesses had been responsible for levying taxes in ways that were well considered and fair, putting the money to use here, to run Virginia to the benefit of both the colony and Britain.

"But the French and Indian War cost the king a pretty penny. Parliament decided to pay off England's debts by taxing us. First came the Sugar Act taxes;

then the Stamp Act, which imposed a fee on all printed paper—newspapers, legal documents, even playing cards.

"We have no members of Parliament elected here, speaking for us in London. It's taxation without representation. Most unjust, completely against the British constitution.

"If Parliament forces us to pay taxes, without our agreeing to it first, what arbitrary rule might come next? Besides, it was through our sweat and tears that the colonies grew. No member of Parliament I know has braved the ocean, Indian attacks, unknown disease, and a wilderness to build this new world. Why should they profit from work they have not done?

"The latest insult is to force us to pay an import fee on tea and to purchase it solely from the British East India Company. The tax itself is not much—but it's the principle of the matter, Nathaniel, the principle! Boatloads of that unwanted tea sailed into Boston. The people of Boston refused to unload it. Men calling themselves the Sons of Liberty dressed up as Mohawk Indians and dumped out every bit of that tea—ninety thousand pounds into the harbor.

"Now England is going to blockade Boston's port until the town agrees to pay for the tea. Nothing—no foods, no goods—will be able to come in or out of the city. The people could starve. British troops control the city. Anyone caught promoting protest—engaging in sedition, as is the legal term—will be sent to England for trial. That's a passage to the hangman, if ever there was.

"When our Virginia burgesses heard of these Coercive Acts, they called for this day of fasting and prayer. It is to show that an attack on one of our sister colonies is an attack on all British Americans. These men are on their way to say prayers. That's all. But Governor Dunmore sees our standing by our Boston brethren as a challenge to the king's authority. So Dunmore dissolved the House. He banned their meeting.

"See that man there?" Basil pointed to a dignified, heavyset gentleman in front of the procession. "That is Peyton Randolph, Speaker of the House. Well, I suppose I should say 'was' speaker. When the governor dissolved the House, Mr. Randolph led the burgesses straight to the Raleigh Tavern and kept right on meeting. They have called on Virginians to give up tea and to not buy anything shipped here from England. They've suggested a congress of all the colonies, so that representatives from Georgia to New Hampshire can unite, making our voice stronger. Very clever, that move is.

"The burgesses may even urge us to stop selling

our tobacco to England. The thought is that completely cutting off trade would pressure the king to stop this madness.

"Breaking off trade altogether could ruin planters and merchants, the people who hire me to teach their children. . . ." Basil wrung his hands in worry. "Well . . . such methods worked once before to push Parliament into repealing the Stamp Act. Hopefully they will again. Everyone is trying to keep the disagreement polite so that reconciliation can come quickly."

Basil watched a moment longer before adding, "Still, I fear this business will tear friends and families apart. Evidently it was Mr. Randolph's brother, John, who advised the governor that a quiet day of prayer and fasting was a prelude to more dangerous defiance. He is the attorney general to the governor. Some say it was on John's word that the governor dissolved the House. I wonder what those two brothers have to say to each other today."

An extremely tall, very serious, and very strong-looking man, who dwarfed all the other burgesses, caught Nathaniel's eye. "Who is that, master?"

"Who?"

Nathaniel pointed.

"Oh, that's only George Washington. A surveyor and planter. Now, let me see if I can find Patrick Henry.

That's the voice stirring up patriotic zeal." Basil stood up in the riding chair and scanned the crowd.

Nathaniel recognized the name as that of the father of the youth who'd purchased Vixen. He waited with curiosity.

"Odd. Unlike Henry to not be in the middle of this," Basil muttered. "A most controversial man who argues the most radical of points. Why, he's even defended Baptists!"

Basil nearly fell out of the carriage with looking. Nathaniel stroked the horse to keep her still. "He'd be dressed almost like a parson, Nathaniel. He's a rather plain fellow in appearance, really. No one can argue his affect on people, however, or his bravery. It was Mr. Henry who convinced the burgesses to resist the Stamp Act. He insisted we have the same constitutional rights as Englishmen, despite our living in the colonies. He even hinted that the king was becoming a tyrant. Some of the burgesses shouted that Mr. Henry was speaking treason. He is said to have answered: 'If this be treason, make the most of it.'"

"Make the most of it, indeed, Mr. Basil!" A lean, dark-haired youth appeared behind the riding carriage. He grinned merrily. "Another of your lessons, Mr. Basil? Do you ever tire of preaching? At least this lecture is worth the having!" The youth winked at

Nathaniel. He was freckled and dimpled, with huge, chestnut-brown eyes, and there was a good-natured light touch about his teasing. Basil did not seem offended.

"Fie, Ben," Basil matched his banter, "had your lessons equaled your revolutionary rhetoric, you would be a master craftsman in your own right much sooner."

"And miss the delight of bedeviling you, sir? No indeed, reading and ciphering are for old men."

Basil smiled at Nathaniel. "Listen not to this wastrel, lad. This is the very apprentice I told you of, who introduced me to Edan Maguire. Edan had despaired of teaching him his catechism, and so he hired me. The atrociousness of his spelling is equaled only by his lackluster addition!"

"Awww, Mr. Basil, why would anyone be concerned about spelling and adding when we are in the midst of such times! There are so many more important things to be concerned about."

"But Ben, we are trying to redefine our relationship with the crown, to safeguard the rights of Englishmen around the globe, whether colonists or Londoners. 'Twill be accomplished through rational, legal, *learned* arguments."

Ben rolled his eyes and hit upon a way to stop Basil's lecture. "Mr. Basil, for shame, methinks you've forgotten your manners." He nodded toward Nathaniel.

"Oh dear, so I have. Ben, this is Nathaniel Dunn. He comes to join our household, hopefully as an apprentice. Junior to you, of course."

"Huzzah!" Ben threw up his arms in celebration. "That means you get kindling duty, Nathaniel!" He walked around the chair to shake hands. Nathaniel nodded and looked down shyly. "I like the looks of that eye, Nathaniel." Ben lowered his head to inspect Nathaniel's black eye. "Got you that in defense of our liberty?"

Not understanding his meaning, Nathaniel remained mute.

"A silent one, then?" Ben asked. "Not allowed in these times, my friend. Be you Whig or Tory?"

Nathaniel was still perplexed.

"Patriot or loyalist?"

Nathaniel didn't know what the labels Ben was using meant, but he knew he planned to stay out of trouble. He would keep his head down and get by. Choices only brought on abuse from those who didn't agree—especially choices that put one at odds with people in power.

"Leave off, Ben," Basil said gently. "The lad's just

arrived. He knows naught of politics."

"But he best learn, master tutor. Choices must be made. Those who stick by Parliament will not be popular. But those who try to straddle the fence between both, or claim to be neutral, will only be suspected and hated by both sides."

PART THREE

November 1774

Rouse every generous thoughtful mind,
The rising danger flee,
If you would lasting freedom find,
Now then abandon tea. . . .

Shall we our freedom give away,
And all our comfort place
In drinking of outlandish tea,
Only to please our taste?

Forbid it Heaven, let us be wise,
And seek our country's good:
Nor ever let a thought arise,
That tea should be our food.

Since we so great a plenty have,
Of all that's for our health;
Shall we that blasted herb receive,
Impoverishing our wealth? . . .

Adieu! Away, oh tea! Begone!
Salute our taste no more:
Though thou art coveted by some
Who're destined to be poor.

—"India Tea," a colonial protest song

꧁ Chapter Nine ꧂

"GOD'S TEETH! I will not drink sassafras! Does she think me a savage?"

Edan Maguire shoved a cup of the Indian herb drink at Nathaniel. Nathaniel managed to bobble the cup and saucer and save it from crashing to the floor. But hot liquid drenched his new waistcoat and spilled onto Edan's table, just missing a design page of heraldry for a carriage. He winced as the heat soaked to his skin.

"Baaah," Edan waved his hand impatiently. "Clumsy fool! Mop that up. Then go and tell that wench of a wife of mine that I'll have none of this substitute. I don't care that there's a three pence tax per pound. I don't care what these ruffians say about protesting British doings in Boston. I want real tea. Where is the liberty they speak of, when I can't even choose for myself what to drink of a morning?"

Nathaniel hurriedly mopped up the spill, ducking to

avoid being smacked as Edan threw his hands about in indignation. Edan's temper was poker hot when it flared. This morning it was as scorching as the embers in the blacksmith's forge where Edan's smithy made nails for carriage wheels.

Shaking out a copy of the *Virginia Gazette*, Edan went on: "Listen to the Association Resolves of this so-called Continental Congress. They call themselves most dutiful, loyal subjects of the king while calling on us to defy him. Do they really think that by our not drinking tea or refusing to buy English goods the greatest empire in the world is going to bow down and change? They obviously know naught of the lobster-backs. They ought to talk to my Irish countrymen to know what comes of challenging the British crown and its soldiers. I came to this land to be free of such suicidal argument."

He threw the broadsheet newspaper to the ground. "Where am I to purchase the gold leaf I need to guild my carriages if not from British merchants? I will be ruined! These madmen want us to make our own home-spun cloth and . . . and . . ." he spluttered, and picked up the paper to find the exact wording. He read with heavy sarcasm, "And 'to engage in frugality, economy, and industry, discouraging any display of extravagance.' Why, that could include my magnificent work, since riding in one of my carriages makes a man appear an earl. . . . And look here. Next summer, if the British don't do our bidding, we will stop exporting our goods to them—everything but rice. That means every tobacco planter in Virginia could end up in the poorhouse. My business will die!" He slammed the paper to the table.

Sticking out his lower lip, he glared at Nathaniel. "Then you'll be out in the streets, boy, back where you came from. And you and you and you as well." Edan pointed at Ben, then at John Hunter, an indentured servant, and finally at Obadjah Puryer, a journeyman in the trade. The two men worked in Edan's shop in the many stages required to complete a carriage. Ben helped them finish projects, actually doing some of the work under their watchful eyes. Nathaniel had inherited all Ben's grunt labor—sweeping, stoking fires, sharpening tools, and caring for the horses and chickens.

Nathaniel stood silently, never quite sure when Edan's tirades were over and he should go about his commands. Walk away too soon, and Edan would grab him by the collar.

"Well?" Edan roared, throwing up his hands. "What are you waiting for?" He stood up from his chair. "Return straightaways. I need you to crank the wheel for the lathe. We need to carve this piece of elm into a hub today. I've an order for a phaeton from a well-off gentleman, whom I trust will pay speedily." Grumbling, he picked up the slab of wood. "Nobody can do anything around here without my telling them. When I was a journeyman in Dublin—now there's a city—I was grateful to work. I used to . . ."

Nathaniel scrambled for the door. As he passed, Ben crossed his eyes and pulled down his mouth with his fingers to make a grotesque face at Edan's turned back. Nathaniel couldn't believe how reckless Ben was.

But even John was rebellious in mood that morning and whispered to Nathaniel, "Don't worry, lad. They don't call him the Palace Street Puffer for nothing."

"What? What did you say, scurvy scoundrel?" Edan shouted, turning around. He slammed the hunk of wood down. "I'll not tolerate any gossiping among you rabble!"

"We just told him to a-hurry, master!" answered John in a singsong voice.

"Baaah!" barked Edan.

Nathaniel bolted for the safety of the kitchen before he could be questioned. If Edan really pushed him to know what John had said, Nathaniel would have to tell. If he didn't tell, Edan would shake it out of him. He'd hate to get John into trouble. Nathaniel liked John. But better it be John than Nathaniel. Being in trouble with Edan was a deep and wide chasm that Nathaniel would do anything to avoid. So Nathaniel ran, clutching the teacup and spilling more tea all over his waistcoat.

Inside the warm outbuilding he found the most revered servant of the household, Sally, the slave cook. Her status came partly from her formidable bearing, partly from her close relationship with Edan's wife, but mainly from the delicious foods she created and her frank wisdom. She was plucking a chicken, making a little pile of downy feathers. Mrs. Elizabeth Maguire stood beside, holding a book titled *The Compleat Housewife*. Before he could say anything, she spoke with a sigh: "I know, I know. I heard him."

Mrs. Maguire shook her head. "Everyone this side of the governor's palace could probably hear him, more's the pity. Here we are among the gentles he hopes to befriend, and there he is sounding like a fishmonger. What must our neighbors think?" She put her hand to her cheek, flushed with dismay. "Well . . . it's not as if that Mr. Wythe isn't a bit odd himself, now is it? Taking a bath daily? Imagine!"

She checked a small kettle hanging over the fire. "I've already started a pot of chocolate for him, Nathaniel, to replace the sassafras." She stirred something else in the fireplace and took a sip of it from the ladle, wrinkling her nose. "The sack whey is ready for

Mr. Wilkinson, though. All it needs is hartshorn spirits." She added a few drops from a small vial and stirred. "This should cure that cold."

Nathaniel knew Basil would not be happy to receive Mrs. Maguire's sack whey. The elixir of wine, watery milk, and distilled slices of deer antler was disgusting. But she'd read in her book that the way to stop a cold was to lie much in bed and drink such concoctions. She was determined to get him well quickly, and Basil wanted to avoid being bled by a surgeon.

"I can't stand being cut," he had moaned. "Last time they took a whole cup of my blood to balance my humors. So I'll try her remedies. Besides, I'd not hurt Mistress Maguire's feelings for the world. She is very kind."

She was that. A tiny woman, not much taller than Nathaniel, Mrs. Maguire was quiet and thoughtful. She wasn't exactly pretty or dignified. There were too many worries etched into her face for that. Underneath her mob cap, her graying hair was thin and stringy. But she watched to see what people needed and then silently provided it—a matter-of-fact kindness that bred beauty of a sort. A few weeks after Nathaniel arrived at her house, a set of clothes and a pair of shoes appeared beside the rolled-up straw mattress he used in the stable's hayloft.

She'd recently given him the waistcoat as protection against the November chill. He looked down at the striped wool and was relieved to see that the wet spots were drying. He'd hate for her to think he was careless with her gifts. He glanced up shyly at her, but her back was turned. After six months in her household, Nathaniel had come to recognize that her generosity was not born of an outgoing personality, or the beginnings of affection. It was more the simple decency someone might show in taking in a stray dog. Starved for care, it was enough for Nathaniel. Had she been more warm and loving, like his mother, it would have torn his heart out.

Mrs. Maguire pulled the chocolate off the fire. "Basil . . . Mr. Wilkinson . . . has asked me about your sleeping on the floor in his room now that the weather is turning. I told him that is acceptable. The nights will soon be frigid. But you must keep to your morning stable chores, Nathaniel, without fail."

She turned and caught him watching her. As always, Nathaniel averted his eyes. "Look at me, lad. I want to make sure you hear me well." She smiled when he obeyed, but she said pointedly, "Mr. Maguire will not like it if you are late with the horses' oats."

"Aye, mistress. I will not fail."

Sleep in the house? Yet another privilege he had not

dreamed of. He was so afraid that it would all disappear or reveal itself to be a trap of some kind. He tasted meat—mutton, bacon, beef—or salted fish several times a week. He had a pair of shoes and bedding to sleep on. Nathaniel distrusted it all. He couldn't help it.

He was almost glad of Edan's temper, which kept his life rooted to what he had known the past two years—unending labor and unpredictable punishment.

"Please take this upstairs to Mr. Wilkinson." Mrs. Maguire handed the sack whey to Nathaniel. "I'll take this cup of chocolate out to my husband. I need talk with him about this Non-importation Agreement. There is much pressure for Williamsburg's merchants and shopkeepers to sign their names to it. We must do so as well. County committees will check merchants' books to make sure we stick to the ban on imports. The threat is if we purchase or sell any British goods, they will print an ad in the *Gazette* telling townsfolk to break off all dealings with us.

"We cannot afford to be shunned." She turned to Sally and confided, perhaps forgetting Nathaniel's presence. "Mr. Maguire's debt is large. We owe seven hundred pounds for this house. He thought our fortune would be made by following Lord Dunmore to Williamsburg from New York City when the king made Dunmore royal governor here. Edan was convinced that Virginians would be so impressed by the coaches he made for Lord Dunmore that they would flock to our workshop. He insisted on moving us to Palace Street to make our association with the governor clear. We had no need for such a large house."

Clucking in sympathy, Sally kept at her work.

Mrs. Maguire rubbed her forehead. "He is a fine carriage maker. That he is. He is right to take pride in himself. But . . ." She looked out the door toward the shop in back of the garden. "But things have not worked out as planned. And now our Williamsburg neighbors might not like the fact he has done so much work for Lord Dunmore. Edan must come to understand that. Otherwise we could lose everything." She picked up the tray with the pot of chocolate and squared her shoulders.

Sally stopped plucking to warn, "Have a care, mistress."

"Aye," Mrs. Maguire quietly replied. "That I will."

⟡ Chapter Ten ⟡

NATHANIEL PUSHED OPEN the door to Basil's bed-
chamber, carefully holding the steaming and smelly sack
whey. Basil was sitting cross-legged under the window,
his gray hair down upon his shoulders, nightcap askew,
reading a book in the sunlight. When he heard the door
creak, he scrambled to his feet in a comical bolt of bare
legs and flapping pages. He might be old, but he was spry.
He was on his feet and running for the bed in an instant.

But he stopped with an embarrassed snort. "Oh, 'tis
only you, Nathaniel. Methought it was Mistress
Maguire. She has disciplined me severely when she
found me out of bed. But I simply cannot resist
Gulliver's Travels. I've come to the part where Gulliver is
about to—" Basil breathlessly pointed to a passage,
when he stopped himself abruptly. "Oh, forgive me,
lad. I have read ahead of where you and I are. I shan't
spoil it for you." He looked a bit ashamed. "But just

78

wait, Nathaniel. It is so exciting. We'll read again tonight, shall we? Imagine creating a whole universe of little people and naming the nation Lilliput. Where in the world did Swift get that name? Where does a writer come up with such wonderful nonsense?" Basil sighed with delight.

Back in the hot nights of August, when the air felt as if it could sear Nathaniel's lungs, Basil had sat on the back steps to read in the long summer twilight. He'd called Nathaniel out of the stable and read aloud *Robinson Crusoe.* The novel was about a spoiled young man who'd been stranded on a desert island for twenty-eight years, only to find a remarkable courage and resourcefulness inside himself. Nathaniel had never before heard stories other than those in the Bible. He would close his eyes and could almost see Crusoe being swept to shore by the raging sea; teaching his parrot, Poll, to talk; saving the man Friday. The words made such powerful pictures. As Basil read, a door opened to a world Nathaniel had not known existed.

But perhaps the most amazing new universe had been the music. The music! Basil was gone most days, tallying numbers for storekeepers, teaching in homes about the city, repairing musical instruments. But he had still found time to keep his promise to teach Nathaniel to play the German flute.

Nathaniel had surprised himself by learning quickly. The fingerings were easy. All fingers went down over the flute's holes for low C and then the player basically walked up the instrument to go up the scale, lifting one finger at a time, starting with the right pinkie. But balancing it was awkward. The German flute's mouthpiece was held underneath the lips, and then the length of it went up and out to the right. The real difficulty was blowing strongly enough down into the mouthpiece hole to make a note sound. It took a huge amount of air. Countless times, Nathaniel had almost swooned.

But now Nathaniel was actually making melody. So far Basil had taught him three tunes. Basil played and Nathaniel mimicked. When Basil said, "You have an amazing ear, lad, to learn these songs so quickly," Nathaniel had bloomed with pride. He couldn't remember how long it had been since he had taken pleasure in a task. When nightmares about the voyage over the Atlantic or the treatment at the plantation haunted him, Nathaniel simply replayed those melodies in his mind to chase away the ghosts of fear.

Nathaniel knew that was why Mrs. Maguire was fussing so over Basil's cold. He had given her the same gift with the spinet. Through open windows, Nathaniel had heard her playing the small harpsichord that Basil had brought back from the plantation. She'd stumbled and banged through the summer, but now she was working on a hornpipe, where the melody was clear and delicate. He'd heard Basil encourage, "Yes, my dear. That is excellent."

Afterward Mrs. Maguire had come to the workshop with a radiant smile. "Come hear what I have learned, Mr. Maguire."

"I've not time for idle entertainment, mistress," he'd snarled. "You browbeat me into buying that spinet for you. I did so. I've taken this puny boy in exchange for your lessons. Need I do more?"

Her smile had disappeared. So had she. Mrs. Maguire walked back into the house and played and played and played.

Nathaniel shook his head to toss off his daydreaming. *Too close.* You are getting too fond of this old man, Nathaniel warned himself. Your own father deserted you. This old man can, too. He squelched his burning desire to ask what was happening to Gulliver in the land of Lilliputians. Instead, he held out the cup of sack whey.

The stench of it wafted toward Basil. His face fell. "Oh, must I, lad? It is so wretched. I drank the whole lot of it yesterday." He pouted and kept his hands to his side.

Nathaniel pushed the cup at Basil.

"Ah me," Basil took it, held his nose, and swallowed. "Oh, horrible." He took another gulp. "Oh, could hemlock be any worse?" He managed a third swig, his face contorted like a gargoyle's. Gagging and coughing, he spluttered, "That's enough. Enough, I say." He lifted the lid of his chamber pot, releasing another stench into the air, to pour the remainder in. "That's where that belongs." He closed it back up and turned to Nathaniel.

"Nathaniel, lad, may you never be so blessed with a woman's good intentions." He sank onto the bed, his face pale from the ordeal of taking his medicine.

Nathaniel made for the door.

"Lad?" Basil held up his hand to stop him.

"Aye, master?"

"I wish to speak to you about Ben."

Nathaniel waited.

"He reports you avoid his company."

Nathaniel frowned, but said nothing. He didn't avoid him exactly. But when Ben asked him to travel at twilight to meet his friends, Nathaniel did hang back. Ben was very likeable, but he was such a risk taker. Edan had whipped Ben more than once for smelling of ale. Two years older than Nathaniel and tall for his age, Ben at fifteen could slip into the taverns and talk protest. As much as he was drawn to Ben's playful personality, Nathaniel wasn't about to join in those dangerous doings.

"I know he is a bit of a roustabout, but he has a good soul, lad," Basil coaxed, seeming to read Nathaniel's thoughts. "Ben's circumstances are confusing for him. He has several childhood friends at the College of William and Mary. His family was middling gentry. They owned a small farm, and his father made additional money as a joiner, building houses, fences, cabinets. But his father died. Without the income of his father's craft, Ben's mother was unable to keep their family together. Thinking carriage-making would be a steady industry, she apprenticed Ben to Edan. But Ben clearly chafes at the assignment. Although he is a mediocre student at best, I think he longs to be talking patriot philosophy with college scholars."

Nathaniel nodded. "Aye, master, I understand." He had sensed Ben's frustration.

Basil pushed a little harder. "'Twould do you good, Nathaniel, to have a friend."

Nathaniel froze. He had had a friend. Moses. And Moses had been ripped away from him. Since coming to Williamsburg, he'd searched every African face that passed by—it seemed half the city's residents were black. He kept hoping to find Moses somewhere. He'd even slipped away to the market square to see if one of the carts coming in from outlying plantations carried him. But he'd never found him. It made his heart ache thinking of it.

Nathaniel's silence discouraged Basil from further prodding. "Well . . ." he murmured, clearly disappointed. "We shall read on tonight, after your chores, yes?"

Nathaniel nodded, keeping his eyes down and his face blank. But inside, as much as he hated to admit it, he could hardly wait for sundown to visit the Lilliputians.

⚚ Chapter Eleven ⚚

A WEEK LATER, Edan Maguire stood on the lawn of the Capitol, arguing with the most revered man of Williamsburg, Speaker Peyton Randolph. Even Nathaniel could see that Edan was making a fool of himself.

One of the richest and best-educated men in the colony, Randolph had just come home from Philadelphia, where he had been chosen president of the Continental Congress. Calm, tactful, and cautious, Randolph listened to radicals like Patrick Henry and his own cousin Thomas Jefferson. But he kept Virginia's official protests polite, designed to bring about repeal of British taxes and to restore good relations with the king. Williamsburg newspapers were calling him the Father of American Liberty.

Randolph was at the Capitol that cool November day along with hundreds of merchants and planters promising to not sell or use any British goods. While Edan ranted, a dozen townspeople stood nearby, waiting to talk with Randolph. A short distance away was a table to which man after man stepped, took up a pen, and signed the Association Resolves. A gentleman overseeing the process shook the hand of each man as he signed. Observers clapped him on the back in congratulations. The crowd inside the high brick walls of the Capitol yard was growing and getting louder each minute.

Not heeding how many people were listening, Edan blundered on: "But how can the people of Williamsburg so abuse Lord Dunmore when he's just won a war against the Shawnee Indians and claimed all of the territory south of the Ohio River for Virginians to settle?" Edan's face was red. He leaned way too close to Randolph.

Taking a slight step back, Randolph pulled a lace handkerchief from the wide sleeve of his floral frock coat and held it to his nose. Even by the city's standards, Edan's odor was strong. Nathaniel had seen many a lady hold a nosegay up to her face when he passed.

"These resolves have nothing to do with Governor Dunmore," Randolph replied evenly. "They are directed to Parliament to convince it to stop this unconstitutional taxation of us. They do not tax Englishmen at home without representation. Nor should they us. We have made humble and reasonable petitions to the crown. Our letters have been treated with contempt by His Majesty's ministers. We cannot sit idly. Participating in our government, protesting actions we do not like, are fundamental rights of Englishmen. And we are Englishmen, even though we live in the colonies. And so . . ."

"Peaceably?" Edan interrupted. "Do you find boarding the ship of a man who has long been good to the planters of this colony and dumping his cargo into the York River peaceable, sir?" He referred to a "tea party" two days earlier. Following the example of Boston, about twenty men boarded a merchant ship docked in nearby Yorktown. They threw two half-chests of tea from England overboard. The ship's merchant, John Prentis, had printed a groveling apology on the same day the local committee of safety issued a statement that anyone who broke the embargo should "be made to feel the resentment of the publick."

Pointing his thumb toward the Duke of Gloucester Street, Edan went on, "Someone has put a 'liberty pole' outside the Raleigh Tavern. On it hangs a bag of feathers, and beneath it is a barrel of tar. Is that to frighten me into signing this association? Aren't you, sir, being just as coercive as you claim Parliament to be?"

"Hear, hear!" applauded one of those awaiting Randolph, a portly man in a plush, burgundy coat, an obvious loyalist.

"Fie, man, for shame!" cried another. "Such talk makes you an enemy of American liberty."

Two other men took steps forward, one growling, "Perhaps Mr. Maguire should be the first to taste of tar and feathering."

"Peace, gentlemen, peace." Randolph held up his hand. "We must not argue among ourselves. It is important that we make a united stand. That way we will convince His Majesty to repeal these offensive acts. We did the same to protest the Stamp Act, and it worked."

"Aye, that and a little bit of fright put to the stamp collector," whispered one listener to another, who laughed.

Randolph continued: "Mr. Maguire, these resolves call for non-importation, non-consumption, non-exportation—in short, shutting down trade between us and England, getting them in their purse. It is the most speedy, effective, and *peaceable* way to show Parliament we mean what we say. When they see how determined we are, they will have to repeal these oppressive acts. Then we can return to a calm and loving state with our sovereign king. Representatives you elected agreed to these resolves for you. We are bound by honor and love of our country to follow them. Good day, sir." He bowed his head in courtly fashion and turned away.

The knot of men followed, save one, who hissed, "Be forewarned, Maguire. Those who are not with us will definitely be seen as against us." He left, looking over his shoulder threateningly.

Edan stayed rooted, breathing hard in anger. But after a few moments, his coloring changed from red to chalky white. He hung his head. Mumbling about bankruptcy and backwater tyranny, he shuffled off to join the line of signers.

Basil, Ben, and Nathaniel had watched the scene. "Mistress Maguire will not be happy to hear of her husband's tantrum," said Basil. "That made him at least ten enemies."

"Not that he doesn't already have a host of them," quipped Ben. "I've been asked to keep an eye on him and report any disloyal acts of consuming British goods."

Alarmed, Basil turned to Ben. "Report him? To whom?"

"To a few patriot gentlemen who have taken an interest in our ill-tempered carriage maker," answered

Ben. "They are like to be on the committee of inspection to be elected next month."

"Ben, lad." Basil shook his head. "He who asks you to pry into your master's doings and spread gossip is no gentleman."

Ben grinned. "I didn't say I was planning on fulfilling the request, master tutor, but"—he looked at Nathaniel meaningfully—"it would feel good, wouldn't it, to stick it to the old curmudgeon? A little payback for those whippings."

"Ben!"

"Oh, don't worry! You taught me better than that, old sir. I am no Brutus." A passing youth caught Ben's eye. "Oh look, if I'm not mistaken, there goes James Monroe. I knew him at home. I heard he was coming to the college. Nice lad." He darted off, calling, "James! James!"

Basil watched him go. "I worry about that boy," he muttered. But he brightened suddenly. "He remembered about Caesar and Brutus. A miracle! Mayhap I did teach him something. Now there's a story of conceit and betrayal I must tell you, Nathaniel. Back in the time of Rome . . ." A gust of cold wind rattled the trees and shook out the remaining autumn leaves in a tumble of crimson and gold. Basil began to cough violently. Nathaniel wanted to tell him to return home to bed.

"Mistress Maguire's remedies are foul and only so effective," Basil gasped through his coughs.

A girl touched Basil's sleeve. "Posset drink might help that cough," she said. "You curdle milk and ale and flavor it with sugar and spices. That's what Mother gave us."

Basil straightened up. "Ah, Miss Rind." He bowed his head and made formal introduction. "Nathaniel, this is Miss Maria Rind, daughter of the publishers of the *Virginia Gazette*, first her father, and then her mother, Clementina. I have oft placed advertisements in their broadside about my teaching. Maria, this is Nathaniel Dunn, my . . . my . . ." He paused, considered, and said, "A fellow musician."

Maria put her feet into a V and curtseyed at the knee.

Nathaniel had no idea what to do.

"Like this, Nathaniel," Basil whispered. He placed one foot in front of the other, bent with the back knee, and bowed his body over his right arm. "It's to show the young lady what a well-muscled leg you have," he teased.

Maria giggled.

Awkwardly, his face flaming in embarrassment, Nathaniel made the formal greeting.

"Don't worry," Maria told him. "There are lots of things I am supposed to know how to do that I do not." She paused a moment to think. "My penmanship is awful," she offered.

Grateful, Nathaniel nodded.

"Mother simply did not have the time to teach me after Father died and she took up the press."

"I am sorry for the recent loss of your mother," said Basil. "She was a brave lady. Look around you, Maria. Much of today's patriotism is a result of what your mother was courageous enough to print."

Maria's smile was a mix of pride and sadness. "Yes, she was very strong."

Basil explained to Nathaniel, who burned with new embarrassment that he knew nothing of this obviously important printer. "Burgess Thomas Jefferson wrote an eloquent defense of our rights in August, called *A Summary View of the Rights of British America*. Mr. Randolph presented it to the House of Burgesses to adopt, but it was too revolutionary for its members.

"It said that because we had established these colonies through our own hard work, we had the right to make our own laws without Parliament's interference. Mr. Jefferson said that government must be honest, and that it exists only through the consent of the people. He wrote that God gave us liberty at the same time he gave us life. Stirring words, yes?

"But then he went on to say—and this is what many felt bordered on treason—that the king was no more than a chief officer of the people, obligated to serve *our* best interests. Therefore, he was subject to *our* will. Most people were afraid of those words. But not Mrs. Rind. She printed them. And because she did, Thomas Jefferson's ideas traveled throughout the colonies. They were reprinted in cities as far away as Philadelphia. The resolves that these merchants are signing today bear the mark of Mr. Jefferson's belief in our ability and right to govern ourselves.

"It is strange, is it not, that a man who so stumbles when he speaks can write so beautifully. I hear it was the same with his courtship of Mrs. Jefferson, completely tongue-tied but won her heart through his violin playing." Basil put his hand over his heart. "I never had the opportunity to play with Mr. Jefferson; he was a student of Francis Alberti. He and his cousin John Randolph are the best violinists in the city. I wish. . . ."

Basil was about to wander off into one of his stories, but Maria interrupted: "Thank you for your kind words, Mr. Wilkinson. Mother would be pleased by them. Although a woman, she was a bold believer in liberty." Maria sighed. "I wish I could stay to hear them read the resolves, but I best collect my younger brothers before they get into trouble. They left the house without asking. The littlest is only four years old. I hope you will do us the favor of more advertisements, sir. My cousin, John Pinkney, will continue printing our paper. We children are to stay with him."

She curtseyed once more to Nathaniel. "I hope we meet again," she said shyly.

Pale, with solemn dark eyes, Maria was pretty, probably a year younger than his thirteen years. Nathaniel hesitated. Basil elbowed him, and Nathaniel clumsily bowed again as she left.

Nathaniel hadn't managed to speak one word. Maria was a recent orphan. Yet she had the graciousness to be kind to both Basil and him. He began to feel ashamed of the way he always held himself in.

On the walk home, Nathaniel decided to do something he knew would please Basil. "Master, can you explain more about what Thomas Jefferson wrote?"

Basil lit up like a firefly in summer. "Oh, Jefferson was undoubtedly influenced by John Locke and Alexander Pope. These are English philosophers who believe that by nature, man is born free and good, with the right and the ability to choose his own course. And rather than being afraid that we will blunder, Locke and Pope believe man has a sense of reason that will guide him to make the right moral decisions. We are not in need of higher authorities. In fact, those higher authorities—kings, the Church—are often corrupt and foolish. Man's God-given common sense is the best ruler of our actions. Each man is capable of learning and directing his own destiny. Laws of the land should be tailored to allow him to do so.

"This concept of man's capabilities is new, revolutionary, dignifying all of us with an inborn intelligence before only thought to belong to kings, lords, priests, and the mighty." Basil stopped walking and put his hand on Nathaniel's shoulder. "It includes you, Nathaniel."

Nathaniel looked at the old tutor blankly.

Basil patted his shoulder and repeated: "That includes you, lad. Believe it."

No, he had spent so much time being directed by others that he had no faith in himself or in any promise of freedom. Basil's words rung like a distant bell in Nathaniel's head, but he couldn't yet heed its call.

⁓ Chapter Twelve ⁓

"THERE, GIRL. THAT'LL feel better." Nathaniel straightened up to pet the carriage mare.

He'd been packing a poultice into her hoof. With the weather turning cold, the ground had stiffened to rock hard. Edan had taken her out to pull one of his finest chairs up and down the streets of Williamsburg, hoping to spark some interest in purchasing it. Keeping the horse at a smart trot to show how light and fast the carriage was, the pounding against the road had chipped up her hoof and made her limp.

The horse nudged Nathaniel, her hot breath warming his face. He smiled and held still, enjoying the horse's gentle affection. Ever since he had protected her against Basil's bad driving, she had been attached to him.

"I wager the Indians have names for people like you. He-who-speaks-not-to-people-but-charms-animals."

Ben's voice made Nathaniel jump. He hadn't noticed Ben standing in the stable door.

"Or Basil probably knows some old fable by what's-his-name—Aslop?—about a lowly stable boy who takes such good care of a donkey that the king makes him a duke or whatever they became back in Greece." Ben clapped Nathaniel on the back and laughed good-naturedly. "Now if this old mare can get you to talk, surely I can as well. Hmmm? What say you, Nathaniel?"

Ben's humor eked a smile from Nathaniel.

"Aha!" Ben put his hands on his hips as if to crow. "The lad dost smile!"

Nathaniel blushed.

Ben eased his teasing. "I mean nothing by it, you know, Nathaniel. Let us be friends. I can use all the allies I can find in Edan's shop. In these changeable days, all we colonists are in need of friends." He put his hand on Nathaniel's shoulder and Nathaniel did not pull back—like an easily spooked horse grateful for a sure-handed trainer. "There's a bit of fun I want you to see in town, Nat. Come along."

It was early evening. Nathaniel's chores were done. Basil was late coming home from his rounds, so it was unlikely there would be music or reading that night. But in town? "I . . . I don't like taverns, Ben," Nathaniel murmured, thinking of the trouble he'd witnessed in the ferryman's inn and of the thrashings Ben had taken for frequenting Williamsburg's.

"No taverns tonight, lad. This is a bonfire—a bonfire celebrating the triumph of King James over Catholic rebels. A company of boys I know have organized it."

"You mean Gunpowder Plot Day?"

"Aye, Nat. The very same! Basil will be so pleased that you know your English history." Ben sobered abruptly. "I'm sorry, Nathaniel. Of course, you know that. You just came over the sea, didn't you? Did they celebrate gunpowder day at home?"

Nathaniel nodded. Commemorating the defeat of Guy Fawkes and his Catholic lord conspirators had been an annual event in Yorkshire. Each November there had been a bonfire and dancing in the village. His mother had always held tight to his hand and taken him home when the revelers began enjoying their ale a bit too much, burning a huge stuffed straw doll—an effigy of the plot's leader. That's about the time the celebration turned nasty and almost superstitious prejudices against people with different religious beliefs flared.

"Then you must come for certain. You will be our expert." Ben put his arm around Nathaniel's shoulders and propelled him out of the stable, through the back of the Maguires' small orchard, onto Nassau Street. "I must admit, Nat, that I know little of the thinking behind the holiday. Just that it celebrates foiling a plot to destroy the English constitution."

"Well," Nathaniel hesitated, trying to remember the historical reason for the festivities. Like so many annual revels, the initial reason for the event had been overtaken by the party itself. "It had something to do with religion."

Ben snorted. "Didn't all England's troubles have something to do with religion? Let us hope that is something we can change here in America. Freedom to worship God as each person sees fit. I heard Burgess Jefferson talk on it at the Raleigh Tavern."

"But can't people do that already in Virginia?"

"They can. Still, they are required to attend service in an Anglican Church established by the Church of England—like Bruton Parish—at least once a month or pay a large fine. And Baptists, Methodists, Catholics, and Jews are not exactly in the center of things in Virginia, are they? But go back to the gunpowder plot."

Nathaniel searched his memory. "There were Catholic lords who wanted to overthrow King James, I think—the Scottish king after Elizabeth. I think he had been lenient toward Catholic practices at first. His mother, Mary of Scots, had been Catholic. But then he changed his mind. Catholic nobles rented a house in

London that had cellars directly beneath Parliament's House of Lords. They filled it with barrels of gunpowder and were planning to ignite it at the same time they captured King James's son and daughter. The idea was to kill the king, his advisors, and the Protestant members of Parliament all at once. But one of the conspirators realized they'd also kill lords sympathetic to Catholics. He warned one of them to stay away. So the king found out about the plot and arrested all of them."

Ben nodded. "I see. I warrant those involved were treated to the executioner."

"Aye," Nathaniel answered, shuddering at the practice of cutting a traitor open—drawing and quartering—*before* hanging him.

"Somebody should have lit that powder sooner then!" Ben said in a strange mix of laughter and grim seriousness.

Nathaniel was shocked. There was nothing funny about such a joke. Was Ben really so violent? He felt himself begin to recoil from the older boy when Ben sung out, "Here we are!"

They'd come to the edge of town, past the main lawn of the college, where the land spread out in grassy fields. There was a good-sized fire blazing and a large crowd of youths jumping and skipping around it. "Come on." Ben started trotting, and Nathaniel dutifully jogged behind.

"There you are, Ben!" cried out several boys, circling around them.

Night's darkness had come. In the crackling light thrown from the fire, Nathaniel could only see half their faces; the rest were cast in shadows, making their expressions look slightly devilish. They were sweaty from dancing close to the flames. Ben introduced them. "Nathaniel, this is Beverly Dixon, son of the postmaster. This is Robert Greenhow, of the store. Methinks Basil does books for your father sometimes. Am I right, Robert?"

The boy nodded.

"And this is Henry Nicholson and this"—Ben patted the shoulder of a hulking, sour-faced boy—"this is Jeremiah Nowland. Do not let his jolly countenance fool you," Ben teased. "Underneath this friendly exterior beats the heart of a beast." The other boys laughed. Jeremiah shoved Ben off.

"Brought you some tea?" he snapped. "If you didn't, you can't join us."

"I did," Ben answered stoutly, not at all shaken by the youth's threatening voice.

"Prove it. We're all free men's sons. You're just an apprentice. You have no money of your own. Where would you get tea?"

Ben drew himself up tall but didn't respond to the taunt other than to pull a sack from his waistcoat. "I have tea," he answered calmly. But there was a cold anger in his voice.

Nathaniel gasped. He knew where that tea had come from—it belonged to Edan.

"Huzzah!" The boy named Beverly cheered, breaking the tension. "Your turn then, Ben. Come throw it into the fire." He pulled Ben close to the flames and held up his hand to still the group. They stopped and listened.

Mimicking older men, Beverly held onto the lapels of his coat and planted his feet wide apart. He cleared his throat dramatically and took on a deep, pompous voice: "Gentlemen, herein we accept into our association of Protestant schoolboys, the presence of one, Benjamin Blyth, who will proclaim his loyalty to Virginia's resolve to not consume tea subject to tax by the crown. By throwing said tea into the fire, we show our allegiance to American liberty as well as to the good old English constitution! Huzzah!"

The boys picked up the chant: "Huzzah! Huzzah!"

Ben threw handfuls of tea into the fire, creating

little flares and sizzles in the flames. The boys began dancing round the bonfire, chanting an old rhyme Nathaniel recognized:

"Remember, remember the fifth of November,
Gunpowder, treason, and plot.
I see no reason why gunpowder treason,
Should ever be forgot!

"Guy Fawkes, guy, t'was his intent
To blow up the king and the parliament.
Three score barrels were laid below
To prove old England's overthrow

"By God's mercy he was catch'd
With a darkened lantern and burning match.
So, holler, boys, holler boys,
Let the bells ring.
Holler, boys, holler boys,
God save the king!"

Only Jeremiah stood, watching Ben with a smoldering malice to match the fire's. He turned on Nathaniel. "Got you tea?"

Nathaniel vehemently shook his head no.

"Then back out of the circle. You don't belong."

Nathaniel retreated. He watched from the shadows, confused. It made no sense to him that the boys would protest England's tea tax by celebrating a past king's victory over a man who was protesting oppression of Catholics. Nathaniel thought on the distrust still held against Catholics back home in England. They weren't allowed to vote or inherit property. The few Catholic families he knew of in Yorkshire disappeared from view around Guy Fawkes Day. Wasn't that even more unfair than a tax on tea?

No, none of it made sense. He resolved to keep clear of it, despite the fact the boys were obviously having great fun.

On the way home, Ben was flushed and excited.

Nathaniel did like Ben. He worried for him. If Ben had stolen that tea, he was in for it. "Ben?"

Ben stopped. "The lad speaks! Huzzah!"

His loud merriment embarrassed Nathaniel. He fell silent again.

"Oh Nat. I am sorry." Ben stopped short. Nathaniel couldn't see his face in the gloom, but he knew Ben meant the apology. "My teasing gets me into trouble all the time with people, like that arrogant boy Jeremiah. My own fault with him, really. This summer I was in town for Edan and passed through market square. The boys were playing cricket. I stopped to watch for a while. Jeremiah was playing in the field. He kept trying to hit the wicket from way out there. He should have thrown it to a player closer in. He was just showing off. So they asked if I knew how to play. I answered that I did, having watched how that lad had fumbled things. A joke. But he didn't take it that way. He's been an enemy every since. . . . What did you want to say, Nat?"

Nathaniel hesitated then blurted: "Ben, where did you get that tea? Did you steal it from Master Maguire?" He didn't explain that his concern was for Ben's safety.

In the darkness, Ben's voice came back offended. "I may be only an apprentice, Nathaniel, but I am no thief. All the boys went about town asking citizens to donate their tea to our bonfire to show their resolve to abstain from British goods. I convinced Mistress Maguire to give it to me when I told her we'd be having a gunpowder plot bonfire. I told her 'twould be better for her to face the ire of her husband than the ill-will of the town."

"Ben!" Nathaniel knew just what giving away Edan's remaining tea supply would cost her in his foul temper and curt language.

"'Tis true," Ben said defensively. He began walking in quick strides. "The Maguires are being watched. They are disliked because of his close bond with

Governor Dunmore. She needed to show support for our cause." He walked even faster. "Besides," he muttered, "it was the only way I could join up with the boys tonight. They're going to start a company of boy volunteers and drill on the green like the militia does. I can't miss it, Nathaniel. I can't. I want to be part of the fight. For a fight is coming, no matter how much they talk on reconciliation and goodwill for the king. Right now in Boston, British lobsterbacks occupy the city and crush the people. It's a pot waiting to boil over. It'll come, mark my words. And I am going to be in it. All Americans who have any self-respect should be."

Nathaniel had been almost running to keep up with Ben's long-legged stride. But he slowed and let Ben stalk off ahead, realizing that given time, with his dimpled smile and genuine, easy manner, Ben could probably charm the fur off a bear. He'd get the wool off a lamb—like Mrs. Maguire or himself—in a minute. Nathaniel was going to be very careful of what he allowed Ben to talk him into doing.

PART FOUR

January 1775

Goody Bull and her daughter together fell out.
Both squabbled and wrangled and made a great
rout. . . .

The old lady, it seems, took a freak in her head,
That her daughter, grown woman, might earn her
own bread. . . .

The daughter was sulky and wouldn't come to,
And pray what in this case could the old woman do?

In vain did the matron hold forth in the cause,
That the young one was able; her duty, the laws;

Ingratitude, vile, disobedience far worse;
But she might e'en as well sung psalms to a horse.

Young, forward, and sullen, and vain of her beauty,
She tartly replied that she knew well her duty,
That other folks' children were kept by their friends,
And that some folks love people but for their own
ends. . . .

Hello Goody, what ails you? Wake woman, I say,
I am come to make peace in this desperate fray.

Adzooks, ope thine eyes, what a pother is here!
You've no right to compel her, you have not, I swear. . . .

Come, kiss the poor child, there come kiss and be
friends!
There, kiss your poor daughter, and make her amends.

—Colonial political words set to "The World
Turned Upside Down"

ꙮ Chapter Thirteen ꙮ

"THE TIMES AND this town completely perplex me, Nathaniel. Here, lad, hold that mirror higher. I cannot see to tie this cravat. Aargh!" Basil tore the long linen tie from his throat, nearly choking himself as he did so. He began again to wrap it around his shirt collar. "Isn't it odd that all Williamsburg's leaders—many who are defying Parliament and harassing anyone drinking tea—are heading to the Governor's Palace tonight for a ball honoring *the queen's* birthday? My students have talked of nothing else all week long. Their households have been uproars of preparation. All the ladies have pulled out the silk dresses they are supposed to give up in favor of homespun cloth. How quickly principle gives way for a party!

"But I do suppose the ball will ease tension. No sane person wants this disagreement between us and Britain to grow. Look how easily the British bottled up Boston.

"Aargh!" He ripped the tie from his throat again. "I have to tie this wretched thing correctly or I won't be able to breathe to play." He closed his eyes and took a deep breath, exhaling slowly to calm himself.

This time he managed to thread and weave the long tie correctly as he spoke. "Of course, the evening is advantageous to me. This is the first time in years that Mr. Pelham has invited me to play flute to his harpsichord for dancing. There is to be an oboe, a French horn, and two violins as well. It will be thrilling to play in a real ensemble again! And it is a happy occasion, after all, since Governor Dunmore is also celebrating the christening of his daughter. Clever of him to name her Virginia, don't you think? That certainly charmed the city. That and his parading back into town last month as conqueror of the Shawnee. I hear he might even have some of his Indian captives there in native dress to entertain his guests. The man is wily. All these displays make citizens forgive what a disagreeable braggart he is.

"Hold the mirror up again, lad, so I can see to this hair. I suppose I should have a wig, but then I would have needed the barber to shave my head. It does make one so cold in the winter."

Basil had washed his hair. Now strands of it stood out every which way as he brushed. He rolled his eyes.

"I am not made for court, Nathaniel. In appearance or conversation. I find it too confusing—our leaders calling the members of Parliament villains at the same time praising Lady Dunmore for her beauty and wit. It is hard to know what opinion is safe."

Nathaniel nodded, agreeing with Basil. It was hard to know what was safe to say or do these days. No matter what the choice, you were sure to offend someone. Conversations with Ben, for instance, were nearly impossible since Ben saw everything in black-and-white absolutes. Anything short of revolution was cowardice or betrayal to him.

Basil put down the brush with a snort, giving up. "Of course, it's not likely that any of the guests would speak to me tonight in any case. Tonight I am simply one of the household servants and slaves."

Out of a box he pulled a gray queue, a long, thick braid of hair, neatly finished with two large black ribbons, a cheaper alternative to a wig. Basil tied the hairpiece on his head with a string. "This cost me a month's wages. It's made of yak hair from Tibet. Goodness knows what human hair would have cost." He stroked it a moment. "Soft, though. Now powder to hide the string."

With a large puff, Basil dusted his head, making a snowstorm of white powder.

111

"*Kerrrrr-ccchoo*! Oh dear, we will have to get this powder off the floor . . . *kerchoo* . . . hand me that rag, Nathaniel . . . *kerchoo* . . . *kerchoo* . . . *kerchoo*." The queue nearly fell off Basil's head as he wheezed.

Nathaniel watched in astonishment. He'd seen fine gentleman thus dressed and powdered, but he'd never before seen the process.

Finally free of sneezes, Basil laughed at himself. "Who needs snuff when one has powder, eh, lad? Know you the song 'The World Turned Upside Down'? They've changed the words to politics recently, but the original words went . . ." He thought a moment, then sang, "'*If boats were on land, churches on sea, if ponies rode men and if grass ate the cows . . . if summer were spring and the other way round, then all the world would be upside down.*' That's how I feel all dandified—completely out of sorts. But, my music will make me a place of belonging. They won't be able to dance without me!"

Basil took a blue wool coat from the bedstead and shook it out before putting it on. It was pleated and long, down to his knees. "There, how do I look?" he asked Nathaniel.

Still like a grasshopper, all arms and legs, thought Nathaniel, but he answered, "Very comely, master."

Basil smiled. "Aye?"

"Aye, sir."

There was a large crash downstairs and the sound of something rolling along the floor. Basil sighed. "Mistress Maguire has been so upset. She's been dropping things all day. She is disappointed not to be invited to the ball. You would think the governor could invite the Maguires since there is only one house between this and his palace gate. Even though the Maguires are from the middling class, this house is as fine as many belonging to the landed gentry.

"But Lord Dunmore obviously follows the European code—only those *born* to privilege may enjoy it. He forgets that America was founded as the land of opportunity, a new world where everyone has the chance to pursue a better life. Work hard and prosper and welcome to the upper class. But tonight, all those ideas seem to have been put away. Tonight, we revert to the old ways."

Another crash and clatter.

Basil sighed. "I had better make my way to the palace, lad. I think my preparations make her feel worse." He picked up the satchel in which he carried his recorder and Nathaniel's German flute. "Wish me good fortune, Nathaniel. Tonight I play for the mighty. And with your flute, I will play all the better." He made a flourishing bow to Nathaniel, as if he were governor, only to catch one of his pleats on the door handle, yanking the door to *thwack* his backside.

"Ah me," mumbled Basil as he made a more humble exit.

Nathaniel almost laughed out loud.

Through the bedroom window, Nathaniel watched Basil walk up the green to the governor's palace. To see Basil go all the way through the ornate gates—with its lion and unicorn statues and royal seal—past the liveried footmen awaiting carriages, Nathaniel pressed his nose to the windowpane. The coldness of the glass startled him into pulling back. Seeing he'd left a nose print, Nathaniel hurriedly polished it away with his shirt sleeve.

Nathaniel stepped back to marvel for the hundredth time at the huge windows, six panes tall and three panes wide. As awe-inspiring as the governor's mansion was, the Maguires' two-story clapboard house had seemed a king's castle to him. With plaster and paint on the inner walls and glass in the windows, the Maguires' home was beyond anything Nathaniel had ever imagined living in. His own cottage in Yorkshire had been cozy, warmed with firelight and his mother's love, but it had been just one large room with a loft. There was nothing to decorate the stone walls. They were the same on the inside as the outside. The floor was dirt; the windows merely open holes, closed up with shutters against the cold.

Night was falling, darkening the room quickly. Nathaniel lit a tallow candle by the small fire flickering in the bedroom's hearth. Resting the pewter candle-holder beside the pitcher basin on the table, he pulled a trundle bed out from underneath Basil's. Having it, too, was an unaccustomed treat. In Yorkshire his mother had stuffed a bedding tick with goose down and sweet-smelling lavender for him, but it lay upon the cold, dirt floor.

He paused, remembering how once, when he was about five years old, a garden snake had crawled into the house and his very bed for warmth. His father had snored through the invasion, refusing to wake. It'd been his delicate mother who'd beaten the snake to death with a fire tong. Then, with her usual calm, she'd rocked Nathaniel back to sleep, singing. He'd never told his mother that she had so astonished him with her sudden ferociousness that for a while he'd been quite afraid of her!

He took off his stockings and breeches, folded them carefully to place on the closet shelf, and quickly slid under the blanket in his shirt and bare feet. Snuggling in, he pulled his mother's Bible out from under his pillow and hugged it to his chest. They might have been poor, subject to garden snakes, damp cold, and hunger, but his childhood cottage still seemed a safer place to

Nathaniel. There he had his mother's love and his parents to make decisions. He knew what to expect. Here the world indeed seemed upside down, on the brink of such upheaval—an upheaval that could swallow up people like Ben and tear apart the little bit of stability Nathaniel knew. What would Basil do if fighting came as Ben predicted and longed for?

Nathaniel closed his eyes against his fear. He imagined playing his flute while his mother listened, her bright blue eyes dancing with joy. He slipped into peaceful Yorkshire dreams.

❧ Chapter Fourteen ❧

"NATHANIEL?" A HAND shook his arm gently.

Dreaming of home, Nathaniel put his own hand over it and sleepily murmured, "A little longer, Mother, please. Sit you awhile beside me."

"Poor lad," said the voice. "It's me—Basil." He cleared his throat and said more loudly: "Nathaniel, I need you to arise."

Nathaniel's eyes popped open. Waking and realizing that it was Basil, not his mother, Nathaniel pushed Basil's hand away. He saw the hurt expression on Basil's face, but he couldn't help the rage he felt that the old man stood where he wanted his mother to be. Even his dreams had to be interrupted—even asleep he wasn't allowed to stay at home where he wanted to be. He bit his tongue to keep from shouting at Basil, at the world: "Why did she have to die? Why did I have to come here?" For a moment his ice-blue eyes glinted with hatred.

Basil sat on his heels. "I understand that look, lad," he said softly. "Someday, perhaps I will explain why." He then spoke in a more matter-of-fact tone. "Never look at Edan that way, Nathaniel. It will earn you a whipping." He stood. "Now, we must do something for Mistress Maguire. Get up and dress quickly. Come down to the parlor."

Dawn was seeping into the house as Nathaniel hesitantly entered the parlor. He'd never before been in the formal room with its painted floor covering of black-and-white checks and its blue-gray chair rails. Beside the polished walnut spinet sat Mrs. Maguire in a high-backed chair. Her eyes were red and puffy. She'd obviously been crying. "I just wanted to hear the music and to see what the ladies wore," she was lamenting to Basil.

"Yes, my dear, I understand. We can play a piece right now, though, as if we were royalty ourselves. And you are a far lovelier person than any of those grand dames in their white lead makeup and paste-on beauty marks. There was one lady whose wig was so big and so weighted down with feathers and jewels that it fell right off during a country dance."

"Oh no, Mr. Wilkinson, you make up stories to make me feel better."

"No, mistress, 'tis true, very. We musicians had a

hard time playing through our laughter. At that point, I'm afraid that all the gentles had had a bit too much rum punch."

He spotted Nathaniel. "Come in, lad. It's all right. Mistress Maguire and I have been practicing this piece by Handel, but it wants a flute and violin to her keyboard. I will play violin and you your flute."

"Nay, master!" Nathaniel cried. "I know not the work."

"Aye, but you read music now. You've worked through all the songs in my flute tutor. We will play the adagio movement, which is slow and simple in melody." He put his arm around Nathaniel's shoulder and drew him out of Mrs. Maguire's hearing. "She plays only so well herself, Nathaniel. This way she will have company in her mistakes. 'Twill make her feel better to help you through it. Understand, lad?"

"But could we not play the Stamitz duet we've learned already for her to hear?"

Basil shook his head. "'Tis one thing to listen to music being performed—a wondrous experience, yes. But it's quite another to brave playing it yourself. It is far better medicine for the soul. Let us do that for her, yes?"

Nervously, Nathaniel blew an A note for Basil to tune his violin. The three instruments only matched intonation so well, but Basil did his best to blend with both the spinet and flute before nodding at Nathaniel to begin. Nathaniel looked at the sheet of lines and black notes before him. When he realized that he was the lead instrument, the first melody voice instead of Basil, the little dots of notes swam before his eyes. Four times Mrs. Maguire played the opening chord that Nathaniel was to follow while he stood dumb, staring at what suddenly seemed a foreign language.

"It's all right, lad," coaxed Basil. "Concentrate."

Nathaniel swallowed and glanced over at Mrs. Maguire. She was staring hard at her music as well, just as unsure. Nathaniel very much wished to please her. She had been so kind. But why was Basil pushing him to try this—performing this piece without practice? This was too hard, too big, too sudden a leap.

"Let us begin again, Nathaniel," Basil said reassuringly. "After all, nothing ventured, nothing gained, eh?"

Nathaniel considered. A person couldn't do something if he didn't even try. Basil was right about that. Nathaniel's recent change in fortune had shown him that even when things seemed hopeless—set like stone in sorrow—there might be a way out, a possibility of change. Still, Nathaniel didn't trust change or braving to hope that it would last. Instead, he expected failure or betrayal—it safeguarded him from disappointment.

But surely this sheet of music was a small enough challenge, wasn't it? One to his head and fingers, not his heart. Couldn't he manage to drum up the courage to play this simple string of notes? Suddenly impatient with himself, Nathaniel felt a desire to shake off his shield of timidity.

He put the flute back to his lips. "Aye, sir." Nathaniel nodded. "I'll try."

Pleased, Basil smiled. "I will count a measure of preparation . . . one, two, three . . ."

Mrs. Maguire rolled out the notes of the chord. This time Nathaniel stepped in with his melody—only five notes in the first phrase, held out long, then trilled, then turned to momentary dissonance, then neatly resolved. Pause, and again. He and Mrs. Maguire's notes circled one another in a slow, dignified turn of song. A measure of rest and then Basil joined in, his line echoing and following Nathaniel's, like birds calling to one another: *answer me, answer me.* The music was an incantation to speak, to express, without having to find the right words, without having to brave eye-to-eye conversation. Even the most shy, the most timid, could take flight—soaring in independent voice, blending together in harmony, then out again in solo. It was a dialogue of sound, of emotions that could remain undefined, and it unlocked something in Nathaniel.

When the adagio ended, Mrs. Maguire had a glow about her as alive and warm as the rose-colored sunrise filling the room. Nathaniel felt bathed in light as well, as a glimmer of confidence dawned inside him.

They played on—a sonata for violin and keyboard by Corelli, another for flute and keyboard by Abel. Now more sure of herself, Mrs. Maguire picked the composer Henry Purcell. It was only when Basil and Nathaniel put down their instruments to listen to her that they realized Edan had slipped into the room in his robe and nightcap. He was sitting in a corner chair. His usual scowl was missing and his eyes were half closed in pleasure. He was even tapping his foot in time with the lively rigadoon his wife was playing.

Tugging on Nathaniel's sleeve, Basil motioned for them to leave. They tiptoed out of the room. The Maguires seemed not to notice.

"A moment of harmony like that," Basil whispered, "is a sacred thing to be relished. Would that it could last. Or that the colonies and England could find the same."

"Perhaps the king and Mr. Randolph should play duets together," Nathaniel murmured.

Both Basil and Nathaniel were startled by Nathaniel's attempt at political wit. They stopped short in the hallway and gazed at each other in surprise. Nathaniel smiled shyly. Basil absolutely beamed.

ೕ Chapter Fifteen ೖ

THE REST OF January passed quickly and quietly. The excitement of the governor's ball vanished. Williamsburg residents disappeared into their burgundy, green, and mustard-colored houses against the cold. Smoke drifted up from their hearths into the pepper-gray skies, the backyard gardens lay barren, winds rattled through the leafless orchards, making a hollow, haunted moan. Those who did walk the mile-long Duke of Gloucester Street did so in businesslike hurry, their woolen capes wrapped snugly around them, their faces so bundled they could take little notice of passersby. Darkness flooded the streets by the late afternoon, and the nights dragged by, lit by tiny, scattered dots of candlelight. There was an air of waiting throughout the town—waiting for spring, waiting to see what would happen next between the king and his colonists.

Mornings dawned icy. When Nathaniel scurried to the stable to feed Edan's horses, milk cow, chickens, and hogs, he often skidded along the path, white with thick-glazed frost or sprinklings of snow. He liked being out as the sun rose, though, to hear the rooster's crow echo through the silence of Palace Green, answered by one, then another neighbor rooster making his own audacious cry to the world. Prodded by these small, arrogant bundles of bright feathers, the town stirred and woke itself. Cows lowed; horses nickered and snorted to clear themselves of sleep. Here and there a door opened and shut as someone came out to feed them. These sounds punctured the crisp air and carried far, a reveille of town life.

By the time he'd finished feeding the livestock and pulling up water from the well for them and the household, Nathaniel's face and hands were red from the cold. He'd gratefully race to the workshop and stir the embers of the great fireplace there to reawaken the warmth of the previous day's fire and feed it with new kindling. His next job was to sweep up the wood shavings that littered the shop's floor and gave the place a wonderful smell of freshly cut wood. Only then would he venture into the kitchen to collect his breakfast of cold ham and corn bread from Sally.

Usually Nathaniel would sit by the shop's hearth to

eat and be long finished before John and Obadjah, Edan's indentured servant and journeyman, came sleepily stumbling down the stairs with Ben. The three shared the room above. But toward the end of the month, Nathaniel discovered them already up and arguing. Obadjah was telling John that he was a fool. John was saying something about the town of Richmond. Ben was babbling about change and begging John to wait for it. They snapped silent when they saw Nathaniel.

Obadjah scowled and brushed past Nathaniel to go to the kitchen. Ben trotted behind, promising to bring back a biscuit for John.

John grinned at Nathaniel. "Morning, lad. Frozen your fingers off yet feeding the swine?" He reached over to count Nathaniel's fingers, purposefully omitting one. "Good God, only nine. Let me count again. Eleven. My oh my. Where did you pick up the extra?" He held up one of his hands, with the thumb tucked behind his palm, making it appear missing. "Hey, give back me thumb!" John joked.

It was a game you might play with a younger child to great effect. Most boys Nathaniel's age would find it quite stupid. But Nathaniel liked John in spite of his resolve to not become attached to anyone in the Maguire household. John had a jolly insolence about him. Along with Ben, he was constantly mimicking Edan's fussy bustle when the master's back was turned. John was a small man, and his thick hair naturally stood up in spikes, much like the hedgehog wigs that gentlemen paid good money for. With such a sassy wit and physical appearance, John had an elflike quality about him. Nathaniel marveled that in his bondage he could be so lighthearted. He wouldn't exactly call him friend—as he had Moses and was beginning to call Basil and Ben—and yet Nathaniel enjoyed John's company.

Moses. With Basil, the flute and books, decent food and clothes, Nathaniel hadn't thought much about Moses recently. He felt a twinge of guilt. He had stopped searching the faces of Williamsburg for Moses. Where Moses had ended up was a mystery. Nathaniel prayed that his situation had improved as much as his own had.

"Hand me one of the spoke shaves, eh, lad?" John settled onto a stool behind the long, thick worktable. Nathaniel went to the back wall where tools were hung—saws, chisels, clamps, files, and felloes, thin curved pieces of wood that served as patterns for portions of the wheel rim. He picked the shaver he knew John preferred.

Each worker—except Nathaniel, who answered anyone's needs—had a specific task within the shop. Back home in London, John had been a wheelwright. It was his job to chisel the wheels, their spokes, and the hub or nave. The hardest part was then putting the three together. John had to carefully cut a mortise, or hole, into the wheel section or hub, then whittle a tenon in the spoke end to make it fit snugly into that hole. He was clever and fast.

Edan's blacksmith then fired the iron hoop to encircle the wooden wheel to protect it against the bumps of Virginia's dirt roads. The blacksmith also produced iron axles that held the wheels together, steel springs, the risers and steps. Obadjah's job was creating the body of the carriage, the delicate Windsor chairs or the wooden and leather closets for closed chariots and coaches.

As the master craftsman, Edan did little hand labor. He drew designs, created the paintings that might decorate the fancier products of the shop, critiqued work, helped tighten joists or finish hubs, and pushed for speed. It had been a long and impressive climb from his own apprenticeship in Dublin. As a result, Edan expected the same kind of drive and focus in his workers that he had had in his youth. He saw no need for compliments to motivate. And having created his own wealth in his own lifetime, Edan was desperately afraid of losing it.

Nathaniel was watching John shave away transparently thin slices of oak to fashion a spoke. "Look here, lad." John pointed to a bump in the wood. "Hardest thing there is . . . to make wood flat. Its natural state as a tree is to bulge and grow as sunlight directs it—not what we tell it."

Once more he pulled the shaver down along the length of the stick of wood, popping his wrists up a bit at the bump to try to nick it out. He ran his finger over the smooth surface and considered a moment. "Well, that's close to perfect. Good enough to stop." He added it to his growing pile of finished spokes.

"That's really the trick of it, Nathaniel, coming to understand when we are close enough to perfection to stop whittling. If we don't recognize when something has become as good as our human hands can make it, and keep fussing over it, we're like to ruin it completely by our meddling. Carve too long and the wood becomes so thin it snaps, worthless. It's the same with life—at some point we have to decide whether a situation is good enough to accept or if we must risk all in the hopes we can hone it better." John drifted off in thought and said more to himself than Nathaniel: "Just like making a spoke . . . "

Nathaniel could sense John was trying to tell him something. He started to press for more when the door to the shop flew open. There stood Edan, swaying, holding a large green bottle.

Glancing up, John's face changed to caution and then to the expressionless mask all servants knew how to put on when their master was in foul mood. "And then, lad," John muttered, "there are times to break that spoke and completely start anew."

✑ Chapter Sixteen ✑

UNSTEADILY, EDAN STEPPED through the door and stomped to his desk. He sat down with a thump, crashing the bottle to the tabletop. He turned to stare out the window with a loud sniff, rubbing his nose with his coat sleeve.

"Keep your head down, lad," John whispered, "and get to work."

Grabbing the broom, Nathaniel began sweeping the shavings John had made. He picked up tools that had been left lying about and hung them. He brought in and stacked kindling, making as little noise as possible to avoid attracting attention.

Not knowing he was there, Obadjah and Ben made the mistake of reentering the shop, calling out to John that there was trouble afoot. John shook his head at them, but it was too late. Edan swung around and fixed his temper on them. "What say you, curs? Trouble? Whose trouble?"

Obadjah hesitated, his mind obviously racing to find something to claim as trouble other than the obvious— Edan himself.

Ben came up with a ruse first: "I . . . I . . . I . . . I hear that the *Virginia Gazette* . . . yes, the *Gazette* . . . the *Gazette* printed a letter from Parliament that forbids our importing gunpowder. . . . The redcoats clearly fear our arming ourselves. . . ." Then he couldn't help himself: "It's outrageous, sir, that's what it is. How can we continue to tolerate such tyranny?"

John and Obadjah rushed to interrupt Ben, knowing his patriot indignation would infuriate Edan.

"What will happen if savages attack Williamsburg and we have no gunpowder?" John moaned, throwing his hands up dramatically. He made a face at Obadjah to prompt him to chime in with something.

Obadjah looked confused, then babbled, "Or . . . or . . . or pirates. That's right—pirates! Pirates could make their way up from North Carolina and kill us all in our sleep!"

For a moment, Edan looked baffled. The news of Parliament forbidding powder imports was two weeks old. Some people had been in an uproar over it, but most Williamsburg residents were unruffled, knowing that the brick octagonal magazine in Market Square was loaded full of gunpowder and several thousand Brown Bess muskets.

"I know that!" roared Edan. He squinted at Ben. "You will not be one of these idiot patriots. Hear me? If I find you participating in treasonous activities or standing about talking trouble, I will . . . I will," he blustered, "I will do such things to you that you'll wish you'd never been born."

He shouted at all of them: "I am trying to stay neutral in this mess so that anyone—loyalist, patriot, innocent bystander like me—who wants a carriage will still come to me. If politics prevent business, I'm done for. I may have signed that Non-importation Agreement, but I did so under unjust pressure, I tell you."

Nathaniel held his breath, watching Ben, fearing he would argue. Ben looked down, but his face flamed red with hatred. Obadjah nodded obediently. John's grip tightened on the tool he still held.

"Get to work!"

"Aye, master," they all muttered.

Obadjah set to mixing paint. Ben helped. Obadjah had recently completed a chair to sit atop a riding platform. With ten delicately rounded spindles in the back and curved arms, the Windsor chair could easily grace a house, much less a carriage. Obadjah had painstakingly painted the chair a deep forest green. Now he was about to add a yellow trim stripe to accentuate the bit of paneling he had carved at the base of the chair.

As a journeyman, Obadjah had completed his apprenticeship and was almost a free man. Within a year, his labor for Edan would be done. Then he could set up his own shop. He had been saving money toward that day, wearing threadbare clothes and broken-open shoes that exposed his blue woolen stockings. Unlike John, who was owned by Edan during his indentureship, Obadjah received a small commission for his work. As he'd fashioned the chair, he'd talked constantly about the four pounds that Edan would owe him upon its completion.

Obadjah carefully measured golden lumps into a bowl and crushed them into powder with an apothecary mortar and pestle. Ben poured in thick, sticky oil while Obadjah stirred.

"Have a care not to waste that," barked Edan, taking a sip from his bottle.

"Yes, sir."

Edan swung back around to look out the window. It was sooty from the fire's smoke. "Clean that," he shouted at Nathaniel.

Nathaniel found a clean cloth and water. As he passed Edan, he caught the strong, sweet scent of cherry brandy. Nathaniel knew that the Maguires had a large supply of brandy, gin, rum, and cordials for sale. He had often been sent down into the cool, dark cellar to retrieve bottles for customers. There was nothing unusual in it. Many Williamsburg tradesmen sold things from their homes that were completely different from their main craft. The organist and jailer Peter Pelham, for instance, sold ivory combs, buttons, and shoe buckles. Mrs. Maguire also took ladies' measurements for a New York City stay maker.

But Nathaniel had never seen Edan drink any of that liquor before. Many a person consumed ale at midday meal, but certainly no God-fearing person was drinking at this early hour. Something must be terribly wrong. He wished he could escape to the house and find Basil. Basil always seemed to know what was afoot.

Edan continued to mutter: "Have to sell them cheap. And for cash only. That's all there is for it. A pox upon that man. All dressed in his finery and wanting the fastest carriage possible. How can he order a phaeton worth seventy-five pounds and then once I've built it say he can't pay?"

Nathaniel gasped. That phaeton had taken them weeks to complete and was a gorgeous thing. The two-man seat was leathered and soft, perched atop the front two wheels. With larger back wheels, the phaeton could move like lightning when drawn by four good horses. Edan had carefully painted the wheels and body in burgundy and gold, giving it a rich appearance. It was not something that an ordinary townsperson would just walk in and purchase. It was meant for show and the rich.

Edan looked over to John and Obadjah. "What have we in the storage house?" he asked.

"Excuse me, sir?" Obadjah answered.

"What carriages have we completed and are awaiting purchase?"

"The new post chariot, and a number of chairs, single and double. And, of course, the phaeton," John spoke up. "That be our best work this year, sir."

"Aye," Edan said with self-pity. "Aye, some of the best work I've ever done." He took another drink and sniffled again. "The *gentleman*"—he spat out the word—"won't pay. He says the coming embargo of tobacco will bankrupt him. He can no longer afford the phaeton. Two others who owed me more than a hundred pounds between them have sailed for England without warning, saying they fear for their property and their lives among these blackheart rebels. And I doubt that Norfolk shipping merchant will pay me for his chair, either, since he deals mostly in English goods that now no one will buy.

"That's near three hundred pound I'm owed, never to be had thanks to these accursed patriots. I might as well burn the shop for all the good my hard work does me." He looked as if he might cry.

Silence hung like the tools on the wall—sharp, potentially dangerous—as Edan sniffed and swigged.

Finally, anxious about his own future, Obadjah couldn't stand the suspense. "Master, you will still pay me for this chair I've just done? My time with you is up this summer. I have plans to set up my own shop and I—"

"Plans to set up shop, eh? Steal my business, eh?" Edan heaved himself up. "Like that ungrateful Canadian living near the madhouse who left my employ then besmirched my name whenever he had a chance? Must I deal with yet another dog I've trained nipping at my heels?"

Enraged, Edan reached for an axe hanging on the wall.

Safe in a corner by the window, Nathaniel froze in terror. John jumped back from his stool, knocking it over. "Look out, Obadjah," he shouted. "Run, Ben!"

Ben bolted toward the door, but Obadjah stood rooted by his precious chair, paintbrush in hand.

In six long, staggering strides, Edan reached him.

Heaving up the axe, he brought it down with a crash, splitting the beautiful Windsor seat in half, splinters flying.

"That's what it feels like to work hard and be cheated." He swung the blade again and cracked the chair back down the middle.

"Betrayed!" He sliced a chair arm in two.

"Promises broken!" He hacked at the legs. "Dreams destroyed!"

"Stop!" Obadjah finally screamed. "Stop it!"

Edan kept swinging the axe. John rushed to pull Obadjah back. With a brave lurch, he pushed Edan so that he stumbled and fell into the table. "Go to, sir. Enough!" he shouted.

Stunned, breathing hard, still clutching the blade, Edan suddenly seemed to sober. He looked at the axe in his hand, frowned, shook his head, and then slowly took in the scene of the room, as if seeing it for the first time. The chair, its wreckage, John, Ben, Obadjah. When he turned to look at Nathaniel, Edan dropped the axe to the floor and covered his face. "Don't look at me with those eyes!"

After a moment, he lifted his head. He seemed ashamed, disgusted, confused. In a hoarse voice, he croaked, "I . . . I am sorry. . . . I don't know what came over me. . . . I . . . " With a sob, Edan rushed from the shop.

That night, John Hunter ran away.

PART FIVE

February 1775

When Britons first by Heaven's command,
   Arose from out the azure main,
This was the charter of the land,
And guardian angels sung this strain:
   Rule Britannia, rule the waves
   Britons never will be slaves.

To spread bright freedom's gentle sway,
   Your isle too narrow for its bound,
We trac'd wild ocean's trackless way,
And here a safe asylum found.
   Rule Britannia, rule the waves,
   But rule us justly, not like slaves.

While we were simple, you grew great;
  Now swell'd with luxury and pride.
You pierce our peaceful, fine retreat,
And haste t'enslave us with great stride.
    Rule Britannia, rule the waves,
    But rule us justly, not like slaves.

With justice and with wisdom reign,
  We then with thee will firmly join,
To make thee mistress of the main,
And every shore it circles thine.
    Rule Britannia, rule the waves
    But ne'er degrade your sons to slaves.

For thee we'll toil with cheerful heart.
  We'll labour but we will be free.
Our growth and strength to thee impart,
And all our treasures bring to thee.
    Rule Britannia, rule the waves.
    We're subjects, but we're not your slaves.

—American words to British patriot song
"Rule Britannia"

Chapter Seventeen

"**HERE, LAD.**" Mrs. Maguire handed Nathaniel a scrap of paper. "Go to the *Gazette* office. Ask that they publish this notice." She started to give him a coin to pay for the advertisement, but held it back to her chest, looking at him pointedly. "There will be change. Bring it straight back to me."

"Yes, mistress. That I will," Nathaniel reassured her.

Her eyebrow arched, she placed the coin in his hand and closed his fingers around it. "Straight back."

"Aye." He nodded and scurried out into the street.

The household had been in an uproar since John's running off. Every servant was viewed with suspicion. After witnessing how violent Edan could become, all of them were trying to avoid being interrogated by Edan about John's whereabouts.

Nathaniel had found the charred remains of a note in the shop's fireplace the morning John disappeared.

It read: "Edan Maguire, carriage maker, has authorized John Hunter to travel to Richmond to deliver a chaise." The ink was blotted and smeared. John obviously had been trying to forge a pass to get through the slave patrols that kept watch for runaways. He must have thrown this one out to make another, cleaner one.

Nathaniel was staring at the note, wondering what to do with it, when Ben came up from behind. Ben snatched it away. "Not thinking of handing that over to Master Maguire, were you?" he'd snapped, without any of his usual good-natured jests.

"N-n-no." Nathaniel was no telltale. "But what if master questions me? What am I to say? If he thinks I know something—like about this pass—he might beat me to know it."

With disgust, Ben took a step back from Nathaniel. "Then let him beat you. Are you really that weak? I thought you were just shy and mightily abused in your past, Nathaniel. I didn't figure you for a plain and simple coward." He crumpled the paper in his fist. "If you tell Edan about this, he'll know exactly where to find John. If John's caught, for each day he's run, a month is added to his indentureship. Captured after a fortnight out, and there's a year more on his bondage. If you tell about this pass, you're locking chains on John. You must stand by friends. Would you also betray me so easily for fear of a harsh word?" Ben's voice was full of contempt, his expression the same he might have when tossing kitchen slops to the pigs.

Nathaniel hung his head. He just wanted to stay out of trouble, that's all. Why should he stand up for someone else? His own father hadn't protected him. But still, seeing Ben's reaction, he was ashamed. Nathaniel knew his mother would never have placed her own welfare above someone else's, especially someone she cared for. "'Love bears all things . . .'" she'd have said. And Basil had stepped in to save him from the blacksmith without even knowing Nathaniel.

Nathaniel looked up at Ben with his eyes full of self-hatred and sorrow. What had he allowed himself to become?

For a long, withering minute, Ben glared at him. Then, slowly, as Nathaniel held his gaze, Ben softened. He sighed with impatience. "You must learn to stand by your friends, Nat. We must all steel ourselves. After the Continental Congress met, someone drew a picture of a snake cut up into segments. Each segment was named for a colony—Virginia, New York, Pennsylvania. Underneath it there was a caption: 'United we stand, divided we fall.' It's true. We have to stick together in Edan's shop just as sure as the colonies need to bind fast. John could no longer endure Edan's moods and tyranny—just like the people of Boston. Someday soon they are going to crack under the lobsterbacks and fight back. When they do, Virginia will follow.

"I had hoped that John would stay to join in our fight. But he chose to run now to secure his own freedom instead. That's all right. Liberty called to him in a different voice than it does me." He was quiet, as if convincing himself not to be disappointed.

After a moment Ben continued, "Ten years ago, before he died, my father helped lead Virginians against the Stamp Act. Patrick Henry and Spencer Monroe—the father of my friend James—wrote out a petition protesting the tax's violation of our rights. My father helped them collect signatures to it. He also convinced our neighbors to not purchase anything that carried the British stamp. I was only six at the time, but I remember my father risked jail doing so. But it was worth it. By banding together, we forced Parliament to repeal the Stamp Act.

"My father would never run away from trouble. So I won't either. I'm going to stand right here and demand that we be treated justly. We are in the right no matter how hard the redcoats bear down on us. That's the real mistake the British have made—trying to force us."

He closed his eyes and recited: "'The God who gave us

life gave us liberty at the same time. The hand of force may destroy but cannot disjoin them.' That's what Mr. Jefferson said. I memorized it. Don't you feel it, Nat?"

Ben seemed very tall suddenly.

Nathaniel felt like a worm. The thought of escaping or demanding his release from indentureship had never occurred to Nathaniel. He hated to admit it, but once . . . no, twice . . . he'd thought of freeing himself a completely different way. He'd thought of throwing himself into the York River to end his misery at the plantation. It was Moses who had seen him on the cliff and called him back. After all the good fortune that had befallen Nathaniel since, that thought now did seem gutless and foolish.

Seeing Nathaniel so thoughtful, Ben patted his shoulder. "There's a good lad." Ben threw the forged pass into the fire and waited until it turned into a blackened ash that drifted up and out the chimney.

As the paper disappeared in flames, Nathaniel resolved to burn the information it held from his mind as well, making it impossible for him to reveal it no matter what Edan did to him.

Ben continued to stare into the flames. "That reminds me to visit James at the college. When his father died, James's uncle was able to send him to William and Mary. When my father died, I was sent here to labor for Edan Maguire." He picked up the tongs and began jabbing at the fire. "I'll prove that I'm just as good as those who can still afford frilled shirts and new boots. I may only be an apprentice, but I can do my part."

Outside on the street, Nathaniel realized he now held another piece of paper that could endanger John. His walk to the *Gazette*, published by Maria Rind's family, would be a short one—right onto Palace Green, left at Bruton Parish Church, and then just past the courthouse, the magazine, and Mr. Chowning's Tavern. The wintry day was bone-chilling, yet Nathaniel slowed to read the notice:

> *Run away from the subscriber, in Williamsburg, an indented servant man, named John Hunter, a native of London, about five feet high, speaks very quick, and has a comical, sly, squinting look, and a bushy head of hair; had on, when he went away, a dark, drab short coat. Whoever secures the said servant in any of his majesty's gaols, so that I may have him again, shall have ten shillings, or twenty shillings for bringing him home.*
>
> *I suspect he may be lurking somewhere about Richmond."*
>
> *E. Maguire*

Twenty shillings! There'd be many a man who'd hunt John down for twenty shillings. Oh, how Nathaniel wished he could simply lose the note on his way to the newspaper.

He stopped abruptly in the middle of the street. Several carts nearly ran over him. If Nathaniel could only purchase John some time, John could lose himself on the frontier. West beyond Richmond rolled the Blue Ridge's mysterious wilds. That's clearly why John was heading that way. There was little need for wheel-wrights in the outpost of Richmond.

What would Ben do with this advertisement?

He certainly would not stand by idly as Nathaniel would like to. Would he throw it out? Rewrite it? He'd likely do something bold and stupid that would only land them all into a cauldron of trouble. What about Basil? Basil's courage seemed to come out in the face of unkindness. Bringing John back was unkind, wasn't it? Certainly. But how could Nathaniel betray Mistress Maguire, who had been nothing but kind to him?

Nathaniel rubbed his forehead with frustration. This was precisely the kind of daunting and dangerous choice he had never, *ever* wanted to make.

He stood agonizing over what to do, quivering with cold and confusion. There was no way that he could avoid delivering the advertisement. If he did, the

Maguires would simply write a new one and take it themselves, more than like, no longer trusting Nathaniel with the errand. But—Nathaniel finally felt a solution hit him like the February wind—he could at least stop potential bounty hunters from knowing to look for John in Richmond.

Breathing hard with nervousness, Nathaniel tore off the bottom of the notice and Edan's suspicion that John was "lurking about Richmond." This way people might start looking for him at Norfolk wharfs or even the borders of North Carolina—giving John enough time to vanish into the mountains.

Nathaniel would just pray that Edan wouldn't notice the omission. He refused to think about what would happen if he did. Nathaniel walked on. Feeling both strong and absolutely terrified, he had the vague recognition that the decision to help John completely changed the way he navigated the world. Like Gulliver, Nathaniel had stepped onto a foreign land with no familiar compass to guide him.

∽ Chapter Eighteen ∽

THE RIND-PINKNEY VIRGINIA GAZETTE was printed in an impressive, two-story brick home. Like many of the houses in Williamsburg, it was rented by the owner to tradesmen who lived and worked their craft in the same building. As he knocked on the door, Nathaniel heard voices and the thumps and bumps of business being done inside. Maria opened the door. She blushed when she saw Nathaniel, who stood gawky and silent, letting the cold air rush through the door to rattle Maria's skirts.

When he realized she was shivering from the frigid blast, Nathaniel reached up to tip his round hat as he'd seen gentlemen do in respect to ladies in town. But instead he knocked it off his head to her feet. Terrified it would blow away, he dove for it, nearly tackling her. When he popped back up, hat in hand, they almost cracked heads.

A brood of children saved him from his embarrassment by suddenly emerging from inside, crying, "Who is it, who is it?"

"A . . . a . . . subscriber?" Maria provided Nathaniel's answer.

"Yes, miss. I have brought a notice from the Maguires. One of their servants has run off."

"Goody!" The littlest one clapped his hands and danced about.

Maria shushed him and reddened again. Nathaniel guessed that her family was having money difficulties as well. With five young orphaned children to care for, Maria's cousin, John Pinkney, had his hands full. Nathaniel knew that a number of people rented rooms in the house to cut some of the family's housing costs. He wondered too if the paper's strong voice for freedom was losing them readers.

"Come in," said Maria. "There is still time to set type for this issue."

Nathaniel followed Maria into a room crammed with tall, wide printing presses and stacks of paper. There, her cousin Pinkney, an apprentice a few years older than Nathaniel, and a slave were preparing the Thursday broadsheet.

Pinkney was pulling out individual letters from rows and rows of tiny lead squares in a compartmented wooden box. One by one he placed them along a long iron ruler. He squinted as he worked. When Nathaniel drew closer, he could see why. The letters were no bigger than a black carpenter ant, and backward!

Seeing how puzzled Nathaniel looked, Pinkney laughed. "It is confusing having words in reverse. I must lay out the entire sentence like that—backward—spelling a word like 'the' as 'eht.' That's because when we press the paper down onto the galley, the printing reverses the image. I really have to mind my ps and qs because they appear almost identical reversed."

He wiped his inky hands on his apron and reached for Nathaniel's note, obviously glad for a break. "Ah, perfect! I had a hole in this column. I'll place your notice in between the one about a strayed horse and the one about a found slave."

Pinkney counted up the letters and spaces in the notice. "Maria, can you take care of payment, please?"

"Yes, of course." She gestured for Nathaniel to follow her into the next room, which was filled with books and pamphlets for sale. "That will come to three bits, Nathaniel." She caught herself and blushed again. "Is it all right if I call you Nathaniel?"

Maria's dark, soulful eyes met Nathaniel's. "Oh my," she whispered, probably not realizing she spoke aloud, "what beautiful eyes."

Nathaniel felt like telling her she could call him by whatever name she wanted. But instead he cleared his throat and stammered out, "Y-y-y-yes."

Her smile was sweet. "You may call me Maria then."

Nathaniel ducked his head and stuck out his hand with the coin, hot and sweaty from his nervousness. Maria weighed it and cut the coin in quarters, giving back one triangle slice to Nathaniel.

"Thank you, miss, ah, Maria." Nathaniel began to back out of the room, squishing the brim of his hat.

"Would you like to see your notice laid out?" Maria stalled his departure.

Nathaniel nodded. They entered the pressroom again. By now one of the pages was completely composed in a frame. The apprentice was applying ink to the type by "beating" the laid-out letters with leather balls stuffed with wool on sticks that he had smeared with black ink.

Pinkney wasn't quite finished laying out Edan's notice. "Your master always writes long," he commented. "A year or two ago he had quite a battle with an old journeyman of his in our newspaper. I remember a lot of name-calling and a challenge between them to each make a carriage and then let the public pick the best. A contest to decide who was the better artisan. But nothing came of it, as I recall. A bit of a hothead, is he not?"

Nathaniel didn't know what to say. Criticize his master in public? He might risk punishment to help John, but gossiping about Edan was simply foolhardy.

Maria frowned at her cousin and changed the subject. "Here, Nathaniel, I have learned to read backward. I can tell you what this notice says, if you like?"

Nathaniel nodded, grateful to avoid answering about Edan.

"Let's see." She puzzled a moment. "'d-e-t-t-i-m-m-o-c. Committed . . . to the public jail, a . . . y-a-w-a-n-u-r . . . runaway . . .' Wait a moment. Watch this, it's like magic." She reached under the counter on which Pinkney worked and pulled out a small mirror. She positioned it to reflect the type, now reading forward in the mirror. Slowly, for she was not a fluid reader, she spoke: "'Committed to the public jail, a runaway slave named Moses, says he belongs—'"

"Wait, did you say Moses?" Nathaniel's heart started to beat wildly. In America, there were many Africans named Moses, he knew. But could this be his friend? He fought the desire to grab the mirror from Maria.

"Yes." She nodded.

"Please," he urged her, "please read the rest."

"'A runaway slave named Moses, says he belongs to a plantation in Surry County on the James River, but will tell no more. He is unusually tall, close to six feet, very muscular and strong. . . .'"

Yes, that's right, thought Nathaniel. *Incredibly strong.*

"'On his forehead is a scar shaped like a crescent moon. . . .'"

Nathaniel gasped. It had to be Moses. He snatched the mirror from Maria to finish: "'. . . a scar shaped like a crescent moon; had on when he was taken up a mint-colored broadcloth coat, double-breasted scarlet waistcoat, and a pair of buckskin breeches.'" Nathaniel remembered those clothes. They were Moses's Sunday clothes. "'His owner is desired to apply for him, pay charges, and take him away. Peter Pelham.'"

Peter Pelham. That meant Moses was in the Williamsburg jail!

Nathaniel managed to shove the mirror back into Maria's hand before he was out the door, running.

⹂Chapter Nineteen〞

THE WILLIAMSBURG JAIL was a grim place. On the opposite side of town from the Maguires' home, just north of the Capitol, the prison was surrounded by a tall brick wall. Within the exercise yard behind it, pirates, thieves, murderers, debtors, and runaways might be let out of their cells to walk for a few minutes—their view limited to the red bricks holding them in, the filth and dirt at their feet, and the sky above. Until recently the insane had been housed there, too. Their screams and pleas for mercy or to the phantoms that plagued them pierced Nicholson Street, strangely mixing in with the everyday sounds of passing carts, cows, gardening, and conversation among neighbors.

Attached to the prison was a two-story house. There lived the jailer—the acclaimed organist of Bruton Parish Church, Peter Pelham—with his wife and their flock of children. Pelham regularly took a prisoner to church to pump the bellows that operated the organ while he played. It was to his front door that Nathaniel ran. A sour smell of sewage, trampled mud, and rotting garbage hung about the place. Mrs. Pelham answered Nathaniel's knock, balancing a baby on her hip and soothing a sniffling toddler clinging to her apron.

"Please, ma'am," Nathaniel asked, panting from his run. "You hold a slave, named Moses. May I speak to him, please?"

With a weary face, Mrs. Pelham looked him over. "Have you come from his owner to claim him? You'll want more strength than is in you, child, to get him back to his master. He put up quite a fight when the sheriff brought him in."

"No, ma'am. I'm just a . . . a . . . a friend," he blurted out the word.

Mrs. Pelham frowned. Nathaniel realized too late that whites were not supposed to be "friends" with slaves, especially one who had run away and caused trouble for the jailer. But he sensed compassion in her. "I used to work with him before. We . . . we were . . . we spent a great deal of time together then."

"Where do you belong now?"

"To Basil . . ." He corrected himself. "I work in Edan Maguire's shop."

"The governor's carriage maker?"

Nathaniel hesitated, not knowing whether that bit of information would help or harm his hope to see Moses. But there was no way around the answer. "The carriage maker, aye, mistress," he muttered.

Mrs. Pelham nodded, seemingly impressed.

"Up . . . want up," the small child whined, holding his hands toward her. She sighed and somehow managed to gather him up and balance him on her other hip. "I'm not sure that Mr. Pelham would allow this, but he's at the church right now. Come. I will leave you with him for a few minutes. I've my young ones to tend to. When I come back, though, you must leave straight-aways."

Nathaniel followed her out of the wintry sunlight, through a large room, down stairs into darkness. He put his hand along the wall to steady himself and felt dampness and moss growing along it.

"Here the rascal is." Mrs. Pelham put down her children, who both began wailing, to pull a large key off the wall. She unlocked a heavy wooden door.

Nathaniel gasped. Inside, lying facedown on straw was Moses, chained to the wall by leg irons.

"He is too strong," Mrs. Pelham said softly. "He needed to be contained." She handed Nathaniel a bowl filled with a nasty-smelling salve of turpentine oil. "His face and arms are bruised. I was afeared to try putting it on his cuts. Mayhap he'll let you." She disappeared, carrying her infants, their cries escorting her retreat.

Nathaniel tiptoed in, more out of fear of the place than of making noise. "Moses," he whispered. "It's Nathaniel. Wake up, Moses."

Moses lifted his head. Nathaniel bit his lip to keep from crying out in dismay. Moses's eyes were nearly swollen shut they were so bruised. His mouth was split open on one side. There was no recognition in his bloodshot eyes.

"Moses, don't you know me? It's Nathaniel, from the York River."

Moses looked at him blankly.

"Let me put this balm on that cut, Moses. It wants physick to heal." Nathaniel scrapped up a dollop of the sticky salve and spread it on Moses's chin.

"Nathaniel?" Moses finally spoke in a raspy voice.

"Aye, Moses. What happened? Why did you run away?"

"I could stand bondage no more, Nathaniel. I could not. My new master teach me to pilot boats, up and down the James River and into the Chesapeake Bay. He were kind enough, but the hours on the tides, they spoke to me. You feel so free on the waters, Nathaniel. That river comes and goes, pulling, going the way it wants. And on the bay I could see to the ocean and the way to my homeland. If the waters have their own mind, why can I not?"

Moses was sitting up straight now, his voice growing stronger as he spoke. "There was a good woman among us, name of Lucy. She finished what you start. She taught me to read, Nathaniel. She's a slave, too, but she lived in Williamsburg when she were young. Her master sent her to the Bray School, where they learned black children, free and slave, to read. So, she been teaching me. She used the good book to learn me, Nathaniel. I learn about Moses, the man my mama call me for. I learn how he show up the pharaoh and set his people free. Why didn't you tell me about Moses, Nathaniel?"

Nathaniel hadn't even connected his friend with the biblical hero. Perhaps in those days, when Nathaniel was so sad, so beaten down, he couldn't contemplate the Old Testament story of escape and salvation. "I'm sorry," Nathaniel said, although as he looked at Moses in chains, he wondered if his friend had been well served by the knowledge.

"Moses"—Nathaniel choked out the words—"did

your master do this to you?"

"Nay, Nathaniel. It was the slave hunter. A foul man I pray God punishes."

Nathaniel looked about the cell. All it held beside the chains and the straw was a bucket of water. A barred, open window let in a trickle of sunlight and an ocean of cold. He began to shiver, a chill washing into his bones and heart.

"Cold, boy?" Moses asked. "You never was hardy enough." He tried to reach out to rub circulation back into Nathaniel's arms, but his chains clattered and stopped him. "But you look better than when we was parted, Nathaniel. Where you be?"

In ease and luxury by comparison, Nathaniel thought. He was suddenly flooded with unchecked gratitude toward Basil. And wasn't it just like Moses, as he lay locked in prison, to worry over Nathaniel. He told Moses about Basil and Edan. Moses nodded, pleased. "Near the governor palace, you said?"

"Yes."

"How close?"

"One house down. Before you reach the brick house belonging to Mr. Wythe."

Moses thought a moment, as if memorizing the location.

"Moses, what will happen to you now?"

"They take me back."

"What then?"

Moses shrugged. "Twenty lashes for the last man what run. That's all."

"That's all?" Nathaniel gasped.

Moses smiled and then winced, holding a hand up to his battered mouth. "A lash may cut my skin, but it can't hurt me no more, boy. Not now my mind be free."

Footsteps approached. Mrs. Pelham appeared. "I've just been told that his master is sending for him tomorrow. Best say your good-byes."

Nathaniel fought off sudden, childlike tears. He struggled to ask: "Can I do something for you, Moses?" But he knew there was no helping Moses here, today. But in the tomorrows ahead? Surely those calling for liberty for themselves would think to include slaves like Moses in their cause—if patriots took up the fight, if Moses could stand bondage until then.

Moses shook his head. He gestured to Nathaniel to come closer and whispered into his ear. "The Lord will show us the way to the promised land. I'm going to follow. You do, too."

That night without warning, without quite realizing

what he was doing, Nathaniel caught up to Basil and hugged him around the waist from behind, darting away again, out the door to the horses before he could see the old man's joy.

PART SIX

April 1775

Come, join hand in hand, brave Americans all,
And rouse your bold hearts at fair Liberty's call;
No tyrannous acts shall suppress your just claim,
Or stain with dishonor America's name.

Our worthy forefathers, let's give them a cheer,
To climates unknown did courageously steer;
Thro' oceans to deserts for Freedom they came,
And dying, bequeath'd us their freedom and fame.

The tree their own hands had to Liberty rear'd.
They lived to behold growing strong and revered;
With transport they cried, Now our wishes we gain,
For our children shall gather the fruits of our pain.

Then join hand in hand, brave Americans all,
By uniting we stand, by dividing we fall;
In so righteous a cause let us hope to succeed,
For heaven approves of each generous deed.

—"The Liberty Song," words set by patriot
John Dickinson as a parody of the English
song "Heart of Oak"

✑ Chapter Twenty ✑

"OH, TO HAVE been there, Nathaniel!" Basil sighed. "To have heard him! His words were so stirring that one of the men leaning through the window of the church to listen has requested to be buried underneath that window when he dies."

Basil had wandered out to the stable to find Nathaniel to talk about Patrick Henry for about the hundredth time. For the past weeks, the town had discussed little else than Henry's March twenty-third speech to the Virginia Convention. The fiery Henry had demanded that the colony raise troops to defend itself in case Britain used military force to stop their protests. At first he was dismissed. Despite the harsh occupation of Boston, despite the British warship anchored at Burwell's Landing just outside Williamsburg, leaders like Peyton Randolph stubbornly held on to the belief that reasonable legal arguments plus the trade embargo would convince the king to recognize American rights.

But Henry wouldn't give up. He thundered that the colonists had done all they could to avoid fighting. They had "petitioned, remonstrated, and prostrated themselves before the throne." Still, Parliament refused to listen and only sent navies and armies to suppress them. "If we wish to be free . . . we must fight!" he'd shouted.

Basil had been to the Raleigh Tavern and heard bits and pieces of Henry's already legendary speech.

"They say no one stirred as Mr. Henry spoke, they hardly breathed, listening to him. Can you imagine having that kind of effect? It's the power of words, Nathaniel, the power of words! Never forget it."

Nathaniel smiled as he brushed to pull away the horse's itchy, hot winter fur. Although his back was turned to Basil, he knew the old tutor's eyes were glossy with an awed rapture. Basil was like that about words.

"A man who'd witnessed it acted out Mr. Henry's speech. Mr. Henry said we must replace 'the illusion of hope' with 'the lamp of experience.' He went on: 'Gentlemen may cry peace, peace, but there is no peace. The next gale that sweeps from the north will bring to our ears the clash of resounding arms! Our brethren are already in the field.'

"Then Mr. Henry slumped, with his hands crossed before him as if shackled, and cried out, 'Why stand we here idle? Is life so dear, or peace so sweet, as to be purchased at the price of chains and slavery? Forbid it, Almighty God!'

"Mr. Henry held his arms up toward heaven like this"—Basil reached for the sky—"and ended: 'I know not what course others may take; but as for me, give me liberty, or give me death.'" Basil pulled out each word of the last sentence like a drumbeat.

He dropped his hands. "Oh Nathaniel, what a man! What a mind! What a speech!"

Somewhere during the course of Basil's description Nathaniel had turned, currycomb quiet, himself spellbound by Patrick Henry's dramatic call for action, just as Virginia's lawmakers had been. In the end, Henry's impassioned words pushed the Virginia Convention to muster two regiments of infantry. Everywhere men were beginning to gather rifles, muskets, even Indian tomahawks to join up.

Flushed with inspiration, Basil remained motionless, staring off into air. "The recruits will wear hunting shirts as uniforms at first. On those shirts, men are embroidering Henry's words: 'Liberty or death.' Think Nathaniel! Those words will march straight into battle and be the banner that steadies men under fire. Those words may create a new nation—a nation of hope, of fairness, of equality!"

He lapsed into silence. Nathaniel turned back to the horse but he, too, was lost in thought—about the choice Patrick Henry was calling for. About the choice Moses and John Hunter had made.

A chance that Obadjah had taken as well, on the very day that Patrick Henry stirred so many souls. Perhaps encouraged by John's escape, Obadjah decided he also had had enough of Edan's tirades.

Absentmindedly, Nathaniel laid the currycomb on the horse's neck. It stamped its hoof impatiently, waiting.

Liberty or death. Is life so dear as to be purchased at the price of chains?

What had happened to Moses when he was returned to his owner? Had John made it to liberty? There had been no word of him. Hopefully escape would be easier for him and for Obadjah, men of the same skin color as European noblemen. When poor Moses had fled, it had been easy to spot him. There were freed Africans in Virginia, yes, but they were few. Moses must have stood out like a comet in the night sky.

Nathaniel began to brush the horse again.

Basil broke into Nathaniel's musing. His voice was changed, the enthusiasm over Henry's oratory gone. "How old are you now, lad?"

Nathaniel stopped his combing. He hadn't thought about that in the longest time. If it were April . . . "What month is it, master?" he asked.

"April, mid-through."

"Aye?" Nathaniel suddenly remembered small celebrations of his birthday—his mother finding honey to make sweet cakes, her hugging him and whispering that the day of his birth had been the most glorious of her life. Even his father had managed a few compliments that day, led by her example. He had always wanted to please her.

A new thought came to Nathaniel about his father—a thought that made him freeze mid-stroke. Would his father ever consider running from his indentureship as John and Obadjah had? If he did, would he come take Nathaniel?

In a torrent of confusion, Nathaniel looked at Basil. Would such liberty be worth the price of leaving Basil, his books, his music?

Basil's voice barely came to Nathaniel through the storm suddenly raging in his mind. "How old are you, lad?"

Nathaniel merely stared.

"Nathaniel?" Basil prompted.

His father would never come. Never. Why would he? Nathaniel shook off the idea and tried to focus on

Basil. "Excuse me, sir?"

"I asked how old you are."

"Oh! Fourteen, master. Just. On the fourth of this month." The day had passed without Nathaniel even recognizing it.

"Why, happy birthday, lad!" Basil said happily. Then in hushed voice, he added, "I am glad you are so young."

"Why, master?"

"We may be washed in blood, lad, if it comes to war. King George has thousands of well-trained troops, plus Hessians he purchased from German princes. Those mercenary soldiers are ruthless. We have but a handful of militia, only a few of them experienced, and that in the French and Indian War, mostly under British commanders.

"There was a great deal of discussion about this last night at the Raleigh Tavern. No one knows who we'd have to command an army against the British. Take George Washington, for instance. He's the Virginian with the most battle experience. He fought in the French and Indian War, but he has never led more than a regiment. The British Army thought so little of him that they refused to give him an officer's commission.

"But," Basil added, "there were several men there

last night who said that Washington has a calm courage about him that they would follow straight into Hades."

Basil sighed. "Most of our fighters will be farmers and yeomen. You, thank the Lord, will be too young to bear a gun. The one to worry on is Ben. If I know that hothead, he's already plotting how to get his hands on a musket."

Ben had, in fact, discussed the very same several nights back with some of the boys from the bonfire. Ben had gathered them in the stable, including Nathaniel, as if he were sure to want to join in. Ben had said the gunpowder magazine housed plenty of muskets and that no one would notice if they took a few. He joked about dressing up like Indians—as they had in the Boston Tea Party—to raid the magazine, which the boys laughed about excitedly. That's when Nathaniel left with the excuse of feeding the chickens. He didn't want any part of stealing muskets.

Basil shook his head in disapproval of Ben. "You keep an eye on our young friend, Nathaniel. He is too impetuous. He knows naught what war means. As rousing as Mr. Henry's words are, as just as is our cause, I do wish . . . mayhap . . . let us hope that Mr. Henry has been premature in his warnings."

★ ★ ★

But Patrick Henry was not. At that very moment, riders were galloping south from Massachusetts, spreading the news of a deadly skirmish between American minutemen and British troops at Lexington and Concord.

That night, Lord Dunmore and twenty royal marines struck against the people of Williamsburg.

୭ Chapter Twenty-one ୨୦

FLAM-FLAM-FLAM-FLAM.

Nathaniel's eyes popped open. What was that sound? He rubbed the sleep from his eyes and strained to see through the darkness. Across the room Basil snorted, still slumbering.

He must have been dreaming. Or Basil's snores had awoken him as they so often had during the winter. He turned over.

Rat-a-tat-tat. Rat-a-tat-tat. FLAM-FLAM-FLAM-FLAM.

Nathaniel sat up. Those were drums! He jumped out of bed and ran to the window. In the waning moonlight, he saw men running down the street toward Market Square.

"Alarm! Alarm!"

Scanning the rooftops, Nathaniel looked for flames. When a house caught fire, townspeople rushed to pass buckets of water to prevent flames from spreading and burning down entire blocks of buildings. But he saw none.

"The redcoats! The redcoats!"

Rat-a-tat-tat. More drums, more shouts.

Nathaniel scrambled to pull on his stockings and breeches. "Master!" he called. "Master Basil, something is amiss. Get up."

"Eh? What's the matter, lad? Go back to sleep." Basil groaned and stretched and rolled over with another snort.

Nathaniel could hear Edan and Mrs. Maguire stirring downstairs. He'd have to hurry the old man so that he could get out of the house before Edan might prevent it. He pushed on Basil's turned back. "Master, I think we've been attacked! Master, you must get up!"

FLAM-FLAM-FLAM-FLAM. To arms, Williamsburg! To the magazine! Alarm! Alarm!

"Master Basil!" Nathaniel pleaded.

Basil propped himself up. "What is it?"

Rolling drums answered before Nathaniel could.

"Good Lord!" Basil tumbled out of bed. "Grab my coat, lad!"

The two of them clattered out the door, down the stairs and onto the green as Basil pulled on his clothes. His long gray hair flew about his head as they trotted. Other men dashed by them, stuffing their shirttails into their breeches as they rushed. Women in nightcaps, wrapped in shawls or blankets, peered out from behind their open front doors.

The entire town was up, running, afraid.

Nathaniel and Basil joined a crushing crowd in the Duke of Gloucester Street between the magazine and courthouse. Jostling one another, trying to hear, people shouted questions and answers, anxiety and anger bubbling, building to a boil.

"What's the matter? What's happened?"

"They've emptied the magazine of our gunpowder!"

"Who?"

"British marines! They came to town in the night and stole more than fifteen barrels of the colony's gunpowder!"

The man with that information was quickly engulfed, illuminated by dozens of lanterns. He tried to shield his eyes.

"What? Say again, man."

He repeated the news. It rippled through a hundred people, passed by indignant bellows.

"But that's ours!"

" . . . to defend ourselves against Indian attacks and slave uprisings . . ."

"And takeover by the Royal British Army!"

"That's right!"

"Let's after them!"

"Aye! Aye!" The crowd erupted into a guttural chant. Many in the mob carried muskets, gardening hoes, workmen's axes—whatever they had been able to grab as they raced to the alarm. They held them in the air and shook them threateningly, knocking one another about in their excitement. Nathaniel was nearly squashed by a bull of a man beside him. He instinctively grabbed for Basil's coat sleeve, but Basil had been washed aside in the storm surge of infuriated people pushing roughly to be on the move.

A shrill voice kept calling until finally it stilled the mob. "Wait! Wait! It's too late!"

It was the same man. Again he became the center of a swarm. "They've already made it back to the *Magdalen* at Burwell's Landing."

"How say you?"

Frustrated calls of "We can't hear!" "What did he say?" echoed through the multitude.

He held his hands up imploringly and the crowd gradually silenced. "This was a well-planned theft, lads! He knew our watchmen had gone home to their beds, the lazy sots. He had the schooner and the marines waiting."

"He? Who?"

"Lord Dunmore! He must have ordered it. He has

the key to the magazine gate. They used his wagon and came from the palace stable yard. Mayhap he had the marines there for days waiting for the right opportunity. It's obviously to prevent us from arming as Patrick Henry called for."

At this, the crowd roared. Dawn was breaking, and its gentle light fell on faces clouded with disbelief and disappointment, faces twisted in rage and vengeance. "Treacherous villain!" "To the palace!" "Dunmore will answer for this." "We'll hold him hostage until he orders the powder's return." "Aye. Let's to it."

Reignited, the mob bumped and shoved and turned itself to march toward the palace. Gathering on the green, with muskets in hand, was Williamsburg's company of volunteers, organized the previous year to fight with Dunmore against the Shawnee. Shouldering their muskets, they too, moved forward to join up against the man who so recently led them.

"Nathaniel! Come here, boy!" Basil and Nathaniel swam toward each other, elbowed and pushed. They fell together, and Basil dragged them out of the tide of rushing people.

"Good God," murmured Basil. "I think we might witness an assassination. If this gets any more out of hand, we must back out of it, lad. Who's to say that Dunmore hasn't fortified himself with armed marines?

From behind his wall, they could shoot into the crowd and slaughter dozens."

Just as Basil spoke, Nathaniel spotted Ben at the mob's tail end. Pointing, he called out to him, "Ben! Come back!"

Ben waved before he squirmed his way further into the crowd, his excited grin plain to see.

As the feverish horde began to gain direction and speed, a refined voice called out, "Peace! Hold! Stand down, gentlemen."

Voices echoed the call to "hold" and the crowd paused, looking back toward the courthouse. On its brick steps stood three men.

"Shsssh. It's Peyton Randolph. Quiet, lads. Listen to Mr. Randolph." The crowd slowly shushed itself.

Basil and Nathaniel inched to the crowd's perimeter.

"Who are the other two gentlemen, master?" Nathaniel whispered.

Basil stood on his tiptoes to see. "Mayor John Dixon and the colony's treasurer, Robert Carter Nicholas. Cool heads, both. Let us listen."

" . . . write a petition, asking for return of the gunpowder," Randolph was saying.

"Nay. We've petitioned enough!" a man with a musket shouted. "Patrick Henry is right. Parliament never listens! Look how they hold down Boston. Parliament has already declared Massachusetts in rebellion and clearly plans to crush it. Virginia might be next. Maybe that's what this gunpowder theft is leading up to!"

"Aye, aye," murmured many. "Maybe." "Yes, maybe so." "Maybe more marines are marching toward us right now to occupy our city!" Panic crackled through the mob, like heat lightning through a summer sky.

Peyton Randolph held his ground. "This is not Massachusetts and this petition is not going to Parliament." Accustomed to unruly debate in the House of Burgesses, Peyton remained composed despite the heckling. "This is to a governor many of you know personally. . . ."

"That we do! We know him as a scurrilous drinker and boor!"

A few men laughed. Randolph ignored them. "Give us leave to write a petition and deliver it to the governor immediately."

"Never mind more paper and polite niceties," countered another man. "Let us take the governor before he slips away to a ship as well."

"He will not desert his wife and children," answered Mayor Dixon, playing off the popularity of Lady Dunmore.

The crowd mumbled and argued among itself until

finally one man shouted, "Gentlemen, Mr. Randolph is about to leave for the Second Continental Congress in Philadelphia as our representative. That august body of leaders from all thirteen colonies has elected him their president. I think we can trust Mr. Randolph and our town counselors to pen a persuasive petition to Governor Dunmore."

Randolph and the man bowed at each other.

"What say you?"

For a moment, there was silence. Then several seconded the motion, persuading the rest. Randolph and Dixon withdrew into the courthouse to write hastily. The crowd remained rooted, watching the courthouse doors like a cat at a mousehole.

✑ Chapter Twenty-two ✑

"I CAN'T BELIEVE they are writing yet another petition!" Ben found his way through the mob to Basil and Nathaniel. He was trailed by four boys, including the foul-tempered Jeremiah. They were impatient and itchy. Like horses denied their morning feed, thought Nathaniel. He nervously realized that Edan's carriage horse was probably twitching about in her stall wondering where he was with her oats.

"Haven't they figured out that their petitions and arguments only give the redcoats more time to plot?" Ben fussed. "Words are the weak weapons of fat, old men."

His friends laughed. The boy named Beverly chimed in, "They probably are in there napping for all the courage they have."

Frowning, Basil turned on Ben and spoke with

uncharacteristic vehemence. "For shame, Ben. For shame, Beverly. Is not your father inside as well?"

Beverly hung his head, but Ben sighed and rolled his eyes. His reaction infuriated Basil. He caught Ben up by a buttonhole of his coat.

"These men have risked the hangman for years with their words. And it is their words that have inspired all of us to believe enough in our rights as human beings to speak up and demand justice. For generations, nay centuries, mankind has held that we must do the bidding of a king, no matter how idiotic, how tyrannous he was. Words have taught us that he is—how did Mr. Jefferson put it?" Basil hesitated a moment and then went on, "'That kings are the *servants* not the *proprietors* of the people.' This crowd is born of such words, ennobled by such words. I am no longer just a poor musician, a lowly servant, because of words. I am a man guaranteed by my very nature to have rights, to have dignity. I stand tall because of words."

Basil stopped abruptly, realizing that he had raised a fist and was shaking it at Ben. Ben's chin was lifted, his eyes rebellious. He was grinding his teeth so hard as Basil spoke that his dimples appeared and disappeared repeatedly. He was obviously aware that whoever was near enough to hear was listening to Basil chastise him.

Basil dropped his hand but ended forcefully: "If Mr.

Randolph wants to pen a few more words, I am for it. We owe him that respect, Ben."

At that moment, Randolph, Dixon, Nicholas, and several other town aldermen emerged. Ben had opened his mouth to make some retort, but upon seeing them turned expectantly toward the steps of the courthouse. So did everyone in the crowd.

Mr. Dixon began to read, and it was immediately obvious that the mob's reaction would be a mixture of Basil's and Ben's.

We, His Majesty's dutiful and loyal subjects . . .

"I'm not feeling the might bit dutiful meself right now," sneered a listener.

"Shhhhhhh, listen." His neighbor elbowed him.

. . . humbly beg leave to represent to your Excellency . . .

"Excellency of what—deceit?" heckled another.

. . . that the inhabitants of this city were this morning exceedingly alarmed . . .

"Now there is a fact!"

. . . that a large quantity of gunpowder was, while they were sleeping in their beds, removed from the public magazine and conveyed on board one of His Majesty's armed vessels . . .

"Yes, that's right." "Well said." Heads began to nod.

. . . we therefore humbly desire to be informed by your Excellency, upon what motives, and for what particular

purpose, the powder has been carried off in such manner . . .

"If that's not an act of war, what is?"

. . . and we earnestly request your Excellency to order it to be immediately returned to this magazine.

Dixon ended, looking up and squinting into the now bright morning sunshine. "Come, friends," Mr. Randolph called. Without waiting for a response, he and the other officials began walking to the palace. The independent company of volunteers fell in behind them. Silenced by their belief in Randolph, the crowd followed dutifully. It came to a halt in front of the Wythe and Maguire houses. The town officials went on alone to the palace gate and disappeared inside.

Nathaniel saw Edan and Mrs. Maguire standing on their front stoop, and slipped behind Basil to hide from view. He knew from Edan's scowl that he would punish Nathaniel for being part of this march if spotted. He looked for Ben to forewarn him. But Ben had disappeared with his friends.

"That petition should have had a little more teeth to it," grumbled a well-dressed man, standing beside Basil.

"Remember the proverb, sir: Civility costs nothing," Basil murmured.

"True." The gentleman tipped his hat to Basil. "But here's another one: 'Blessed is he who expects nothing, for he shall never be disappointed.' Dunmore will not return the gunpowder. I've hunted with him and gamed with him. He stops at nothing to win. I would not be surprised to learn he cheats at cards. He also has a terrible temper. If anything he will see this mildly worded petition as an insult. 'Twould be better to grab him by the throat and shake the powder out of him."

The man turned out to be right.

Acting almost as if it was beneath him to answer, Lord Dunmore stated he had taken the gunpowder to protect it from being stolen by slaves. Dunmore claimed there was a slave uprising brewing in nearby Chesterfield, Prince Edward, and Surry counties. His action was merely one of concern for the well-being of the colonists. He continued that the magazine was ill guarded by the colonists, vulnerable to seizure, and that there had been sightings of slaves around it after dark—that was why he had chosen the middle of the night to clean it out of powder.

Dunmore promised—if an emergency arose—that he could return the gunpowder to Williamsburg within half an hour's time. However, for the time being, he said, it would remain aboard ship. Given the fact the townspeople were so upset, Dunmore did not think it wise to put gunpowder into their hands.

With that, he dismissed Dixon and his council.

It was with some difficulty that Peyton Randolph and Mayor Dixon persuaded the crowd to go home and go about their jobs. But disperse they finally did. Perhaps their anger had been cooled by the wait, their lack of breakfast, and the realization that their only other option was to go ahead and seize the palace and the governor. Despite the company of armed volunteers standing before them, and their indignation, the crowd of Williamsburg citizens wasn't quite ready to storm the home of the king's man.

But tempers remained hot. That night another crowd gathered when rumors coursed through the town that the marines from the *Magdalen* were coming again. Again, when no actual redcoats were seen, the city elders and Mr. Randolph convinced the townspeople to go home.

The next morning, Dr. Pasteur made a call to the palace. Enraged with what he called the city's insolent response to his rightful taking of the powder, Dunmore told the doctor that if the town insulted him any more, he would declare freedom to the slaves, arm them, and "reduce the city of Williamsburg to ashes." He commanded the doctor to give that message to Peyton Randolph and the town council: "I have once fought *for* the Virginians, and by God I will let them see that I can fight *against* them."

Within hours, most everyone knew of the governor's threat.

It was also reported from house to house, from person to person, from shop to shop that Patrick Henry had collected one hundred fifty marksmen and was marching to the Capitol from Hanover to recapture the stolen gunpowder.

"See," Ben had said excitedly. "A man of action. When he says 'liberty or death,' he means it!"

Dunmore was completely game for giving Patrick Henry exactly what he asked for if liberty was not to be had. He renewed his threat to destroy Williamsburg if Henry came any closer than Ruffin's Ferry, thirty miles to the west.

No one doubted that the defiant Henry would stick to his word. Likewise, no one doubted that the wrathful Dunmore meant what he said as well. Anxiously, Williamsburg awaited their head-to-head clash. A number of prominent families fled the city.

Then, on April twenty-seventh, an exhausted rider careened into the city, carrying the report of Lexington and Concord.

There, in Massachusetts, eight days earlier, British general Thomas Gage had ordered seven hundred redcoats stationed in Boston to march into the countryside to capture colonial stockpiles of weapons. A silversmith named Paul Revere learned of the plot and spread the word that the redcoats were coming. Seventy minutemen flocked to Lexington Green to face off with ten times their number. Someone fired a shot. After a confused volley, eight Americans lay dead, ten wounded.

The British continued to Concord, where they destroyed the colonists' depot of weapons and supplies. On their march back to Boston, however, New England patriots dogged them, shooting from behind trees and boulders. Two hundred and fifty British regulars were killed or wounded.

The argument between the parent and its child now was sealed with blood.

The timing of Dunmore's theft of Virginia's gunpowder with Gage's destruction of Massachusetts's weapons seemed too coordinated to be coincidental. Virginians could no longer deny the inevitable. The war of words was giving way to a war of bullets.

The *Virginia Gazette* summed it up: "The sword is now drawn and God knows when it will be sheathed."

✑ Chapter Twenty-three ✑

AT DAWN A few days later, Nathaniel lingered over haying the horses, slowly shaking the dried grass to separate it into airy mounds. It was so peaceful in the gray-lit barn. He hated to leave it. The whole town was on edge, awaiting the showdown between Patrick Henry and his militia and the governor and his marines. The tension within Edan's workshop was nearly unbearable as well. With only Ben and Nathaniel left, Edan's paranoia festered. His tirades about the colonists and their conspiracies were filled with more and more curses.

Ben's attitude worsened Nathaniel's jitters. He'd become blatantly reckless. Nathaniel had found him standing in the street, scribbling on a paper, right in front of the Maguires' house.

"How do you spell 'guard'?" he asked Nathaniel when he approached.

"I don't know," Nathaniel answered. "*G-a-r-d*? What are you doing?" He peered at Ben's messy writing. It was hard to decipher, but Nathaniel could make out "Shawnee" and "musket." He gasped. "Are Indians coming?"

"Nay," Ben answered without looking at Nathaniel. He kept writing. "The governor is arming the palace with them."

"But the Shawnee are his hostages. Basil says he shows them only to his dinner guests."

Ben smirked. "Basil doesn't know anything. Look up at that window." He pointed to a second-story corner window of the governor's palace.

Nathaniel looked. "I don't see anything, Ben."

Ben glanced up and frowned. "Well, he was there a minute ago. A great huge savage holding a musket. Look there." He gestured to another window. "See that slave?"

This time Nathaniel could indeed see an African servant looking out the window. But what of it?

"They're keeping guard," Ben spoke impatiently, reading Nathaniel's thoughts. "I followed one of Dunmore's maids to the market and asked her how things were inside the palace. She told me that the governor had dozens of muskets loaded and he had shown all the men servants how to fire them."

"Why are you writing that down, Ben?"

"To give this information to the right people. We're watching to see what Dunmore will try next."

Nathaniel couldn't believe how foolhardy Ben was being, acting as spy for the very people Edan raged about. He was like a flint that could set off a wildfire with one strike. "You better stop, Ben. What if Master Maguire sees you?"

"So what if he does?" Ben dismissed Nathaniel. "What Master Maguire thinks or does is of little consequence in what is about to happen. Besides, I've given a report on him as well that should silence him soon enough." And with that, Ben stalked away.

Worrying over that conversation, Nathaniel had nearly jumped a foot when a swallow shot out the barn door just above his head. Normally the swifts' darting flight in and out of the eaves never startled him. Now a rustling in the hayloft sent a tingle along the back of his neck. He paused in his work, cocked his head, and listened. Nothing. He must have been imagining it. He shook his head to steady himself.

He poured fresh water into the trough. Wait. There it was again. Louder. Too large a sound for mice or birds. Nathaniel's hands began to shake a bit. He listened. Once more it came.

Slowly, Nathaniel reached for the pitchfork. It probably was a mother raccoon trying to nest in the straw, a dry, warm place for her young. But that could be dangerous. Raccoons loved to pick up bits of oats dropped from the horse's feed bin. And a mother raccoon was very aggressive. It could bite a horse and sever tendons. Nathaniel would have to run it off.

Holding the pitchfork, he climbed the ladder. Somehow in a flash of shadow and movement, up and out of the straw, a huge, strong body arose and pinned Nathaniel to the floor, pressing the fork's prongs against his throat. Gasping, Nathaniel stared into the eyes of a very angry African.

"Please," he whispered. "Let go."

"Not a word, boy, or I'll push this fork right through you."

"Aye," Nathaniel whimpered, fighting off a wrenching cough from the pressure of the pitchfork and the man's arm across his chest.

"Wake up," the man hissed. There was more rustling in the hay. "Hurry. The household is up. I've got one here."

Another figure rose behind the man atop Nathaniel. He was enormous too. Wait a minute. Nathaniel focused through the gloom. Wasn't that . . .

"No, no, no. That's Nathaniel. Get off." With two easy lifts, Moses pulled the man away and Nathaniel to his feet.

"Sorry, boy." Moses brushed him off.

His companion glanced nervously over his shoulder and said, "How'd we fall asleep? We best move on. Fast."

Moses took Nathaniel by the shoulders. "You got money?"

Nathaniel nodded. He had his one precious shilling that Patrick Henry's son had given him. "Why? What are you doing here, Moses? Did you run off again? Oh Moses, what will they do if they catch you this time?"

"That's why I need money."

"But why did you come back into Williamsburg, Moses? There are slave patrols all over town. And they're really watching because Lord Dunmore said there was an uprising."

Moses rubbed his forehead and sighed heavily. His companion sneered and spat. "We came because we hear the governor promise to free the slaves. And that Williamsburg folk were after him. So me and Robin and a couple others left the farms to help. Went straight to the palace last night to say we stand with him. His men turned us away and locked the gate." Bitter disappointment and confusion puckered his face.

Roosters began to crow.

"We gots to go, Moses." His friend tugged urgently on Moses's sleeve. "I told you this was a fool idea.

This boy ain't got money."

Moses spoke in a tumble. "Since the governor turned us away, we heading to the Chesapeake, Nathaniel. Last month we was delivering and picking up at the Norfolk docks. I met a Captain Collins. He say the British navy was looking for men what know the Virginia waters. My master was right there, so there was naught I could do then. But word all along the river is now's the time to run.

"There's a boatman say he sail me right up to the *Magdalen*, what the captain command. But I gots to pay him, Nathaniel. A whole pound. A pound for me and a pound for Robin, here. You know where we can find two pounds, boy?"

Nathaniel took off his shoe and pulled the shilling out of it.

"I need more than that, boy." Moses looked at him hard. "I was glad to do it, Nathaniel, but I save your skin onct or twice, didn't I?"

Nathaniel hung his head. "More than once or twice, Moses," he whispered. He stuck the shilling back into his shoe.

"I need you now, Nathaniel. I need your help. There must be money somewhere about this house. Please." For the first time Nathaniel could remember, Moses looked frightened and vulnerable. He had to help.

Full light was coming on strong. He'd have to hurry. There was only one place Nathaniel knew he could get his hands on money quickly, without getting caught. That was the small tin box Basil kept under the foot of his mattress.

Changing the ad about John's whereabouts had given Nathaniel new pluck. And God knew Moses was a true friend who deserved his loyalty. He didn't stop to consider or to worry about consequences. Within five minutes, Nathaniel had slipped into the house, fished out two pounds from Basil's meager savings while he snored, and sent Moses out into the growing light of day.

Patrick Henry did not halt his march at Ruffin's Ferry, as Lord Dunmore ordered.

Enraged, Dunmore sent his wife and children to safety aboard the HMS *Fowey*, a warship just off Yorktown. The captain of the *Fowey* announced that he would bombard Yorktown if any harm came to Lord Dunmore.

Under those threats to the populace, Henry finally halted at Duncastle's Ordinary, about fifteen miles west of Williamsburg. But he sent some of his men to kidnap the governor's receiver general to force payment for the stolen gunpowder. Retaliating, Dunmore promised to spread devastation as far as he could reach. With several British warships and marines at his command,

Dunmore could certainly do it.

Once again, Peyton Randolph and other moderates scrambled to reach a compromise. Under pressure from them, Henry accepted 330 pounds for the gunpowder. He vowed to use the money to buy replacement gunpowder. Warning his troops to remain vigilant, he sent them home. Henry himself turned northward toward Philadelphia, to take his seat at the Continental Congress, already in session.

Firing a parting shot at Henry, Dunmore declared him an outlaw. He warned Virginians "not to aid, abet, or give countenance to the said Patrick Henry."

But Henry was too popular, too much the symbol of eloquent, steel-hard bravery, too much the voice of liberty. People turned out in legions to cheer and protect him from arrest. One after another, their fifes and drums playing, county volunteer troops escorted Henry across their borders on his trip north to Philadephia. When Henry reached the Potomac River, separating Virginia and Maryland, the ferryman fed him and rowed him over for free. Only a few Virginians accompanied Henry across since it was easy to see the flags and bright colored jackets of the Maryland volunteers awaiting him on the other side.

Once Henry was gone, calm somehow returned. It was the homecoming of the beloved Lady Dunmore that seemed to reassure Williamsburg the most. She would talk sense to her belligerent husband, said townspeople. And surely Dunmore would not recall his family if he planned more treachery.

Dunmore even reinstated the House of Burgesses and called it to reconvene in June. Although some feared it was merely a trap to arrest colonial leaders, others hoped it meant Henry's daring had convinced Dunmore to cooperate. A kind of wary optimism hung about the city and quieted its streets.

That was when Nathaniel's life erupted.

"Nathaniel," Basil called to him one evening about the time they typically played flutes together.

"Yes, master?" Nathaniel sensed from Basil's stern tone that what he had been dreading was about to happen.

"I am missing money, Nathaniel. Know you of it?"

Nathaniel swallowed hard and lied: "Nay, master."

Basil stood silent, watching him carefully. Nathaniel tried to keep his eyes steadily on Basil's. But he began to squirm, and his gaze dropped.

Basil sighed heavily. Then he spoke in hoarse sadness. "I think the weather is warm enough for you to resume sleeping in the stable."

Nathaniel felt a stab in his heart that made him dizzy. But he managed a feeble, "Aye, master."

Tell him! Nathaniel's mind screamed. *Tell him why.* But Nathaniel didn't trust Basil to protect Moses. Didn't trust him to understand. Still, didn't know how to trust.

He picked up his few possessions and made for the door.

"Wait," Basil spoke.

Oh please, thought Nathaniel. *Please don't banish me this way.* But still he did not speak, did not offer the old man any explanation.

Basil handed him something wrapped in a linen cloth. "Happy birthday, Nathaniel," he said, and turned away.

Alone, up in the hayloft, Nathaniel unwrapped the package. Inside were two gifts: a book, *The American Instructor or Young Man's Best Companion*, and a wooden fife. Flipping through the book, he found exercises in reading and arithmetic, ways to improve himself and his opportunities. Ways to groom his God-given reason and intellect to make his own destiny, just as Basil had told him. Tearfully, Nathaniel put it aside.

With shaking hands, he held the fife to his lips and blew a high-pitched note, a sound he knew called soldiers to duty, a sound that sang of liberty. He knew Basil had meant it to be a symbolic as well as musical gift.

Nathaniel dropped his face into his hands and sobbed. Basil would never feel the same about him, now that he thought Nathaniel was a thief and liar. Oh, if only he had explained. The sorrow he felt was almost unbearable. Because this time Nathaniel knew that his trouble, his loss were his own fault. He could not blame it on an unjust fate, or the brutality of his masters. His situation was born of his own actions, his own choices. *He* was responsible.

If that's what liberty meant, it was a cruel and hard price to pay for it.

PART SEVEN

June 1775

Come join hand in hand all ye true, loyal souls,
'Tis Liberty calls, let's fill up our bowls,
We'll toast all the lovers of Freedom's good cause;
America's sons will support all our laws.
　Our firelocks are good:
　Let fair freedom ne'er yield.
　We're always ready,
　Steady, boys, steady,
　By Jove we'll be free
　Or we'll die in the field.
Though the lords and the commons may rail in the
House,
At our patriot assembles, we don't care a souse;

We'll keep cheerful spirits, nor mind their commands
The sun of fair liberty will shine o'er our lands.

—A liberty song composed at a town meeting
in Chester

৩ Chapter Twenty-four ৩

"IF MASTER SEES you doing that, you'll catch it, you know."

Nathaniel glanced up at Ben. For the past week, Nathaniel had been slipping into the shop even earlier than usual to use the pen and ink on Edan's desk. "Do you see him coming?"

"No, but it's well past his time," Ben answered. He watched Nathaniel finish a capital *D*, with an elaborate curlicue at its top and a perfect backstroke at its bottom. "Very nice, Nat," he murmured. "You could be an excellent secretary or bookkeeper with that penmanship."

"Really?"

"In fact"—Ben puffed himself up and jokingly threw out his chest and lower lip—"you can be my secretary when I am elected to the Continental Congress. Or mayhap when I am governor of Virginia." He grinned.

"Yes. I like the sound of that. You and me running Virginia, Nat. What say you?"

Nathaniel blew on the letter to dry the ink, ignoring Ben's fantasies. The older boy was so full of himself these days. But he did linger on one thing—being a secretary or bookkeeper. Nathaniel hadn't really given a thought to the advantage good cursive might give him for a trade once he was free of his indenture. He was simply trying to win back Basil's friendship with it.

When Basil had sent him to live again in the stable, Nathaniel thought he might die of the ache in his heart. Basil had not sought him out to play music at night or to read from his novels ever since. Nathaniel had lain in the hay in the stable's loft and listened to Basil playing his violin or his flute, all alone. There were no jaunty jigs or quick-paced allegros with their dazzling run of notes or bravado of trills. Basil played melancholy tunes, one after another.

Selfishly, Nathaniel took hope in their sad sound that Basil was missing his company, too. But he knew that part of it was Basil's deep disappointment in him. Unwittingly, Nathaniel had fulfilled the prophecy of the abusive blacksmith, from whom Basil had saved him—Nathaniel had indeed robbed Basil as he slept. So in the stable Nathaniel hid, despairing, until the evening light of May lasted long enough to prompt him to pick up the book Basil had given him. Nathaniel wound his way through its words.

In Basil's gift, he had found an idea. Perhaps if he completed the spelling and arithmetic exercises in the book, Basil would be proud of Nathaniel's effort. Mayhap it would rekindle Basil's interest in him as a student. Basil loved to teach—to teach anybody who would listen, really. Nathaniel realized it was his best chance.

The problem, of course, was how to record his work. Most pupils used chalk on slate hornbooks, erasing their work after their tutor approved it. Nathaniel had none. And certainly he could not afford the purchase of paper, pen, and ink. But one night he came up with a solution. The loft's floor could be his tablet! Nathaniel took a piece of chalk from Edan's desk, justifying that bit of thievery by the end result and the hard work he did about the place.

Hour after hour Nathaniel lay on his stomach, scratching spelling words and math problems onto the planed pinewood. He covered them all with hay, to keep them from smearing away and to keep his project secret from Ben, who came up at night sometimes to tell Nathaniel about his gallivanting about town. Nathaniel didn't want anything ruining his surprise for Basil.

What Nathaniel was writing now was a thank-you note for the book and fife. With it, Nathaniel could approach Basil to start a conversation. Then he would invite the old tutor to the stable to see his work.

For that note, he had taken a sheet of Edan's paper and was using his ink and quill pen. He knew it was dangerous. But he was almost finished. The *D* he had just completed was part of his signature. Only three more letters—*u, n, n*—to write.

But today was not the time. Edan would come into the shop any minute; Ben was right. Nathaniel carefully folded the paper along creases he'd made the previous days and tucked it into his waistcoat.

"You should have come with me to the illumination last night," Ben chided Nathaniel. "There's no use sulking in the loft."

"What was it for?" Nathaniel had heard the church bells and seen that every household window glowed with candlelight.

"It was to honor Peyton Randolph. He's back from Philadelphia for the session of the House that Governor Dunmore called. But nobody trusts that Scottish snake. General Gage has authorized the lobsterbacks to arrest and execute rebel leaders. There's a wanted list, and Mr. Randolph is on it. Williamsburg's militia escorted Mr. Randolph to the safety of his house last night, fearing Dunmore might try to arrest him on the road. We boy volunteers were there, too, to greet him."

So that was the commotion Nathaniel had heard. The Randolph home was two blocks away from Edan's house. In the loft, as he puzzled over a long set of sums, Nathaniel had heard a low roar of huzzahs. But that was not such an unusual sound in Williamsburg these days. Ever since Dunmore and his British marines had emptied the magazine of its gunpowder, volunteer militiamen had been drilling on the open ground of market square.

More and more out-of-town frontier marksmen were arriving too, clad in homespun hunting shirts that fell to their knees and covered leather leggings. They were weather-beaten and hardy, crude in their language and manners. One had terrified Mrs. Maguire the other morning when she'd tripped over him, sleeping in their orchard.

"You should have seen us, Nat, oh, we were so grand! Robert Greenhow got a copy of *The Manual of Military Exercise as Ordered by His Majesty* from his father. We've been practicing all its drills. We marched right up to Mr. Randolph's front door and everyone there said—"

At that moment Edan stomped through the door. He was breathing hard and holding a hand up to his chest, rubbing it, as if trying to push something away from his heart. He shuffled to his desk, sat down with a thump, and took up his pen. Ben and Nathaniel pretended to be busy.

After much scribbling and muttering, Edan grunted to Nathaniel, "Take this notice to the *Gazette*. All the high and mighty burgesses are in town. Several owe me money. This should scare them into paying me." He shoved the slip of paper at Nathaniel and barked at Ben, "About work, boy."

"What would you have me do?" Ben's question was earnest, and for once free of sass. "We've no order, sir."

Indeed, new work had ground to a halt. And it wasn't just due to the disappearance of John and Obadjah. With the embargo hurting everyone's purse and the Continental Congress cautioning against frivolous purchases, nobody was buying large items such as carriages. Edan's finances were decaying rapidly.

Edan threw his head back and laughed a guttural crazed sound. "No work?" He grabbed at his chest again, bending over and coughing. "Dreams will ruin you. Customers will misuse you. People will turn on you." His unnatural laugh continued. "What can you expect from a pig but a grunt?" Edan stumbled out of the shop toward the house, chanting, "A grunt, a grunt, a grunt."

Ben stared after him. He held his hand out toward Nathaniel. "Let us read that notice."

I request those gentlemen that are indebted to me pay me immediately that I may thereby support my credit and be enabled to carry on my business. The many disappointments I have met force me to let those gentlemen know that unless they discharge their respective balances this meeting, their names will be inserted very shortly in all the Williamsburg papers, that the world may know how tradesmen are treated in Virginia.

E. Maguire

Ben let out a long whistle. "That'll get some backs up." He grinned and added, "That might spur the committee to finally take action they speak of, which in turn should push Edan to go home to Ireland. Then we'll be free, Nat! Free!" He did a little jig.

Nathaniel was completely baffled. "What are you talking about, Ben?" The apprentice was acting as crazed as Edan.

"Oh, nothing," Ben answered mysteriously. "You know, if there's no work, I think I'll just meander down to the store to see when the Greenhows think we'll drill again. Hop to the *Gazette*, boy," he teased Nathaniel, snapping his fingers, once again imaging himself the congressman.

Not knowing what else to do, Nathaniel put on his round hat and followed orders.

᥊ Chapter Twenty-five ᥌

ROUNDING THE CORNER of Edan's house, Nathaniel emerged to a commotion on Palace Green.

"Get control of them, confound you!"

Two perfectly white horses attached to a luxurious, open carriage were rearing, jostling the gentlemen inside about wildly—enough for one's powdered wig to be down over his eyes and the other to be dumped to the carriage floor, his feet straight up in the air. A shoe went flying.

"I'm trying, my lord," the liveried slave on the driver's seat said apologetically, but his urgent shushing was doing nothing to calm the horses. Harnessed together, they had to quiet together. But as the two animals knocked each other about in agitation, their panic only rose. Simultaneously Nathaniel and the driver recognized that the horses were about to bolt. "Lord save us," the driver prayed.

Holding out his arms, Nathaniel stepped in front of the horses. "Whoooooa, boys . . . bea-u-ti-ful boys."

One horse reared, the other lunged out as if to strike Nathaniel. He jumped to the side, but kept talking. "Eeeeeasy, beauties. No need to run off, boys. Eeeeeeaaa-sy." The horse nearer Nathaniel paused in its flailing.

The driver echoed Nathaniel's crooning. "That's right, fellas, eeeeeasy." He pulled back on their reins hard and firm, all the while his voice a chant of calming.

The horses settled down to simply snorting and quivering and tossing their heads. The danger was past. The slave tipped his hat in thanks. Nathaniel nodded back. "What set them off?" he asked.

The driver pointed down Prince George's Street, the small lane that ran between the Maguire and Wythe houses. In the distance was a cloud of dust. "Runaway horse," he muttered. "Chestnut demon, saddle still on, stirrups flapping, making it wild." He leaned over and added in a softer voice: "Musta dumped some fine gentleman on his rear end."

He grinned. Nathaniel did too.

"Enough idle chatter! If you can't control these horses better, I'll sell you to a West Indies rice plantation!" shouted one of the passengers.

"Wouldn't make no never mind to me," muttered the driver under his breath. He faced forward and became a statue of servitude.

The man with the wig askew resumed his seat and straightened his appearance. "You there. Boy."

Nathaniel pointed to himself. "Me, sir?"

The man spoke contemptuously: "All these colonials are idiots, I swear. Yes, you. Hand me that shoe."

Nathaniel picked up a huge slipper that looked very like a lady's shoe. With a bow, he handed it up to the man. The man snatched it, not bothering to look at Nathaniel, much less thank him. "Drive on," he shouted.

As the carriage rolled away, Nathaniel heard: "What do you think the response of those provincials will be to my speech? I nearly choked when I said, 'the king has no object nearer his heart than the peace and prosperity of his subjects in every part of the dominion.' A good lashing is rather what they all need in my opinion. . . ."

The carriage rolled out of hearing. Nathaniel resumed his walk.

"You just saved Governor Dunmore's neck, lad," said a passerby. He winked. "Next time leave well enough alone!"

★ ★ ★

The Duke of Gloucester Street was packed with horses and people, as it always was at public times, when the House convened or the courts were open. Overnight the town became a crowded city, with all the self-importance and bustle of a place that changed people's lives and fortunes. Nathaniel was bumped aside by many a well-heeled gentleman until he arrived at the *Gazette*. One of Maria's brothers let him in and took him to the little office where she was writing as a lanky, freckled, red-haired man dictated.

She was flushed. So, too, was the gentleman, who was trying unsuccessfully to dust himself clean. His rumpled but well-cut blue coat and pants were caked with mud and filth. He smelled a bit of manure. He was a tumble of thoughts, as if his mind raced too fast for his tongue to keep up.

"I have never been thrown like that. Unseated in front of all those people. The conservatives will make hay of it, I warrant. Please don't accept any tale of it, Miss Rind, if someone tries to print a ridicule. . . . And what of my saddle and all that is in my saddlebag? My clothes, my papers, my . . . Oh, no . . . my kit! My pocket fiddle! The one with which I wooed Mrs. Jefferson. I always travel with it to remind me of her when we are apart. . . . How will I ever . . . Oh, it cannot be. . . ." The man flopped down into a chair, his long legs stretching across the room, it seemed, he was so tall. In anguish he concluded, "I am undone." He hung his head.

"Oh Mr. Jefferson, someone will find your horse. You'll see. But we need finish your notice, sir, so that my cousin can set the type."

"Yes, yes. That is all we can do, I suppose. Where were we, lass?"

Maria read: "Strayed, from the city of Williamsburg, a chestnut mare, about fifteen hands high. She has the head of an Arabian and . . ."

"And the disposition of a harpy," Mr. Jefferson muttered. "What possessed me to purchase her from Mr. Henry, I will never know. His silver tongue, I'd say, that convinces a man to do anything!"

Nathaniel's ears pricked. Could it be? Could the horse be Vixen? Surely Mr. Jefferson's runaway horse was the one that set off the governor's carriage horses. And surely the description and behavior fit the wild Vixen.

Mr. Jefferson was mourning: "How will I explain the loss of my violin to my beloved? She will chide me, sure. . . ."

"Yes, sir," Maria murmured. "What else shall we say, sir?"

Still slumped over, Jefferson continued to dictate:

"all-over red, with a thick flowing tail, slightly ash in color. The contents of the saddlebag are not expensive, but precious to the owner. . . ."

Maria was scribbling madly to keep up.

Mr. Jefferson rose. "Ah me. Is that how I wish it to read? Is admitting the contents are important to me a mistake? Let me read over the text, please, Miss Rind, to collect my thoughts."

Hesitantly, Maria handed him the paper. He bowed formally as he took it. "I thank you." Looking down, he squinted, and then frowned. "Child," he said gently. "I am afraid I cannot read this."

It was Maria's turn to hang her head.

Nathaniel startled himself by stepping forward. "I can transcribe your words, sir. May I?"

Tears of embarrassment in her eyes, Maria looked at Nathaniel gratefully. Jefferson caught the exchange and smiled slightly. "Yes, lad. I would be beholden to you."

Nathaniel picked up the pen, ready.

"Whosoever returns the mare to me shall have as reward fifty shillings."

Nathaniel's head popped up. "Fifty shillings!" he couldn't help exclaiming.

"Hmmm. Perhaps you are right, lad. In for a penny, in for a pound. I should offer more given how desperate I am to secure the return of my saddlebag. Hang the horse. Let us add this: 'Return of the saddlebag and its full contents intact shall bring an additional thirty shillings.' There. Think you that will spur people to look for her?"

Nathaniel forced himself to concentrate on writing down the words he was so excited. Spur people to look for Vixen? Rather! Eighty shillings was four pounds. With four pounds, he could replace the money he'd taken from Basil and still have extra. A fortune!

Hands shaking in impatience, he handed the slip of paper to Jefferson. The tall man smiled and nodded. "Well written, lad. The spelling is exact. Well done." He looked down looked at Nathaniel, clearly assessing his modest clothes. "Who has taught you?"

Nathaniel hesitated. "I have been teaching myself of late, sir."

Jefferson's eyebrows went up. "Then you are the very kind of citizen in whom I am putting my faith, lad. The Greek philosopher Epictetus said that only the educated are free. I firmly believe that if we enlighten the populace, tyranny will die. Because the people will know they deserve better."

"Thank you, sir," Nathaniel answered hurriedly, not really taking in Mr. Jefferson's words. His mind was consumed with the promise of four pounds.

Without waiting another moment, he was out the

door and dashing, hurtling down the street as fast as he could. Nathaniel would find Vixen before anyone else knew about the reward for her. If he did, he could right his world.

He completely forgot the advertisement he was supposed to place in the *Gazette* for Edan.

⟨ Chapter Twenty-six ⟩

VIXEN HAD BEEN heading west toward the College of William and Mary. Darting around people and carts, Nathaniel calculated where she would finally stop to graze. She could run full speed for at least half a mile, and canter the rest of it. After that she might trot another. That would get her far past the college, thankfully, out from the clutches of robed students who might catch her, out to the beginnings of farms and swamplands.

It was about a half mile from the *Gazette* offices to the college's Wren Building. Winded by then, Nathaniel slowed to a jog, noting the clock in the cupola of the beautifully symmetrical brick building. It was half past twelve already. Nathaniel knew there would be the devil to pay for not returning to Edan's shop. But he was determined.

In the sandy road he saw dozens of hoofprints and

wagon ruts, nothing to really help him track Vixen. No, wait. A few yards ahead were deep hoof marks, far apart, darker in color, not yet bleached by the sun or sifted with the tread of passersby. Some horse had recently taken this path at a racing pace. He prayed that it was Vixen and not one of the governor's messengers.

He trotted on, looking from side to side to see if she had detoured off the road for a morsel of grass.

Fifteen minutes later he climbed up onto a split-rail fence and scanned a horizon of knee-high corn, tobacco beginning to unfurl its voluminous leaves, watermelon vines spreading into carpets. No horse in sight.

He walked on, passing muddy streams and overgrown woods. From tangled, thick bushes he plucked honey-suckle blossoms, their sugary nectar easing his thirst.

Twenty minutes more. He came across an orchard, a pen of hogs happily sunning themselves, a ram-shackle hut of a farmhouse.

Another fifteen minutes. At a neater farm, a pair of fat plow horses rolled to rid themselves of the itch left from their harnesses. Nathaniel checked the newly turned garden, scanned the hay fields beyond. Nothing.

Dejected, Nathaniel flopped onto the roadside. He'd searched for an hour. That meant he'd covered around four miles. He couldn't imagine a horse not stopping by now to find water or clover—no matter how crazy it was. He'd missed Vixen somehow.

He backtracked, zigzagging along the road.

By the time Nathaniel neared Williamsburg enough to see the Wren Building's white cupola in the distance, he was almost crying in frustration. Gauging time by the sun, it was around four o'clock. The midday meal was over. Edan would definitely be in the shop. Nathaniel's hard work would earn him nothing save a whipping. Maybe he should just turn tail right here and run to the frontier rather than face what surely awaited him in Williamsburg. With all the trouble brewing in the colonies, no one would care about a runaway boy. Given Nathaniel's mistakes, Basil wouldn't. Would he?

Nathaniel sighed. The truth was he cared, even if Basil might no longer. Basil was the closest thing he had to a guardian and friend. He had to go back.

Please, please, please, Nathaniel thought. *Please let me find her.*

A piece of white paper fluttered across the road, rattling and turning somersaults. Another tripped along behind. A third wrapped itself around Nathaniel's ankle. He reached down.

"We must consider alternatives to the frenzy of revenge spawned by the news of Lexington and

Concord. *I beg you to write a petition of peace. Your eloquence would convince . . .*"

Nathaniel flipped the page over. *"To Thomas Jefferson, esquire."* Huzzah! On the other side of the fence a book lay open on the ground. Stuffing the letter pages into his pocket, he picked up the book by Sir Isaac Newton. Down the hill, a silk stocking hung from a wild rose. One of the pockets of the saddlebag had obviously opened and was spilling as Vixen moved. The litter should lead him to her. Gratefully he scampered, picking up bits and pieces of Mr. Jefferson's belongings.

Nathaniel found himself on the edges of a vast reserve of rolling hills and groves of trees. A herd of cattle milled about, some curled up under shade trees, others dealing with frolicking calves. In the distance, atop a hill, cresting the tree line, were the massive, tall chimneys and the gilded weather vane of the governor's palace. Nathaniel recognized that he was trespassing on the sixty-acre park belonging to Lord Dunmore. Of course, Vixen would choose to graze in a place that could bring a jail sentence to him if caught.

He crept from tree to tree until he spotted her. She was lathered in sweat. Her saddle hung akimbo. Cautiously, Nathaniel inched toward the mare. Her head snapped up and her nostrils flared at his approach, but she was too weary, and too happy in meadow grass, to run off. Nathaniel caught her easily.

Coaxing her to a stand of redbud trees to hide them from view, Nathaniel repacked Mr. Jefferson's things. He was relieved to find the fiddle case safe inside the bag. He sat down to await twilight. To get out of the governor's park undetected and down Palace Green to the tavern where Mr. Jefferson was lodging, he'd need darkness and the distraction of people hurrying to their dinner. He tried to keep his mind off the retribution that would await him for his day-long absence.

Four pounds, four pounds, four whole pounds, he repeated to himself over and over.

"May I speak with Mr. Jefferson, please?" Nathaniel stood at the door of the tavern, holding onto Vixen tightly. Inside, he could hear men talking and laughing and the shuffle of chairs being pulled about as dinner was being set.

Within a few moments Jefferson appeared, sleeves rolled up, carrying a pen and a sheet of paper in the other hand. He dropped both with an exclamation of joy upon seeing Nathaniel.

"You found her!" Reaching for the saddlebag, Jefferson startled Vixen and set her to dancing and snorting. Nathaniel held on to her as best he could and calmed the horse and man, saying, "The violin is inside, sir. She had scattered many of your belongings, but the fiddle stayed safe. I think I found everything else."

Jefferson stepped back. "Lad, you are an interesting case. Did you teach yourself to handle such horses as well as write?"

Nathaniel puzzled a moment. Who could teach someone else to calm a horse? But he answered, "I suppose so, sir."

"There, you see. Just my point," said Jefferson. "The nobility of the common man. Completely able to rule himself."

"Sir?"

"Ah, forgive me, lad. My head is full of philosophy and argument. I am in the throes of writing a reply to the governor's welcoming address for the burgesses. Hard work, writing. It is so important these words be diplomatic yet firm, guarded yet concise. . . . Nothing I have scribbled thus far suffices. . . . Hmmm." He thought a moment. "I help myself think by playing violin. Now that you have returned it, I shall be able to concentrate far better."

Carefully he undid the saddlebags and called for the tavern keeper to take Vixen to the stable. "Thank you, lad. I have a fine stable at home, at Monticello. My best mare, Allycroker, has just foaled a colt by Young Fearnought, one of the greatest blooded stallions of Virginia. I purchased this willful chestnut from Patrick Henry, hoping she'd mother good colts as well. What say you to coming to Monticello to help train her, lad?"

"I . . . I cannot, sir," Nathaniel spoke hesitantly. "My time is already purchased."

"I can match the fee, lad. Who owns your time?"

No, no, no, thought Nathaniel. *I don't want to be taken away again, even by as great a gentleman as this.* But he didn't know how to say it. He looked up at the tall, imposing man, shadowed by the tavern's lanterns. Perhaps he could simply change the subject. "Please, sir," he said awkwardly, "may . . . may I, please, have those four pounds you offered for the horse's return?"

"Oh yes! Quite so," said Jefferson, shaking his head as if waking himself. From his pocket, he pulled the treasured pounds and counted them out into Nathaniel's outstretched hands.

"Thank you, sir!"

"No, the thanks are to you, lad." He patted the case of his violin. "I am grateful beyond words." He paused and sighed. "I do wish I could leave the noise of this tavern and go to my cousin's house. John and I always played duets together when I was in town. But his politics are my enemy these days, I am afraid. Know you my

225

cousin John Randolph, the governor's attorney general? A staunch loyalist. After all we've shared and all the affection we bear each other, it is almost impossible for us now to share an evening. It saddens me greatly. Of course, it must be far worse for his brother, Peyton. . . . Well, I am indebted to you." He bowed formally. "I think it would have broken Mrs. Jefferson's heart had I lost the violin which first won it. Your name, lad?"

"Nathaniel Dunn."

"Godspeed, Nathaniel." Jefferson bowed again and then added with a smile, "By the way, Nathaniel. I surmise the lovely Miss Rind is a bit fond of you. My advice is to think of what she loves and play to it, as I did to Mrs. Jefferson's passion for music."

Nathaniel turned as red as Vixen's coat.

"Ah me." Jefferson turned to go back inside. "I can put off my task no longer."

"Sir," Nathaniel stammered, for the idea of an enormous gift to Basil had suddenly come to Nathaniel.

"Yes, lad?"

"Sir, if you truly yearn for a duet, my master, Basil Wilkinson, is an excellent violinist. Lodging at the Maguire house, sir, next to Mr. Wythe's." He pointed down the street. "He is a great admirer of your writings. He is a fine musician, he has played at . . ." Nathaniel paused, unsure if the credential would bring favor or rejection. "He has played at . . . at . . . at the palace."

Jefferson nodded. "I myself played at the palace with Governor Fauquier. Quite a fine musician and educated man. Those were easier times. Thank you, Nathaniel. I know the house. Mr. Wythe was my law professor. Good night."

"Good night, sir." Nathaniel tipped his hat and ran for home, keeping his hand over the waistcoat pocket that held his fortune.

❧ Chapter Twenty-seven ❧

NATHANIEL'S LUCK HELD. Edan had gone to bed earlier in the day with an ache in his chest. Mrs. Maguire had hovered over him all afternoon, mixing an elixir from the leaves of foxglove flowers and coaxing him to swallow it. She even called the surgeon, who charged her five shillings to tell her what she already knew—something was strangling Edan's heart.

Thus occupied, no one noticed Nathaniel's absence. Only Sally mentioned it as she handed him his breakfast corn bread the next morning. "Best save night walking for evening time, child," she said kindly, referring to the evening visits more liberal owners allowed their slaves to make to family members at neighboring plantations. She didn't know where Nathaniel had really been.

It was quiet in the shop. Ben whittled and whistled. Nathaniel glowed with the presence of four pounds in his waistcoat. He also, at dawn, had finished his thank-you note for Basil. Following Mr. Jefferson's advice, he had begun a new project, copying a poem on penmanship from the *Young Man's Best Companion* to give Maria.

> *Hold your Pen lightly, grip it not too hard,*
> *And with due care your Copy well regard.*
> *Join every Letter to its next with Care,*
> *And let the Stroke be admirably fair. . . .*

> *Quit yourself nobly with prudent Care,*
> *Of clumsy Writing and of Blots beware.*
> *Remember strictly what the Art enjoins,*
> *Equal siz'd Letters, and as equal Lines.*

Nathaniel smiled as he copied, thinking how Maria might profit from the directions of the poem. Not that he was fond of her, as Mr. Jefferson, had put it. Oh no. It simply was a kindness. His heart felt so light, he actually began to hum as he wrote, a tune his mother had sung, "'Are you going to Scarborough Fair? Parsley, sage, rosemary, and thyme. Remember me to the one who lives there; she once was a true love of mine. . . .'"

Nathaniel's only worry was how to slip the two pounds into Basil's tin box without being seen. His plan was to simply return the money without comment, since he had never admitted to taking it to begin with. Somehow it seemed best to Nathaniel to leave it all unspoken. Easier, certain. But that would require stealth and opportunity.

That evening, he had his chance. It was a delicious June twilight, the air full of sweet smells and gentle breezes. The kind of rejuvenating night Tidewater people tried to remember during August's firestorm of heat. He had just finished watering the livestock when Nathaniel heard the clear, vibrant notes of two violins tuning.

Nathaniel ran to the open window of the parlor and peeped in over the sill. Mr. Jefferson had come! There he stood with Basil, all flustered and grinning. Mrs. Maguire sat in the corner, smoothing her skirt and gracefully fluttering a fan before her face. She looked completely different from the woman fussing over cold remedies in the hot backyard kitchen. Startled, Nathaniel realized that once upon a time, she probably had been rather pretty.

Nathaniel inched around the house. Once they started playing, he could sneak up the staircase to Basil's room and deposit the money without being noticed. The trick would be getting past Edan's room on the first floor, where the carriage maker was still abed. He took off his shoes and left them under a bush near the back door. He'd have to be very quiet and quick, moving during louder music. It wouldn't do to try during a smooth, delicate adagio, which the creak of a floorboard would interrupt like cannon fire.

Nathaniel waited until the violins were chasing each other in song. Each instrument raced up and down in pitch, whirling about each other like the small white butterflies that spiraled around in the garden. Nathaniel slipped through the door, wincing at its slight squeak, and crept up the edge of the stairs. He stuck to the wall's edge, tiptoeing where the stair plank was nailed and less likely to groan under his weight.

Halfway up, still safe. Round the landing, up three more stairs. He was there!

Breathing hard, Nathaniel fished out Basil's tin box. He pulled from his pocket the money Jefferson had given him. Counting out two pounds, Nathaniel dropped that amount into the meager collection of coins inside and closed the lid. He started to shove the box back under Basil's mattress.

For several long moments Nathaniel hesitated, looking down at the tin box, listening to the jaunty allegro below. Finally, he reached into his pocket and pulled out his remaining money. He dropped all of it into Basil's savings.

Perhaps now Basil could purchase the books he'd

sacrificed to free Nathaniel from the blacksmith one year before. He only wished he hadn't taken off his shoes and could retrieve the shilling he kept there to add to the trove. Nathaniel owed Basil everything. It was only right.

Nathaniel pushed the lid shut with a snap and tucked it back under the mattress. Now he faced trying to retreat out of the house undetected. But he wasn't worried. He suddenly felt strong and free, no longer shackled by indebtedness or deceit. He turned for the door.

There stood Mistress Maguire.

Nathaniel gasped. *Oh no! She'll think I'm stealing.* Nathaniel's mouth popped open to explain, but nothing came out. Mrs. Maguire stepped into the room and closed the door.

"What are you about, boy?" she whispered.

What could he say? How could he explain? The violin music downstairs rose in a crescendo of sixteenth-note runs and Nathaniel felt his own heart race with it.

"I saw you," she said.

Oh, he was lost, done for. Who would believe his story?

"I saw you," she repeated. "I saw you putting money

into Mr. Wilkinson's tin. From whence did you get it?"

Nathaniel shook his head, still silent, feeling himself falling, falling.

"I think you'd rather explain to me than to Mr. Maguire."

There was something about her voice that saved Nathaniel. Something akin to his mother, something that reminded him of the time he'd managed to break every egg they'd collected and spill the precious bucket of fresh milk. "Tell me, my love, what happened," his mother had said. "We mustn't grieve over what we cannot change."

In a torrent of words, Nathaniel told. Told about Moses, told about taking Basil's money, told about tracking Vixen, told about Jefferson and Nathaniel suggesting he find Basil to play violin. Told how his father had not seemed to care about their being sold apart. How Basil had saved him from sure abuse at the hands of the blacksmith. How Basil was building his mind with books and music. Flushed, breathless, he ended and waited, immediately kicking himself for his honesty. Now he was completely exposed, stripped to his soul. And worse, without thinking, he had betrayed Moses.

Mrs. Maguire was quiet for an eternity, it seemed.

Nathaniel's head spun.

Finally she patted his shoulder. "My, that is a tale, lad. Mr. Wilkinson had never explained exactly how you came to be with him. And he never told me that he was missing money. He is a generous man, indeed." She crossed her arms and looked out the window. Below stairs, Jefferson and Basil began the andante section of their sonata, a beautiful lilting melody. She held up a finger and said, "Listen. Isn't it wondrous that man can make such harmony?"

She sighed and then continued softly, "One of the greatest challenges of life, Nathaniel, is deciding to move forward. To live as if each day presents a new, hopeful possibility. To make the decision to leave the past there, in the past. That is the only way to be free of its pain. We must not let past sadness or tragedy or mistreatment rule the way we act today. It takes courage to do so, yes, but we must. I . . . I myself have lost three children. I thought I could never have affection for anyone ever again. And yet, as of late, I have rediscovered that ability."

She turned to him and smiled. "You must learn to trust people who care about you, like Mr. Wilkinson. Go back outside, boy. I will not tell your story. But someday, you should tell Mr. Wilkinson the truth."

Grateful beyond words, Nathaniel inched toward

the door. "Mistress," he whispered, knowing that he was pushing her. "Mistress, please, you will not tell about Moses?"

Mrs. Maguire frowned. "I know naught what is right on that, Nathaniel. Helping a slave run is a crime that could send you to the gallows. I do not want that to happen. And yet, the slave should be pursued. He is valuable property. If we sold Sally, for instance, as Mr. Maguire is suggesting, we could clear a large portion of our debts." She shook her head. "Can you imagine? Selling Sally," she murmured.

For a moment she was silent as the music danced on below. "I must think on what I should do with that information, lad. My instinct is to do nothing. But still, I must consider it a bit. Go on, now."

Nathaniel slipped back down the stairs and out to his loft, feeling free and chained at the same time. He couldn't know that soon events would so rattle the Maguire household that Mistress Maguire would forget completely about Moses.

✑ Chapter Twenty-eight ✑

NATHANIEL DIDN'T NOTICE when paper dropped out of his pocket the next morning. But Ben did. And it would have been far better if he hadn't.

"Pssst, Nat." Ben pointed to the floor behind Nathaniel.

Edan was at his desk, scribbling a design for a carriage they had no order to make. Ben was sharpening chisels and axes, making a piercing, scraping squeal each time he held a blade to the grindstone that Nathaniel was pumping. He thought Edan was paying no attention to them. But he was wrong.

"What is that?" Edan growled, heaving his massive self up.

Nathaniel looked down and gasped. It was Edan's demand for payment that he had forgotten to give to the *Gazette* to publish. Underneath it was the poem he was copying for Maria.

Terrified instinct took over. He snatched up the papers. He bolted for the door.

But Edan pounced. Nathaniel felt himself yanked back by his collar and pinned against the wall. Edan ripped the papers out of his hand.

As he skimmed the top one—his own advertisement—Nathaniel whimpered: "Please, sir, please, I am so sorry. I forgot to give it to the *Gazette*. I . . . I . . ." He couldn't think of any excuse, any story to hide what he had actually done. He wasn't about to confess about Thomas Jefferson, Vixen, and his four pounds.

But it was the way Edan turned over the next page with such calm—as if he were suddenly coming to a vital recognition—that was the most bone-chilling.

In a cold, amazed voice, he said, "I was unaware that you could write. So . . . you must be the one . . . the one to betray me."

Still held against the wall by Edan's meaty hand, Nathaniel shook his head fervently. "Master, I don't know what you mean. I just forgot. Please forgive me. I just forgot to deliver it."

Edan leaned so close that his bulbous nose almost touched Nathaniel's. His putrid breath blasted his face. Keeping his bloodshot eyes fixed on Nathaniel's, he crumpled up the papers and threw them to the ground. He slipped his free hand into his waistcoat and pulled out a letter. "You claim to know nothing of this?" Edan snarled, holding the crackling thick paper up almost as if he were going to ram it down Nathaniel's throat.

"No . . . no sir . . . I know naught."

Edan cackled. "It's a summons—a summons to appear before the committee of inspection. They have demanded to see my accounting books. They want to know if I made the cart that carried off the magazine gunpowder and, if so, when I delivered it. They say they suspect me of being in league with the British Marines because they received a letter claiming I have oft spoken ill of the burgesses and the Non-importation Agreement. Two scurrilous hooligans, so-called patriots, threatened me last evening with tar and feathering as I passed the tavern. All this stems from a letter, a slander.

"I have done nothing wrong. Nothing! I gave up my tea. I haven't ordered items from England. I have stuck by their agreements that I do not like, that can bankrupt me. All I have done is to have an opinion different from theirs. I've taken no action against them. All I want is to be left alone."

He shook Nathaniel, banging him so hard against the wall that pain burst like fireworks through his head and set his ears ringing. "I do all that is asked, and then a letter—a letter from an unidentified assassin—brings me down!" he howled in rage. "It must have been you. I've fed you, clothed you. Why?"

"Master, I don't know what you are talking about. Please, I don't know."

He shook Nathaniel again. "Don't lie to me. I knew when I saw those devil-ghost eyes of yours that you were a viper. It was you!" he screamed. "You! You!" Edan punctuated each "you" by slamming Nathaniel against the wall.

With a crazed, murderous leer, Edan looked over to the tool table, where lay the sharpened axes. His thoughts were clear.

"No!" Finally, Ben reacted. "Mistress Maguire! Sally!" he screamed. He leaped for Edan and landed on his back like a cat. He hung there, while Nathaniel squirmed and kicked, finally breaking free.

Frantically Nathaniel crawled away as Edan shook off Ben and grabbed up a block of wood. He hurled it at Nathaniel. It hit the table with such force that chisels went flying. Nathaniel covered his head against the falling blades and cried, "Please, master!"

Edan seized a turned spoke and rushed for Nathaniel. Nathaniel skidded under the table, darting away from Edan's powerful swings.

"Master! Stop! You kill that boy!" Sally was in the door. She shrieked back toward the house, "Mistress Maguire, come quick!"

With a forceful lunge, Edan caught Nathaniel's foot. Nathaniel desperately scratched at the floor as Edan dragged him out from under the table. Edan pulled him up and held him by the throat.

"Now I have you."

Nathaniel started to close his eyes and turn his head to brace for the blows to follow. He'd been in this position countless times before. But this time something kept him staring at Edan, his head held high, defiant. He prepared himself to hurt, but he did not look away.

Startled perhaps by Nathaniel's boldness, Edan hesitated just long enough for Ben to tackle him, latching onto his knees. Edan let go of Nathaniel to pound Ben with the spoke. But Ben held tight, gasping, "Run, Nathaniel, run for the mistress!"

Nathaniel scrambled for the door, nearly colliding with Mrs. Maguire, who was already darting in. The look on her face was one of horror and disgust. "Edan!"

Edan wavered just enough that Ben broke loose. But Edan reacted swiftly and gripped Ben's arm. He raised the spoke again.

"Edan, stop! Stop at once! You may bully me, but you'll not harm these boys. Stop! Or I will find some way to have you put in the stocks for all our sakes." She was shaking, but she stood firm.

Sally stared at her mistress in disbelief. So did Ben and Nathaniel. It was the first time any of them had heard her stand up to her husband. So astounding was her courage that Edan did stop. He dropped the spoke. They all froze, suspended in surprise, only their frightened, winded breathing breaking the silence.

Then suddenly, Edan screamed. He fell to the ground, writhing and clutching his chest, fighting for each breath. "Elizabeth," he gasped. "Make it stop! Please! Make the pain stop."

For a moment she delayed—a strange mixture of rebellion and relief on her face. A look of something seeing a gate open, a chance at liberty, thought Nathaniel with surprise. Could that really be what he saw in her expression? But it passed, and a resigned sadness, a studied businesslike air, settled over Mistress Maguire. She took a deep breath, knelt beside her husband, and tended to him.

✑ Chapter Twenty-nine ✑

THAT NIGHT NATHANIEL was so sore and bruised he could barely climb up into the loft. He ached too much to sleep. He lay awake wondering what ailed Edan and marveling at Mistress Maguire. He didn't have to wonder who reported Edan's oaths against the trade embargo and the burgesses. He knew it was Ben. That must have been what Ben meant when he'd said he'd done something to make Edan want to return to Ireland.

Around midnight Ben's voice called up the ladder. "Nathaniel? You there?"

"Aye," he replied. Where else would he be? he thought irritably.

Ben swung up the ladder and sat in the hay. The moonlight coming through the manger's open door provided scant illumination. Nathaniel could not see Ben's face, only the dark shadow of his presence.

"I'm sorry, Nat. I was the one who reported Edan."

"I know," answered Nathaniel.

"You do?" He paused and then asked guiltily, "Are you mad at me?"

Of course he was! But should he answer honestly? Nathaniel hesitated. "A little, yes. Master Maguire could have killed me."

"I know, I know." Ben pulled his legs up, wrapped his arms around them, and dropped his head onto his knees. His voice became muffled. "I . . . I . . . I am ashamed that I didn't stop him sooner, Nat. I should have said it was me what sent the letter. I was . . . I was afraid." He sighed and ran his hand through the hay. "I can't believe I was so afraid. What use am I?"

Ben seemed so sad that Nathaniel took pity on him. "Well . . . you were brave enough to get him off me, Ben. Thank you."

There was a long silence until Ben lifted his head. "I suppose that's right. You're welcome, Nat." He was quiet again. "You know, Nat, I think what slapped me into acting finally was seeing you steel yourself for a beating. It made me ashamed of myself. You are very strong, Nat. I just followed your example."

Strong? Nathaniel shook his head. He wasn't strong. He'd taken countless whippings like a dog, tail between his legs. He felt his face turn red, and it was his turn to feel ashamed. "I'm not strong, Ben."

"You're wrong, Nat. You've changed. I've seen it. It was in your face and the way you glared at him."

Maybe. Maybe it was just the sheer unfairness of Edan's wrath that had given Nathaniel strength this time. Perhaps Basil's lectures about his having rights and an inborn intellect and dignity had sunk in without his realizing it. Now he understood what the patriots were all about—fighting against a power that used them unfairly, ruled them with force. Yes, he saw it all better now. He felt it himself. His world of the carriage shop mirrored the struggle between the colonists and the British king.

But there was still one thing that he had to ask— Ben's reporting of Edan seemed, well, spiteful. Of course Nathaniel sympathized with the desire to get back at Edan. Hadn't he loosed Vixen on the black-smith for hitting him? But if Edan got in trouble, Mistress Maguire was hurt too. And she had been too kind to them for that.

"Ben, why did you report Master Maguire?"

"Because!" Ben's voice was defensive and abrupt. "Because he's a tyrant and a bully!"

"Aye, that he is. I'd be glad to put him in chains in a cargo hull and set him adrift in the seas. He deserves it!" Nathaniel, in fact, quite liked the sound of that.

"But"—he tried to keep his own feelings of vengeance in check—"but that means Mistress Maguire. . . ."

"I know!" Ben nearly shouted. Nathaniel heard the sound of handfuls of hay being thrown. "I know. I'm going to go to the committee tomorrow and tell them I was mistaken.

"I had just wanted a way to be free of him, Nat. That was all. I didn't think anyone would tar and feather him, just make him mad enough to go back to Ireland. So many loyalists and merchants are fleeing Virginia, returning to England. Mrs. Rathell just sold off her store's Irish muslins and English silks for a song and sailed back home. She had the sense to know no one would buy her goods in these times. Why do the Maguires have to be so stubborn?" he asked in exasperation.

"I guess they feel America is their home, too," Nathaniel said quietly, recognizing it himself for the first time.

Ben sighed. "Well, I've found another way to liberty. I'm sixteen now. I'm old enough to join one of the Virginia regiments that are forming. Patrick Henry is going to head them. I know that out of loyalty to my father, he'll make sure that I can stay in it even if Edan protests that I am breaking my apprenticeship. Who is going to care about apprenticeships during a revolution? I just need a musket. In fact"—he stood up and brushed off hay—"the boys and I are going to get some tonight."

"What? You're not going to steal it, are you, Ben, because—"

"No, we're going to the magazine. Nobody is guarding it now that the powder's gone. The guns inside belong to the colonists. I'm a colonist. I've a right to one." He moved to the ladder. "I best go. I'm supposed to meet up outside Mr. Greenhow's store. I just wanted to make sure you were all right." Ben swung his leg onto the ladder, then paused. "Nat?"

"Aye?"

"Come with me?" Ben's voice was uncharacteristically vulnerable. "We could use a good man like you. Please?"

Asked like that, Nathaniel could not refuse. He couldn't sleep anyway. Plus, he suddenly had a new interest in the colonists' demand for liberty. He arose stiffly and followed Ben into the eerie, dark streets of a Williamsburg asleep.

The morning would dawn Whitsunday, so there had been the usual celebrations of it in town that afternoon—cudgeling, wrestling matches, pig chasing, and footraces. The boys had been smart to wait until the deep hours of the night to approach the magazine, to allow all the celebrants to go home and be snoring off their ale. Still, the boys tiptoed, guided only by moonlight. Their boastful whispers gave way to unnerved grumblings when they stumbled into one another or tripped over unseen roots and manure.

Nathaniel kept to the tail end of the group, following Ben's back, unable to see exactly how many boys were participating in the raid. A dozen ahead of him, he thought, including Ben's usual cohorts—Beverly, Robert, and Jeremiah.

Ever surly, Jeremiah had tried to run off Nathaniel, complaining that it was enough to suffer Ben's presence, but did they have to associate with an indentured servant as well? "What will you bring next?" Jeremiah sneered. "A slave?"

But Ben had insisted Nathaniel come, bragging on his cool head. "Why, he just stood down Edan Maguire, boys!" Ben boasted. "That's more than you could do, Jeremiah! If I had to choose between you and Nat to be in our company, I'd choose Nat twenty times over. He'll take on a brigade of Hessians for us someday."

Nathaniel protested Ben's boast, but Ben shushed him. "Nat's just being overly modest," he said. "I witnessed the whole thing."

Nathaniel was beginning to get a very bad feeling about this jaunt.

It was a short distance from Greenhow's storefront to the magazine. When they reached the tall brick wall surrounding the octagonal arsenal, the boys grew silent, although the energy of their nervousness could have lit lanterns.

"Anybody in the guardhouse?" one of them whispered.

"No. Home with a bottle, most like," another answered.

"How are we going to get in?" The wall was sealed with a huge double wooden door that was locked.

"I've the key," someone hissed.

"Where'd you get that?"

"Never you mind," Beverly hushed him, taking command. "Give me the key."

The large, heavy key passed from hand to hand until Beverly inserted it in the lock. With a resounding click and groan, the massive doors drifted open.

A few of the boys laughed nervously. They slipped in quickly, as if their break-in was an innocent game of hide-and-seek.

Nathaniel paused, about to turn back—this was insanity—but Ben pulled him inside the magazine yard.

He pushed the huge door closed behind them.

"Come on," Beverly ordered. The boys fell in line. But at the door of the magazine building, they all paused, suddenly skittish.

"Well, here we are, boys." Beverly took in a deep breath. "I hear there are hundreds of blue-painted stock guns and Brown Bess flintlocks inside. Plenty for each of us to have one. They'll never be missed. Then we'll show the militia we're just as good as they, shan't we, boys? Here's to liberty!" Beverly put his hand on the latch.

"Aye!" "That's right!" "Give us liberty!"

All of them save Nathaniel joined in the whispered crowing.

Jeremiah noticed his silence and jeered: "This one's afraid. You lie about him, Ben, just like you lie about everything—your family, your father. I say if this servant is going to join us and taint the integrity of our company, he has to go in first."

All eyes turned to Nathaniel. Before he could shake his head and back away, Ben spoke up. "Shut up, Jeremiah. You're just afraid yourself. I'll go first."

And with that, Ben pulled Nathaniel behind him and opened the door to the magazine.

There was a blinding flash of light and a thunderous *BANG!*

Nathaniel felt himself blown backward, his arms stung by something hot and vicious. Bashing his head against the ground, it took several moments for him to come to consciousness.

When he did, his ears were ringing from the blast. The only sound he could make out was Ben screaming.

∾ Chapter Thirty ∾

"HOLD ON, LAD, I've almost got it."

Nathaniel gritted his teeth as the surgeon dug in his flesh to find a small piece of lead. He thought he might vomit. He was lying in the hayloft, unsure how he'd gotten there. Although, if he thought hard enough about it, he remembered being lifted and carried, an uproar of shouting and a flood of lantern light. All he could figure was that the blast had awoken the town and someone had brought him home.

Basil was there. Nathaniel turned away from the surgeon and his prying needle pinchers to Basil. Basil looked like he was about to cry. But he smiled at Nathaniel. "Brave lad," he whispered.

"There. I've got it. It wasn't embedded far at all." The searing pain stopped.

The surgeon held up a tiny black ball and examined it in the lantern light. "Swan shot," he muttered. "The redcoats must have rammed two handfuls of balls into that spring gun. Diabolical wretches rigged a gun to go off when someone opened the door. I think this time the townspeople really will riot. Lord Dunmore best watch his back."

He began to pack up his things. "You're lucky, boy. You were just nicked. It didn't touch bone. You'll be back to work in a few days. The others weren't so lucky. That boy Beverly still has two balls in his shoulder and one in his wrist."

Trembling from pain and anxiety, Nathaniel lifted his head. "Ben?"

The surgeon didn't answer. He looked to Basil. Haltingly, Basil answered. "Two of his fingers were shot off. He lost a lot of blood. The surgeon did what he could, and now Mistress Maguire is nursing him."

Nathaniel sobbed—hot, bitter tears of regret. Oh, if only he could reverse time. How could they have been so stupid?

Awkwardly, Basil patted him on the head. "I will return, lad. I must see the surgeon away."

Nathaniel fought to stay awake, but he sank into blackness as he heard the surgeon tell Basil that his fee was five pounds. He wanted the money now. He was leaving town. He feared what might happen next. "There's rumor," he said, "that there is powder buried in the magazine yard linked by an underground fuse to the palace. Dunmore could blow up the town in an instant without leaving his dining room. God knows the town is full of panic and false rumors. But if this one is true, Dunmore is probably vengeful enough to do it!"

When Nathaniel awoke, it was late afternoon the next day. Basil was sitting beside him, reading.

He blinked and lifted himself, feeling enormously hungry. But his movement caused a jab of ache in his arm. He flopped back down, groaning.

"There, there, lad, don't try to move yet." Basil stood. "Let me get some porridge for you. Sally has been up here twenty times in the past hour, I think, to tell me that the instant you awake, I am to get some hot gruel for you."

He reappeared with a steaming bowl. He helped Nathaniel sit and watched to make sure he could spoon the liquid himself.

"She's put honey in it to sweeten and no medicine, I promise." Basil grinned. "No one else warrants such treats. You must be her favorite."

As Nathaniel ate, blowing on the scalding liquid before sipping it out of his spoon, Basil's expression of relief changed.

"Lad," Basil cleared his throat. "When I went

to pay the surgeon . . ."

Nathaniel looked up at him with guilt. Oh, to have cost Basil money yet again. He started to apologize, but Basil held up his hand, "Nathaniel, I think I might have misjudged you. I thought you took something when perhaps I just miscounted. I don't know what to think. I . . . is there something you wish to tell me?"

Nathaniel froze, spoon midair, unsure what to say. In the wake of what had happened to Ben, stealing Basil's money for Moses now seemed so long ago. But Basil's sudden surprise made his answering unnecessary.

"Oh, my goodness!" Basil jumped up as if swarmed by ants. He stared at the floor. "What in the world? Nathaniel, what is that?" He dropped to his knees and excitedly began flinging hay aside, like a groundhog throwing dirt as he dug a den.

Nathaniel laughed in spite of his pain, laughed in joy and pride and hope and affection for an old man who could become enthusiastic so easily. "Aye, master. I've been using your gift." Wincing, Nathaniel raised himself up and found the thank-you letter to Basil that he had hidden inside his mother's Bible.

Basil's eyes filled with tears as he read. Embarrassed, he cleared his throat loudly and turned instructor. "Show me, lad, what you have done here."

They sat for an hour, cross-legged, checking

Nathaniel's sums, his spelling. "Oh, well done, lad, well done! I am so pleased. You are a glorious example of all that Mr. Jefferson talked about the night he came—the inborn nobility of the common man, his ability to educate and govern himself. If Mr. Jefferson has his way, we will raise an aristocracy built not on family ancestry but on merit, on intellect, on hard work. If that becomes the measuring stick, lad, then you will be a great man, indeed."

With a catch in his throat, Nathaniel remembered Ben's boast of someday being elected to the Continental Congress. He braved the question that he had been dreading to ask. "Master, what will become of Ben?"

Basil's face clouded. "His right hand may be useless now. Mistress Maguire will keep him here until he is better and then probably send him home."

"But what about the time he owes for his apprenticeship?" Nathaniel asked.

"He won't be able to learn the trade now, with his hand mangled so."

"But . . . but what is to become of him?" Nathaniel asked in horror.

Basil looked out the manger door. "What indeed, lad?" he murmured sorrowfully. "What indeed."

Rage began to boil up inside Nathaniel. But it was Basil who leaped to his feet in a fury.

"I cannot stomach the cruelty, the cunning, the barbarity of the British setting a spring gun like that!" He paced. He thumped his chest. "Such man-made traps are used to kill poachers who might disturb a lord's storehouses. Like rat traps. As if people were annoying vermin to exterminate. Such treachery! Such arrogance! Do the redcoats think we'll sit still while they lay such murderous inventions to maim our sons?" Breathing hard, flushed with ardor, Basil raised his fist and quoted Patrick Henry's cry: "'Forbid it, Almighty God. Give me liberty! Give me liberty against such callous disregard for life, for rights!'"

He turned to Nathaniel with a new idea shining on his face. "Nathaniel"—he straightened his back—"I am going to join the infantry."

"What?" Nathaniel was still agape at Basil's passionate speech.

"Yes, that's it. I am going to join up." The gangly old tutor was lit up from inside. "When we see a wrong that we know we have the ability to correct, we have the responsibility to do so. If men of principle don't fight for an idea they started, who will? I worry that all my lectures set Ben to his reckless acts. I must do as I say. Old men must not send the young to settle their arguments while they sit at home in comfort." He stuck his lower lip out and nodded. "Yes, that's what I shall do. I am going to volunteer."

He stopped and looked at Nathaniel hard. When he spoke again, his voice was quiet, reflective, sad. "I cannot afford to take you with me, Nathaniel. And I would not have you in harm's way. And if I am to fight for liberty, I will hold no one in bondage. I release you—with affection, lad—from the time you owe me. Perhaps I can recommend you to Mr. Greenhow as bookkeeper." He turned to look down at the floor and trailed off in thought. "These sums you have tallied are impressive."

Nathaniel felt as if he had been shot again. Basil was going to leave him?

No, no, no. Nathaniel stood, shrugging off the discomfort in his arm, shrugging off his old ways of simply accepting whatever fate others decreed for him. He felt as if he were shedding a skin he'd long outgrown, that had bound him tight and kept him from growing. It felt wonderful. "Master, haven't you said that as a human being I am completely capable of understanding and determining my own fate?"

"Aye, lad, that is what Pope and Locke have written. I believe it."

"And you are now telling me that I am free of my indenture?"

"Aye."

"Free to make my own choices? Free to make my

own coming and going?"

"Aye, I will write it out and sign it," Basil answered.

The choice was simple. "I am going with you, then," Nathaniel said stoutly. "I want to get back at the British for Ben too." He almost, almost confessed that he couldn't bear the thought of losing Basil.

"Lad, you are too young."

Nathaniel thought a moment about the companies of volunteers he had seen marching on the market green. They didn't move until the fife major and drummer played. The musicians' calls directed the troops. "How old must you be to be a fifer?"

A slow smile spread across Basil's face. "Fourteen."

Nathaniel grinned back.

"Where is your fife, lad?"

Nathaniel pointed to his thin sack of precious belongings.

Basil nodded. "I think you need to learn a few drill calls, then. I saw that Mr. Greenhow had a fife tutor in his store. I will borrow it. We'll begin lessons tomorrow."

PART EIGHT

September 1775

With fife and drum he marched away.
He would not heed what I did say.
He'll not come back for many a day.
Johnny has gone for a soldier.

Chorus: Shule, shule, shule agra
Sure, ah sure, and he loves me.
When he comes back we'll married be.
Johnny has gone for a soldier.

I'll go up on Portland Hill,
And there I'll sit and cry my fill
And every tear should turn a mill.
Johnny has gone for a soldier.

Chorus

I'll sell my rock, I'll sell my reel,
I'll sell my flax and spinning wheel,
To buy my love a sword of steel.
Johnny has gone for a soldier.

—"Johnny Has Gone for a Soldier," American
adaptation of a seventeenth-century Irish tune

❧ Chapter Thirty-one ❧

"READ THAT TO me again, lad." Basil sat on a thick oak tree, downed in a storm that had howled inland up the Chesapeake Bay, stirring the James and York Rivers into raging tempests.

Nathaniel straightened the *Gazette* and repeated: "'Lord Dunmore, it seems, fared but poorly in this hurricane, as, by some accident or other, occasioned by the confusion in which the sailors were, his lordship fell overboard, and was severely dunked. But according to the old saying, those who are born to be hanged will never be drowned.'"

"Oh, well said, well said," laughed Basil, his mouth full of thread and needle. He was sewing—not very well. On his lap was the cutout of a large, blousy shirt. He was trying to stitch together the seams of the sleeves, fumbling with the coarse, Oznabrig linen. "And the next section?"

Nathaniel continued: "'Dunmore has received twenty to thirty more men from British troops in Florida, and soon expects to bring his army to five hundred; with which, we hear, he intends taking possession of his palace in this city that he lately abandoned—if not prevented by those he terms *rebels*.'"

"*Rebels!* Ho ho! That's us!" Basil said gleefully. "Doesn't that make us sound like renegades of legend?" The old man grinned, looking silly and youthful. "Now let's see. I think I have it." He stood to shake out the hunting shirt. But Basil had managed to thread his needle through the sleeve and his pants leg at the same time, sewing them together. The shirt stuck fast to his thigh.

"Oh dear." Basil sat down with a thump, rattling the darkening leaves that still clung to the uprooted oak. He leaned back over his task.

Nathaniel fought off a laugh. So far Basil's career as a soldier hadn't been particularly glorious. He couldn't even sew the frontiersman-like uniform required of Patrick Henry's shirtmen!

The two of them had joined the 2nd Virginia Regiment. They belonged to a company captained by George Nicholas, a young Williamsburg man who had led William and Mary students on a raid for arms into the governor's palace. Shortly after the spring-gun blast in the magazine, Dunmore and his family had fled to the HMS *Fowey*. Fearing Dunmore would soon lead an invasion by marines, Nicholas and his friends emptied the palace of two hundred muskets and three hundred swords. James Monroe, Ben's friend from home, had taken part. When he came to visit Ben and heard Basil rail against the boy's misfortune, Monroe had given one of the seized guns to Basil.

With it, Basil passed muster. With his fife, Nathaniel did, too.

Now they sat in a crowded encampment on fields behind the college, waiting, waiting.

Nathaniel looked around at the men clustered nearby. Many worked on their own purple-dyed shirts, cutting fringe in the shoulder-wide, capelike collar to allow rain to drip off. Others labored over the blue wool "half-thicks" they'd been given to sew gaiters to cover their legs up their thighs, to where the long hunting shirt dropped. They joked and bragged as they worked.

Despite the blustery confidence of the men, Nathaniel knew trouble was coming—real trouble— just like the hurricane that had roared up the rivers bringing destruction and death. Dunmore may have fallen off his boat, and some of the tender ships that followed his larger warships may have run aground in the storm, but the truth was that Dunmore was gaining momentum.

In addition to his well-trained and well-equipped British troops, Dunmore was building a powerful fleet. He had the fourteen-gun *Otter* and the *King's Fisher*, an eighteen-gun sloop. He had also confiscated two merchant ships, the *William*, with thirteen guns, and the *Eilbeck*, with seven. Their tender ships—small boats that carried cargo and passengers back and forth between the shore and the main vessel—were equipped with swivel guns and four-pound cannon. Dunmore was harassing fishing vessels and threatening to bombard riverside plantations and the town of Norfolk.

Plus, in Nathaniel's mind, Dunmore had another secret and potent weapon. For in the *Gazette* was also the news that British naval officers were using Africans as navigators and guides. Nathaniel just knew that Moses was one of the escaped slaves helping the redcoats find their way in the marshy back streams of the Tidewater. His courage and strength would serve the king's forces well. If Moses was fighting for the British to secure his liberty, something wasn't quite right with the patriot cause.

Nathaniel tried to not think about Moses being with the British. Dunmore and the marines he commanded were not to be trusted. Whatever promises they had made Moses, Nathaniel doubted they'd keep.

However, he did think constantly on Ben and his horrible wound. His hand was still bandaged when he came to say good-bye. Mistress Maguire was sending him home. She had contacted Ben's mother, who thought him old enough to try to run their farm and reclaim the family's financial equilibrium. With one good hand and a strong back, he could still manage to do many of the farm's tasks.

"I don't want to be a farmer," Ben complained.

Putting his hand on Ben's shoulder, Basil had spoken gently: "You didn't want to be a carriage maker either, did you?"

"I wanted . . . I wanted . . ." Ben hesitated.

"I know what you wanted, lad. But wanting glory shouldn't be what drives a man to take up arms against others."

Ben frowned. "I do believe in our cause, too, Basil. It wasn't just vanity. I believe in our right to stand up against tyranny."

"I know, lad. Let that be your driving force now. Patience. I have a feeling that this fight may last awhile. Heal. Perhaps one day your hand can hold a musket to defend us. Or better yet, raise your heartfelt thoughts in legislature. Study, Ben. There's the way. Refine your mind with books. You don't need a strong hand to think or speak out to lead others."

Ben stood a little taller. "I'll try, master tutor."

"Oh, oh, let me lend you something, Ben." Basil darted off to his tent.

Ben and Nathaniel grinned at each other, sharing their fond amusement at Basil. Then Ben grew serious. "You keep an eye on the old fool, Nat. He's no soldier."

"No, he's not," agreed Nathaniel.

They stood in awkward silence, not knowing what else to say. Nathaniel had come to care about Ben, there was no denying it. He would miss Ben's jocund humor, his confidence in him, his prodding. He opened his mouth to speak and then closed it. Opened it again, but could only manage, "Take care, Ben."

Ben took a step closer to Nathaniel and looked him firmly in the eye. "You're stronger than you think, Nat. I've learned"—he held up his wrapped hand—"that steady men make better leaders."

Skipping back, holding a book aloft, Basil interrupted. Seeing him coming, Ben adopted a little of his old swagger and concluded loudly for Basil to hear well. "Steady and slow, just like that old tortoise in his race against the hare. Just don't retreat back into your shell, eh, Nat?" He winked at Nathaniel. "Boil some lobsterbacks for me, lad."

Then he turned toward Basil and covered his face in mock horror. "What, old tutor? Not a grammar book!"

Basil ignored the banter. "Not quite, lad. It's Locke's *Two Treatises of Government*."

Nathaniel gasped. He knew how precious that book was to Basil.

Ben did, too. "I can't take that, Master Basil," he whispered.

"Yes, lad, you can. I've probably memorized every line. I shan't miss it. Learn some philosophy to support your zeal. An argument backed with reason, with eloquence, will prove too strong to deny." He put the book in Ben's good hand. "If we win this fight, it may mean we break away from England altogether. Then we must devise a new social contract, a new way of governing. We will need men of thought to create one. Go on home, now, lad. Read. Think."

Ben nodded, turned, and left, looking down at the book as he walked.

Nathaniel had been straining to watch Ben disappear into Williamsburg's bustle when their company sergeant interrupted with astounding news.

"Pay," he grunted.

With hands trembling in surprise, Nathaniel took the first payment he'd ever received for his labor: seven and one-third dollars for the month. He was even more amazed when he found out that Basil, as a private, received less—six and two-thirds dollars! He was so happy, he didn't even mind when the fife major, in charge of teaching all the lower musicians the important camp calls, took half Nathaniel's money as fee for his instruction.

❧ Chapter Thirty-two ❧

IN HIS SLEEP, Nathaniel nodded: "a sixteenth run up G-A-B-C to eighth notes D-D-B-G. Skip up to hold the E long . . . I have it. Keep the tempo with the drummer; don't rush." He rolled over, bumping his head against Basil's feet.

His eyes popped open. He stared into dark, now completely awakened by the smell of damp straw and feet and the snores of five other bodies crammed into a six-and-a-half-foot square tent. The tune he had been practicing in his sleep was still sounding. How was that possible? He rubbed his eyes. Outside the tent flap, something *bump-bumped* and a voice hissed through the tent flap, "Be up, Nathaniel. It's the drummers call. Be quick!"

Nathaniel jumped up, knocking into the sloping canvas of the tent. His tent mates grunted, complained, and went back to snoring.

Of course! That was the duty drummer and fifer playing the call to assemble the musicians. He hurled himself out the tent's flap. Skidding along the dewy grass, he caught up with Ben's enemy, Jeremiah, who by a stroke of ill luck was Nathaniel's company drummer.

"You'll get us in trouble for your laziness," Jeremiah sniped, his drum bumping against his legs as he ran.

Jeremiah had escaped injury at the magazine. But he was Nathaniel's age, still unable to join as a soldier. Almost a foot taller, hefty and mean, drumming seemed a perfect role for him. Yet, he was slow to learn. He blamed his fumblings on Nathaniel playing wrong notes—lies, but ones that Jeremiah made with such vehemence that the drum major often corrected Nathaniel. Nathaniel dared not protest. The major teaching them tolerated no interruptions. He had served in the French and Indian War and believed in the harsh discipline practiced by the British officers. Talking back brought a beating.

Also, Nathaniel was permanently paired with Jeremiah. Each company of sixty-eight foot soldiers had its own set of officers—a captain, first and second lieutenant, and junior ensign—plus one fifer and one drummer. That meant that altogether the 1st and 2nd Regiments had about a dozen pairs of fife and drummers. But they were not rotated. There was no escaping Jeremiah, as a result. If Nathaniel got Jeremiah into trouble, Jeremiah would make Nathaniel pay dearly for it, and have ample opportunity to do so.

In the dim glow of a lantern, the on-duty fifer and drummer stood in front of the commanding officer's tent. There had been frost in the night—the first of the season—and Nathaniel could see puffs of vapor hanging about the fifer's mouth as he blew. Nathaniel knew it would be hard to play his tiny wooden instrument in such cold. He tucked his hands under his armpits to warm his fingers.

Quickly the camp musicians gathered. Together they struck up reveille, telling the soldiers to rise, comb their hair, clean their hands and face, and be ready for the day's duties. It was a quick-tempo walk down the scale from g with a few sixteenth-note embellishments. Nathaniel was still working on those runs, and often substituted a single quarter note in the run's place. Still, his fife's voice pierced the air, much like a rooster's crow, creating a ripple of stirring in the camp.

Within minutes, several hundred men were up and about, scratching, stretching, shouting, stumbling into things. Cooking fires were stirred and rekindled. Men heated up biscuits and coffee. Children darted about, playing soldiers, cared for by the women who'd followed their husbands and did laundry, mending, and nursing. Sutlers opened their wagons for business, offering rum, soap, thread, fruit. Crammed together behind the campus of William and Mary, the encampment had the same bustle and almost the same number of people as the town of Williamsburg.

Nathaniel skipped back through the two long parallel rows of tents. As cramped as it was, he was grateful to be housed in one. The new army was still scrambling to outfit its men. Many were sleeping out in the open. Only those who had brought all their own equipment had shot pouches to carry cartridges or horns to hold gunpowder. Oxen around the area were being shorn of their horns as quickly as possible to supply the rest.

Nathaniel squatted beside Basil and their campfire. They gobbled up the last ham biscuits that Mrs. Maguire had sent them through Sally. They hid what they ate, knowing the other soldiers might make a grab at the tender ham. Already they were all sick of the charred food each tent mess prepared out of the raw meat, dried beans, flour, and vinegar that the army gave them every few days.

Before she'd left, Sally had elbowed Basil and announced, "Master Maguire done died."

Basil had just looked at her, blinking.

"Had a fit. Died. Doctor said it was his heart." She'd leaned close to Basil and whispered, "But iffen you ask me, I don't think he had one." She tapped him on the arm. "You ought to go see Mistress Maguire."

Basil had turned red. Nathaniel thought back on their leaving the Maguire house, when Basil had gently taken Mistress Maguire's hand, bowed, and kissed it as a knight would a lady's. Nathaniel wondered if perhaps Basil would one day court her.

Basil interrupted Nathaniel's musings. "What are you about today, lad? The same?"

"Aye." Nathaniel would have music practice, and then an hour of demonstrating tunes so the troops could memorize the sound and instruction of each call. It was rather important, for instance, that soldiers know the difference between reveille and "To Arms," the emergency alarm to be up and armed against a surprise attack!

"I have fatigue duty," mourned Basil.

That meant Basil would spend most of his day gathering firewood, digging new necessaries, cleaning up the camp. Nathaniel pitied him. None of the men liked it when Nathaniel and Jeremiah played the "Pioneers' March" around 9 A.M. to signal fatigue duty. It was hard and disgusting work. The camp was filthy. Many of the men already had lice and were trying to soothe the horrendous itch brought by the tiny vermin by smearing their bodies with lard. "Well, at least it will get you out of drilling," Nathaniel said sympathetically.

Basil sighed. Nathaniel worried that the tutor's spindly body was too old for such labor. But Basil actually seemed to be growing stronger with the strain rather than weaker. He was particularly thriving in nightfall's camaraderie, when he and Nathaniel entertained their company with music. Basil might start off with more refined fiddling, but by the end the men were singing and joking—adding their own words to songs like "Old King Cole" from the opera *Achilles*: "Old King Cole was a merry old soul, and a merry old soul was he; and he called for his pipe, and he called for his bowl, and"—here the men merrily shouted out words they'd added—"he called for a CUP OF TEA!"

Basil delighted in the patriotic excitement around camp. The only thing missing was his hero, Patrick Henry, who had recently returned to take command of Virginia's regiments.

Despite his complete lack of military experience, Henry had been given the Virginia command because George Washington was in charge of the Continental Army up north, trying desperately to hold off the British in Massachusetts and New York. Many worried that Henry's impatient, fiery tongue—while it did wonders to inspire—might be dangerous with an army behind it. But they could not deny that it had been his words that had stirred so many recruits to join Virginia's forces. Henry wanted a command, and so Virginia gave him one.

Later that day, Basil would finally have the thrill of hearing Henry. But it was not exactly the oratory he expected.

It started off right enough: "Gentlemen, we are now in the service of our people, in the service of justice, in the service of liberty." Patrick Henry stood on a makeshift stage of board and barrels. "Each day dawns with hope. I feel the sun shines brighter as it sees us below ready and determined. My brave people, the very heavens are inspired by our resolve."

Rapt, the thousand men stood hushed, eyes fixed on the small man with the long nose and stern appearance, the man with a voice that seemed to vault to heaven. Henry could probably tell the men they needed to swim across the Atlantic Ocean to fight the British and some might have tried. They leaned forward with anticipation.

"I would expect soldiers in such a noble endeavor to conduct themselves with dignity. Yet . . ." He paused, letting the "yet" resound. "It has come to my saddened attention that some of you are not behaving with the decorum and discipline befitting our cause. The town of Williamsburg complains bitterly of men carousing in the taverns, drinking and sporting with women, haranguing the good townspeople in the streets. Some have torn down fences to fuel fires, stripped the town's gardens and orchards. I have even been told that men practice throwing their tomahawks by hurling them at citizens' doors."

Henry scowled and boomed: "This riotous behavior is to stop at once!"

Looking uncomfortable, the men shifted their weight from foot to foot. Some glanced at one another in surprise and embarrassment.

"There will be no more gambling about the camp. Rolling of dice will bring arrest. No soldier will leave camp without orders to do so. Henceforth, every non-commissioned officer and soldier shall retire to his tent at the beating of retreat, in default of which he will be punished." He paused and added, "Furthermore, men are to stop easing themselves except in the necessary holes!"

That was the end of the inspiring orator's speech. The men were dismissed for three hours of drilling in "woods fighting."

Hugely disappointed, Basil lingered a moment, watching Henry talk with his junior officers. "Ah me," he finally murmured, sighing. "I suppose even an army of ideas has rules and day-to-day chores to attend to."

PART NINE

November 1775

Hark! 'Tis freedom that calls, come patriots awake!
To arms, my brave boys, and away;
'Tis Honor, 'tis virtue, 'tis Liberty calls,
And unbraids the too tedious delay.
What pleasures we find pursuing our foes
Thro' blood and thro' carnage we'll fly,
Then follow, we'll soon overtake them, huzzah!
The tyrants are seiz'd on, they die. . . .

'Tis freedom alone gives a relish to mirth,
But oppression all happiness sours.
'Twill smooth life's dull passage, 'twill slope the
descent,
and strew the way over with flowers.

—American words set to British tune
"The Echoing Horn"

∽ Chapter Thirty-three ∾

"**THINK YOU THE** regiment will march soon?" Maria reached down and picked up a maple leaf from the sea of autumn leaves swirling about their ankles.

"Aye. That's the word of it, soon." Nathaniel scooped up a leaf as well and twirled the five-pointed, bloodred fan to hide his shyness. "Dunmore is causing trouble on the rivers and around Norfolk. We must stop him."

"Yes, I know. Our newspaper is full of the accounts of his plundering."

During October, guided by loyalists, Dunmore had raided up and down the Tidewater area, capturing almost all the cannons and gunpowder patriots had hidden in homes and warehouses. He'd also torched several riverside plantations and villages.

Most recently, Dunmore's ships attacked Hampton, a town overlooking the Chesapeake Bay. The British burned several houses on its outskirts. But they were unable to bombard the town until they had hacked through the fishing boats the townspeople had sunk in the harbor to block the British fleet. That gave the patriots time to beg reinforcements from Williamsburg. Riding all night to cover thirty miles through heavy rain, riflemen of the 2nd Virginia Regiment, plus Culpeper Minutemen, were able to take position in Hampton's brick houses as the British began firing their cannons. Although much of the town crumpled, the brick houses were strong enough to withstand the four-pound cannon balls. Through the barrage, the Virginia marksmen picked off the British sailors on the ships' decks and riggings. Eventually manning their guns seemed like sure suicide, and the British ships withdrew.

Since the Hampton skirmish, the Williamsburg camp had been in an uproar to take the fight *to* the British, rather than waiting to see where Dunmore would strike next. Word was they would soon move out to secure the region's important river towns. The mission was critical.

Dunmore was already strongly entrenched in Norfolk, housed and aided by its loyalists and Scottish merchants. Just off the Chesapeake Bay, Norfolk was the largest seaport in Virginia, possessing warehouses and wharves useful to waging war. More importantly, the city gave Dunmore control of the York and James Rivers where they connected with the Chesapeake Bay and the bay opened to the Atlantic Ocean. If the patriots didn't dislodge Dunmore from Norfolk, all Virginia's towns and ports would be bottled up like Boston. The British would cut the colonies in half.

Nathaniel well remembered his ship of bondage sailing up the Chesapeake Bay. He had cursed its waters then and longed to return to England. Funny that he now wanted to defend it.

"Nathaniel Dunn!" a voice bellowed from the tents. "Drilling soon! Come here at once!"

Nathaniel winced, recognizing Jeremiah's bullying tone.

Maria blushed. "I'll not trouble you more, Nathaniel. But I wanted to give you something, before you left, in thanks for the poem on cursive." After Edan's fit, Nathaniel had recopied it and given it to her. Maria reached into her pocket and pulled out an envelope, neatly inscribed with his name. "I copied it from our newspaper."

As she held it up for him to take, Nathaniel took an awkward step forward and grasped her hand. "Maria . . ." He faltered, paused, and tried again, "Maria, I don't know when I will be coming back. But . . . but . . . well . . . I will be glad to see you then." He held onto her small, pale hand, crushing the envelope.

"Oh," she cried, hearing the stationery crumple.

"Sorry," said Nathaniel, realizing her distress.

He dropped her hand, dropped the letter, stooped to pick it up. Nathaniel tried again. "I hope to see you when I come home."

"Oh, Nathaniel, I just . . . I just don't know. . . ."

Nathaniel's spirits fell like lead in water. Doesn't know? Wouldn't she want to see him? He took a step back, hurt, embarrassed.

"Wait." She stopped him. "I meant I don't know if I will be here. Our printing business is doing worse. We've lost the position of Printer to the Public. It was awarded to Mr. Purdie instead. I might need to be bound out, to support my brothers."

That meant Maria would be entered into servitude akin to Nathaniel's indentureship. He shook his head. "Oh no, Maria, don't let them do that."

"I may have no choice." Maria choked a bit as she said it. "I just hope it can be with a family in Williamsburg so I can still see my brothers and . . . and . . ."—she looked up then, finally, into Nathaniel's eyes—"and you, Nathaniel."

Without warning, she kissed him on the cheek, curtseyed, and ran. Nathaniel's face burned where her lips had touched him. He opened the envelope to see slightly blotted but delicate, careful penmanship of the words:

> *Freedom's charms alike engage*
> *Blooming youth and hoary age;*
> *Time itself can ne'er destroy*
> *Freedom's pure and lasting joy;*
> *Love and friendship never give*
> *Half their blessing to the slave;*
> *None are happy but the free,*
> *Bliss is born of Liberty.*

Nathaniel tucked it into his shirt—just in time to keep Maria's gift from scattering in the wind. From behind, he was shoved—hard enough to hurl him to the ground.

"I called you!"

Nathaniel rolled over, spitting out dirt, to look up at Jeremiah, standing overtop him, his fists balled into threats. "Get up. I'll teach you to not come when I call. As a drummer, I am the more important."

Nathaniel fumed, tensed, felt himself ready to spring. Was he going to have to put up with blows from a boy now too? This boy who had constantly heckled Ben and who was responsible in a way for his maimed hand? How could he hold himself back?

"Get up!" Jeremiah kicked him. "You are such a

weird-eyed weakling. Figures you'd be sotted over that girl. The whole town knows what a failure her family is. Perfect company for you!"

The insult to Maria did it. Nathaniel dove at Jeremiah's knees and knocked him down. The two boys rolled over and over, flaying at each other, without really knowing how to hit their mark in the cloud of dust they kicked up.

"Here! Here now! Stop!" Two large hands took hold of the collar of each boy and hurled them apart.

Somehow Nathaniel and Jeremiah landed on their feet. They were about to go for each other again, but a tall man held up his hands and ordered, "Stand fast, boys, or so help me I will arrest you. Don't we have enough enemies to fight without you scrapping with each other?"

He was young and robust, twenty years or so in age. His fringed deerskin trousers and buck-tail hat marked him as one of the frontier marksmen. On his hunting shirt were embroidered the words "Liberty or Death." His belt held a tomahawk and scalping knife. His appearance was quite daunting. The boys stood fast indeed.

"He started it," Jeremiah whined, pointing at Nathaniel.

"Ah, lad, for shame," said the man. "You bear false

witness. I saw you knock him down from behind after the lass left."

"Did not. He called me a—"

The man shook his head and interrupted. "Save the stories, boy. I'm the eldest of fifteen brothers and sisters. I know hogwash when I hear it. Heed this: lies beget lies. Now be off with you." He waved Jeremiah away.

Nathaniel stood, dusting off his clothes. He knew he shouldn't feel so, but he felt rather proud of himself.

"Hmmm, dust that smirk off your face as well, lad. You must not spar in camp. 'Twill bring you trouble with the officers and with me. I am the drillmaster for my company of Culpeper Minutemen."

Despite the reprimand, the young man grinned at Nathaniel. "I like your pluck, though. That ill-tempered youth is an ox. I am glad to meet a David who would take on such a Goliath." He bowed and tipped his hat, sending the deer tail on it dancing. "Lieutenant John Marshall, of the Fauquier Rifles, is my name. And yours?"

"Nathaniel Dunn, sir."

He winked. "Best to your duty, Nathaniel."

"Aye, sir." Nathaniel rushed off, happy about his letter, happy to have found his courage. He was ready now, ready to fight for liberty. Mayhap Ben had been right about him.

೨ Chapter Thirty-four ೬

NATHANIEL WOULD NEED that fortitude a few days later when his regiment's battle against the British red-coats began.

"It's coming round again, lads. Steady."

Crouched behind a large rock on the riverbank, Nathaniel peeped over its top to watch the riflemen of the 2nd Regiment and the Culpeper Minutemen, lying flat in front of him, take aim at a British warship.

"Wait till you see the buttons on their red coats!" shouted a captain, speaking of the soldiers manning the vessel's cannon.

"Teach them to wear such an easy-to-see target," joked a man.

A chuckle rippled through the ranks as the shirtmen raised their rifles, resting the barrels on the logs or rocks littering the sandy shore. They waited, ready, like the coiled rattlesnake on their Culpeper banner that proclaimed: "Don't tread on me. Liberty or Death."

The patriots were pinned down at Burwell's Ferry, just southeast of Williamsburg. They'd marched there to cross the James River on their way to Norfolk. But just as the first group began rowing against the tide, the HMS *Kingfisher* warship rounded a bend in the river, its sails full, its brow beating up and down against the waves. Firing its six-pounder cannon, the British ship blew holes through the ferryman's house and wharf. The regiment scattered, the men dodging and shouting, hurling themselves behind trees, logs, banks.

Now, they were in a sort of stalemate. A tender boat from the warship kept tacking back and forth within a few hundred yards of shore, shooting at anyone who stood up straight or tried to advance toward the ferryboats. When the tender came close enough, the frontier riflemen shot back.

Stuck in between the American troops on shore and the British boats was a small barge. Its unlucky oysterman had been approaching the wharf to deliver his catch when the skirmish began. After their first volley, the British ordered him to come alongside the warship. Wanting to salvage all the boats that they could for their crossing, the Virginia riflemen shouted at him to stay where he was. Both sides made their point with gunfire. Now the poor oysterman had disappeared from view, probably lying flat in his boat, praying.

Of course, some of the rifleman had other plans for the boat. They wanted its catch. An officer lying atop a pile of crushed shells called out, "I don't know about you, boys, but I'd love oysters for dinner. Let's get on with this! This bed of mine is most uncomfortable!"

"Aye!" many shouted. They, too, were covered with sand and were lying atop rocks and sharp river debris.

"Here she comes," warned the officer. "Ready! Aim. . . ."

The men squinted, finding their mark.

"FIRE!"

CRAAAAACKK. Crack, crack, crack. Two dozen rifles fired.

British gunfire answered with cannon grapeshot.

Lead balls whizzed by—*ping . . . ping, ping, ping*—burrowing into the dirt around them, ricocheting off Nathaniel's rock, snapping off branches.

All around him, Nathaniel heard gasps, curses, and then laughter when the men checked themselves over and realized that they were still alive.

A minute passed as the riflemen reloaded. It was a painstaking process, compared to the muskets, which could be reset in fifteen seconds. First the marksman poured powder into the pan by the firelock, and then an exact charge amount of coarser powder down the rifle barrel. He covered the end of the barrel with a greased patch of cloth, onto which he placed the ball. Then he rammed both in and down, withdrew the ramrod, and aimed.

CRAAACK. Crack, crack, crack. The patriots fired again.

Ping, ping, ping. The British boats answered.

T-wang. A ball chipped a fist-sized splinter off Nathaniel's rock. He dove down, jostling Basil, who huddled beside him.

"Oooooh, the Lord is my shepherd. I'm walking through the valley of the shadow of death, Lord, help me . . ." Basil cried.

"Master." Nathaniel shook him a bit. "Courage." Armed with a musket that only had a fifty-yard range at best, Basil was not expected to be firing. But Nathaniel didn't want the other men to see him so fearful.

Basil kept praying. "I shall fear no evil, I shall fear no evil. . . ."

Nathaniel stared at the little quaking ball of man that was Basil. Nathaniel was afraid too, afraid but strangely exhilarated by each volley he survived. He glanced around at the nearby men. Some were hunkered down like Basil, but most were gritting their teeth, holding firm. No one else was facedown in the dirt.

But something seemed to be wrong with Basil other

than the gunfire. His panic had started on the river. He and Nathaniel had been in one of the first ferry rowboats when the cannonading began. Rocked by the concussion of a cannonball crashing into the water within inches of them, their boat had rammed another, hurtling Basil and several others into the water.

The water in the James was deep, the current murderous. Basil disappeared under the dark waves; surfaced, flailing and gasping; disappeared again; bobbed up; went under. Nathaniel shouted for help. But there was too much confusion. Basil popped up once more, but this time his struggling was far weaker. Nathaniel realized that if Basil went under again, he wouldn't come back up. He snatched up one of the long oars and shoved it toward Basil. "Take hold!"

His action tipped the boat wildly. Men yanked him back to balance it. "No! Help him!" screamed Nathaniel. But the men were concentrating on untangling the boats.

Thrashing and shouting, Nathaniel tried to clamber out of the boat. His hysteria finally alerted one of the men already in the water. The man swam for Basil, grabbed him up, and towed him to the boat. Hands held on to their shirt collars and dragged them along through the waves as the men in the boat rowed with all their might to regain land.

Nathaniel had half carried the old man to this rock while Basil shivered, coughed, spluttered, crying out, "Myra, Myra!"

During the past hour, he'd alternated between crying out for her—whoever she was—and praying in the sand.

CRAAACK. Crack, crack, crack.

Nathaniel braced himself for the Brits' answer.

No return fire.

The regiment waited, each man holding his breath.

Still silence.

A few dared to lift themselves up to survey the river. The British tender was heading back toward the *Kingfisher*. The autumn sun was going down quickly. The British preferred a daylight fight.

"Huzzah!" the men cheered.

"Let's to the oysters, men!" shouted the hungry officer.

That night the regiment threw up a makeshift camp further inland, away from the ferry, out of reach of British guns. In the cold moonlight, American sentries kept an eye on the warship, sleeping on the river. Everyone else slipped into a wary slumber. Everyone, that is, except Nathaniel. He kept watch over Basil.

The freezing waters and the November chill had thrown the old man into a kind of delirium. Nathaniel had tucked his and Basil's blanket around him, but still Basil shivered. He dreamed fitfully, crying out about a frozen-over river in Scotland, about ice skates, about Myra.

After many hours, Basil finally settled into a real sleep. Nathaniel dozed.

"Lad?" Basil's hoarse whisper awoke him in the morning.

"Aye, master?"

"Methinks you saved my life."

"Nay, master, not I."

Basil shook his head. "Aye, 'twas you, I think, sounded the alarm."

Nathaniel shrugged. "I am glad you are better." Then he added the thanks he'd always meant to say before but had not. "You saved me once, master."

Basil smiled weakly. "I made a promise to myself, long ago, Nathaniel, to save anyone I saw drowning before me. No matter what might happen to me. To make up for failing—failing horribly, God forgive me—once before."

He sighed and with a sadness so heavy, his voice

dropped so low Nathaniel could barely understand. "I . . . I had a wife. A beautiful, delicate lass, she was. I was a teacher at a school . . . oh, my life was so blessed. . . . Then the students wanted to try a new sport—skating on ice. We all went out onto the river. . . . The ice . . . the ice seemed so certain . . . but . . . but it was thin and . . ." Basil gasped and dropped his head into his hands. "I fell in trying to save Myra. I managed to pull the two of us out, half frozen, near death. . . . But I let two boys drown to save her. They sank under the ice, calling my name, begging me to help them. . . . I had to tell their parents . . . I had to . . ." He groaned. "My beautiful Myra died from pneumonia. The school dismissed me, the town threw garbage at me as I left." He lifted his head and stared into the darkness. "I ran away. And then I came here."

He turned to look at Nathaniel, pleading in his eyes. "Methought you were drowning when I first saw you, Nathaniel. That blacksmith was a river that could swallow you and drag you under."

"Aye, master, that he was."

Nathaniel's answer seemed to give Basil something he desperately needed. His face cleared a little. "You must really stop calling me 'master.' Basil will do."

"Aye . . . Basil." The name sounded odd on his tongue. Nathaniel knew that it was more likely he would continue to call the old tutor "master," but now it would be a term of affection rather than obligation.

❦ Chapter Thirty-five ❧

THE NEXT WEEK turned bitter cold. The men moaned as they slogged through frigid, slimy swamp waters and puddle-filled roads.

"Lord, my feet ache."

"I wish I had ice creepers."

"My toes are frozen stiff." Only those with good boots or shoes could attach the wrought-iron spikes of ice creepers that elevated their feet out of the cold mud and gave them traction. Most merely wrapped their feet in rags to protect toes that protruded through worn-out leather, to cover holes in their soles, to water-proof their moccasins.

The loudest complaints came from those with "iron bondage"—carrying the heavy cast-iron kettles that each mess of six men needed to cook their food. Whoever had the duty was bruised up and down from the wide, thick pot banging against his legs. His shoulders and arms ached.

"It's not as if we need the wretched thing," Basil mumbled the day he struggled with it. "They give us naught to cook in it."

It was true. On good days during a march, their diet consisted of beef cooked hurriedly on bayonets held over fire—burned and crusty—and fire cakes—a paste of flour and water. Many days, fire cakes were all they had.

Their forty-five-mile trek to Norfolk grew longer than it should have been. Repeatedly harassed at Burwell's Ferry by British ships, the regiment circled northwest—the opposite direction of Norfolk—to cross the James River. The American Colonel William Woodford was under strict orders to protect the troops' limited ammunition. So, rather than continue to spar with the British ships, he took his men to Sandy Point. It took several days to make up the distance that loop cost them.

The lost time also gave Dunmore a substantial victory. The weight of it spread through camp one night, rattling the regiment.

"Heard you the news from Kemp's Landing?" One of their tent mates plopped down beside Nathaniel and Basil.

Basil had just finished daubing a stone with flour

paste and setting it near the campfire to cook. Nathaniel was already eating his fire cake. Charred on the outside, cold and soggy on the inside, it was completely unappetizing. But shaky with hunger, Nathaniel gagged it down.

"Let us hope it is good," answered Basil.

"It's not," replied the man. "Dunmore marched out of Norfolk with a hundred fifty British regulars, loyalists, and runaway slaves. Waiting for them in the woods was our militia from Princess Anne County. We had twice the redcoats' number. We should have held. But we panicked. Our militia only fired once and then was driven back into a creek. A number drowned, the rest fled, deserting our officers, who were captured. The redcoats ransacked the hamlet, scaring the women half to death.

"Dunmore has declared martial law in Virginia, saying that anyone who does not support the crown is a traitor. He's also issued a proclamation offering freedom to any slave or indentured servant belonging to 'rebels' *if* they are capable of bearing arms and join His Majesty's troops. He's made a regiment called Lord Dunmore's Royal Ethiopian.

"Most of the inhabitants around there have signed an oath of loyalty to the king—the cowardly scoundrels. Even the mayor and aldermen of Norfolk signed! They hosted a feast for Dunmore when he paraded back into town. Loyalists wear a badge of red cloth. They say most everyone in the city sports one now. The worst of it is that several hundred of our colonial militia went over to Dunmore. They have been reorganized as the Queen's Own Loyal Virginia Regiment.

"Norfolk is fortified against us. Dunmore has built a fort at the Great Bridge, our only way to Norfolk by foot. We're marching straight into a loyalist lions' den. We're doomed, I tell you."

Everyone silenced. Only the fire crackled and spat as the men nervously looked from one to another.

"I'm thinking it's about time to go home to my missis," muttered one man.

"Aye," grumbled another.

"Oh, pshaw! Nonsense!" Out of the shadows stepped the tall frontiersman John Marshall. He squatted by the fire and held his hands up to its warmth, rubbing them. "Weak minds are easily led and easily changed. We will win the people of Norfolk back. Our cause is just. Know any of you the works of Alexander Pope?"

"Oh yes, sir, I most certainly do," said Basil, brightening. "I used his verse often to teach grammar and morals at the same time."

"Good man. My mother used it to tutor me in the

exact fashion. Master schoolmaster, tell our friends what Pope's main philosophy is."

"Well"—Basil puffed up a bit, preening at the chance to talk philosophy—"in his *Essay on Man*, Pope argues that reason separates and elevates us from the animals. Still, we are only part of the universe, not the focus of it. The point of his I like best is his optimistic belief that evil or what seems to be bad luck is actually part of some overall plan for good."

"Exactly!" applauded Marshall. "Well said, sir scholar. Here is a verse for us to remember tonight, my friends." He closed his eyes and recited:

"All Nature is but Art, unknown to thee;
All Chance, Direction, which thou canst not see;
All Discord, Harmony not understood;
All partial evil, universal Good:
And, spite of Pride, in erring Reason's spite:
One truth is clear, WHATEVER IS, IS RIGHT."

"That's right!" chirped Basil. "Pope believes things happen for a reason that we cannot understand until a future time."

"So we can hope that Dunmore's victory at Kemp's Landing will only increase his conceit and, therefore, his foolhardiness," said Marshall. "He's so contemptuous of us, he won't fear us. He'll act rashly, and then we'll have him."

"Hope, that's the word, hope," Basil replied. "Pope said, 'Hope springs eternal in the human breast.' It's one of mankind's most admirable qualities—his ability to hope and dream of better things."

"Very true," agreed Marshall. "Hope has led us to this fight, hope for independence and a better life, hope in ourselves. Let us remember that, gentlemen."

Encouraged, the crowd about the fire seemed to breathe a collective sigh of relief.

That is, until a rustic fellow, who had inched closer during the discussion, spoke up: "I had one season at school. Didn't learn much. Me wife was the one to always be reading in the Bible, God rest her. But I do remember one saying from Alexander Pope that the master learnt us: 'Fools rush in where angels fear to tread.'"

The man's sour comment squashed the uplift in spirits.

There was something familiar about the stranger's voice that made Nathaniel look at the man more carefully in the glow of the firelight. He wore the fringed shirt and motto of the Culpeper men. His face was badly pocked, making his natural features hard to distinguish. Obviously he'd survived a bad case of smallpox. There was also a long, jagged scar along his hairline that puckered and distorted the skin of his forehead. He had a kind of grotesque appearance. What nature had originally made him was no longer visible.

Nathaniel recognized nothing in his appearance. Perhaps it'd just been the voice that carried the accent of Yorkshire in it that caught his attention. But there was nothing extraordinary about that, really. Most Virginians still spoke with traces of the motherland in their voices.

Marshall laughed heartily. "Another fine quote from Mr. Pope. But you mustn't let your experiences with the Indians on our borders fill you with spite and bitterness about our fellow countrymen. And Providence obviously saved you, my friend, from a scalping for a reason. I think—"

"Stop! Thief!"

Jeremiah came crashing into the ring of men about the campfire. Confused and wild eyed, he tried to push his way back into the dark, but the men caught him.

A fat, red-faced sergeant major thundered into the firelight. "Give it up, boy. You've nowhere to hide now."

"What's he done?" Marshall asked.

"Nothing, that's what," whined Jeremiah. "Nothing at all."

"We caught him trying to slip past the sentinel to come back into camp, Lieutenant," said the sergeant, struggling to regain his breath.

"Was out scouting for loyalist Tories, that's what I was doing."

Marshall looked at Jeremiah and then at Nathaniel, clearly recognizing Jeremiah as the bully he had pulled off Nathaniel. "Tell the truth, lad."

"It is the truth! I was out looking for the enemy."

"You know there is an express order that no man is to leave this camp under the pretense of searching out Tories?" asked Marshall.

"But I had orders!"

"Really? Aren't you a drummer?"

"Yes, I am." Now Jeremiah puffed up like a rooster. "Very important my drum calls are!" he crowed.

"Indeed, they are. That's why you would never be ordered on a search party. First lie. Try telling the truth of it."

Jeremiah stood with his mouth hanging open, thinking. "I . . . I . . ." He started shuffling his feet, as if to run off. Nathaniel couldn't help being glad that Jeremiah was finally being caught in his balderdash. Recognizing that Jeremiah was about to bolt, he stood up and planted himself in the way.

Jeremiah whipped around to hurdle himself into the night and crashed right into Nathaniel. Out of his hunting shirt dropped a roasted mutton leg.

"Oh! Lovely!" Several men dove for the meat.

"Stand off." The sergeant pushed and kicked them away. "He stole that off the miller down the road. Went right into the house, asking for water, and then pinched their dinner." He grabbed Jeremiah by the collar. "You are under arrest, boy."

Marshall shook his head. "Plundering is a court martial offense, boy. You best plan on truthful testimony and begging the court's mercy. Lying will only make things worse for you."

The sergeant dragged Jeremiah, now silent and small looking, away into the shadows. The circle broke up, and Nathaniel pulled out his fife, preparing to play the tattoo—the call to send all men to their tents and to quiet until morning reveille.

"What does a court martial bring?" Nathaniel asked Basil, hoping that justice would finally come to Jeremiah—some public humiliation that would put him in his place.

"Most like a flogging, lad. 'Tis barbaric, but the way of it."

A flogging? Nathaniel had thought he'd be put in the

stocks for a day or two—uncomfortable and embarrassing but nothing like a flogging. A flogging tore flesh away. If Nathaniel hadn't stood in Jeremiah's way, he might have made his escape. Suddenly, Nathaniel felt sick inside.

❧ Chapter Thirty-six ❧

THIS WAS NATHANIEL'S chance, his chance to get even. Jeremiah stood whimpering, hands tied, stripped to his waist, shivering in the cold, helpless. The court martial had ordered twenty lashes for stealing and leaving camp without permission.

"Fifer," commanded the sergeant major. "Five lashes, well laid on."

Nathaniel's fingers tightened on the handle of the cat-o'-nine-tails. Its knotted cords were already wet with blood.

He had known this was a duty of the field musicians—to carry out whippings ordered by officers. Since they stood apart—not really officers, not really soldiers—the camp drummers and fifers could mete out physical punishment without fear of retribution during a battle. Or so was the thought. Others darkly joked that it was good drumming practice. All the musicians knew that if they refused to do the whipping, or did it lightly or half-heartedly, they would be punished by receiving the same amount of lashings as the condemned.

Two fifers had already dealt Jeremiah their five strokes. Now it was Nathaniel's turn.

The sight of Jeremiah's torn back nauseated him. And yet, he clung to his anger. Here was the chance to be revenged, and not just on his latest tormentor. Just once, wouldn't it feel good to be the one dealing out the blows rather than the one taking them? To no longer be the one swallowing the pain and the humiliation.

Nathaniel raised the whip and felt the lashes swing round his head. Jeremiah began sobbing.

"Blessed are the merciful: for they shall obtain mercy." His mother's voice whispered in Nathaniel's ear.

He took a deep breath and readied himself to strike.

But the voice came again, that sweet voice that had crept through the Bible, learning, teaching Nathaniel: *"What doth the Lord require, but to love mercy."*

His raised hand started to shake as he hesitated.

"Fifer," shouted the sergeant. "Five lashes or you will receive the same."

Nathaniel nodded. "Aye, sir." He wasn't about to take a lashing to save the hide of this cruel, arrogant boy. This boy who raised himself up by putting others down. Nathaniel closed his eyes against seeing his blow do its work.

"Let he who is without sin cast the first stone."

Nathaniel had stolen. And from the very person who had saved him from abuse. His mind raced.

What had Mistress Maguire said to him? That to be truly free of its pain, he had to leave the past in the past. It must not rule the way he chose to behave today. Jeremiah was not the merchant, the planter, the blacksmith, Edan Maguire, or even his father who had left him behind. He was just Jeremiah, a stupid, blubbering bully, who was terrified.

Nathaniel had felt similar terror. If he made someone else suffer that kind of agony, then he was just as bad as those who had done it to him. And it would be yet another instance of someone forcing Nathaniel to do something against his will, to do something he didn't believe in. He had changed. He had his own mind. This growing revolution promised that he could use it.

Nathaniel lowered his hand. He planted his feet firmly and looked directly at the sergeant major. "I will not, sir."

"Fifer, you will do as you are told or suffer the same sentence," barked the sergeant major.

"I understand." Nathaniel's voice sounded as if it came from someone else.

The sergeant motioned to two soldiers. Nathaniel was led to Jeremiah's side. As the men pulled down his hunting shirt and woolen scarf, Nathaniel realized that the linsey-woolsey shirt his mother had sewn and he still wore underneath would be bloodied. "Wait, please," he murmured, and pulled the shirt off, folding it carefully. He looked about to the men witnessing the court martial and found Basil's ashen face in the crowd. "Master, will you hold this, please?" he called.

Stumbling through the men, Basil came to him. "Lad," he whispered, his voice quaking, "you needn't take this scurrilous boy's lashings."

No, he needn't. But for some strange reason he couldn't explain, Nathaniel was going to.

The drum major called up the next two fifers—one for Jeremiah, one for Nathaniel. "Five lashes, well laid on!"

Jeremiah sobbed louder. Nathaniel heard the whistle of the lashes as the boy musicians snapped the whip back without a moment's hesitation. He sucked in his breath. He tried to adopt the same attitude that he had always had before—that it didn't matter, he wouldn't feel it, he was beneath caring or feeling anything, almost as if he didn't exist. But Nathaniel was no longer that subservient boy. He cared. He made do instead with sheer stubbornness and the memory of what

Moses had said about the whipping awaiting him—a lash might cut his skin, but it could not harm his mind now that it was free. Armed with that, Nathaniel braced himself.

There was a whine of the whip slicing the winter air as the blow landed. Nine lines of pain seared his back. Nathaniel gasped, staggered, as the earth spun in front of him. He vaguely saw Basil covering his face with his hands.

"Wait! Hold!" John Marshall stepped forward. He had been one of the twenty-four officers sitting in the military tribunal. "I wish to speak for this boy."

"Lieutenant Marshall," warned a senior officer, "you are out of line. This is the prescribed punishment for such insubordination. And the order of twenty lashes for stealing is merciful. Had the drummer been a full-grown man, it would have been forty."

"Yes, sir, I know. But how can we reward the courage of this fifer with a lashing? Isn't this exactly the kind of bravery and resolve we are asking of our soldiers in the face of a superior force?"

The colonel sighed and shook his head. "The consequence for not performing an ordered discipline is a long-standing prescription in the military."

"Yes, but in the *British* Army, sir. The very same army that makes its foot soldiers wear red coats so that when they are shot in battle, their blood will not show—that's how little regard they have for individual human life. I am fighting against such attitude, sir."

The crowd murmured and shuffled, agreeing.

"Marshall, you are spreading sedition. I will not have it."

Marshall put his hands on his hips and looked to the ground for a moment before continuing. "May I argue this boy's case instead? Is not this court martial still sitting?"

The colonel hesitated, and then nodded. "Yes, it is. Proceed."

"Aren't we fighting to allow a man to have a voice in his governance? We're asking our fellow Americans to stop blindly accepting; to speak up for their rights. Isn't the very heart of our struggle to abolish arbitrary judgments of arrogant aristocrats and laws that give no thought to individual liberties? We see that as tyranny. Why should we simply repeat the harsh rules of the British Army? These men are volunteers, choosing to risk themselves to free their country. Look at my shirt, sir. It calls for liberty or death. We risk all for liberty. This," he pointed at Nathaniel, "this is not liberty."

"Lieutenant Marshall, you make your point with eloquence, but you do not convince. If we are to defeat the British, we must have discipline. We cannot have our soldiers thinking for themselves in battle. We can worry about rewriting military law after we have won." He nodded to the sergeant to restart the lashing.

"No. Wait!" Marshall stood fast. "Then let me plead for leniency. For mercy. Let mercy be a check and a balance on our judgment. I have seen this boy"—he gestured to Jeremiah—"beat this one, fifer Nathaniel Dunn, for no reason other than for sport. The fact that Nathaniel will refuse to raise his hand against his enemy, when that enemy is already laid low, should be an example to all of us. Let us be different. Let us make our point swiftly and judiciously, without crushing a man's spirit. Both these boys bleed. I think they have learned well what we desire to teach."

A captain whispered in the colonel's ear. The colonel turned to another officer and talked with him. After a few more moments of excruciating waiting, the colonel said, "Release the drummer and fifer. Bring out the next prisoner and continue."

Back at their tent, Basil washed the welts on Nathaniel's back. "Some of these are broken open, lad. I wish I had not used up my salt ration. I need salt to cleanse these gashes."

"I can help." Nathaniel looked up to see the pock-faced man. His hands were cupped, holding something.

"My mess collected our salt for the boy."

"Thank you, sir. That is generous of you."

The man grunted and knelt. "This will burn, boy. But it will heal. Ready?"

Nathaniel nodded.

The man pressed the salt into the cuts. Nathaniel about screamed from the sting. He doubled over, shuddering, but he only shed a few tears.

"Ah, lad." Basil put his hand atop Nathaniel's head. "You amaze me." Gently he covered Nathaniel with a blanket before standing up. "Thank you for your help." He extended his hand to shake the man's and introduced himself.

"The boy's name is Nathaniel?" the man asked.

"Aye."

"Dunn?"

"Yes. And your name, sir? So that we may know our friend?"

"Smith," the man blurted. "I go by Smith." Abruptly, he turned and left.

Nathaniel paid no heed. Exhausted, he slipped into the deep sleep that comes after trouble is over, and with a clear conscience of having done the right thing.

PART TEN

December 1775

Torn from a world of Tyrants,
Beneath the western Sky,
We formed a new Dominion,
A Land of Liberty;
The world shall own we're freemen here,
And such will ever be,
Huzzah! Huzzah! Huzzah!
For love and Liberty. . . .

Lift up your Hearts, my heroes,
And swear, with proud disdain,
The wretch that would ensnare you
Shall spread his net in vain;

Should Europe empty all her Force,
We'd meet them in array,
And shout Huzzah! Huzzah! Huzzah!
For Brave America!

—"Free America," words attributed to Boston
patriot Dr. Joseph Warren, set to the tune
"The British Grenadiers"

ᴐ Chapter Thirty-seven ᴑ

NATHANIEL'S BACK ACHED. He rolled over, trying to get comfortable, but the marshy, damp ground and the frigid December night air wove a blanket of cold around him. Teeth chattering, he crawled out of the tent and stretched, wincing as the movement pulled taunt the welts on his back. He might as well give up on sleep. He peered into the night, trying to find the figure of Basil, who had sentinel duty. There he was, pacing and stamping along the corner of the Great Bridge Chapel, around which the 2nd Regiment and Culpeper Minutemen, about seven hundred men total, had camped.

Great Bridge. Nathaniel snorted as he made his way across the high saw grass, slick and crunchy with frost. He didn't see what was so great about this place. Twelve miles south of Norfolk, the forty-yard-long wood bridge stretched over the Elizabeth River and was, indeed, one of the few in Virginia. But the places it connected! At each end were islands of land, thrown into the vast sea of the Dismal Swamp, with ink-black waters, rotted trees, vile-smelling mud, and tangles of vines. Walk into that, Nathaniel speculated, and leeches and water snakes would get you quick. Mosquitoes were sure to be vicious in the summer.

Still, the road was the only land approach from North Carolina, the only way for that colony's tar, pitch, turpentine, and lumber to go directly to Norfolk's shipbuilders. As a result, Great Bridge had become a decent-sized hamlet on the southern side of the bridge, with a church, a mill, and about twenty houses in between.

To hold the bridge, Dunmore built a log fort on the Norfolk side, studding it with four-pound cannons and swivel guns. Inside he posted elite British grenadiers plus turncoats of the Queen's Own Loyal Virginia Regiment and Lord Dunmore's Royal Ethiopians. Colonel Woodford estimated they numbered two hundred and fifty.

Despite the Americans' superior numbers, a direct attack on the fort would be sure death. The bridge was only about eight feet wide, the causeway approaching it little more than a narrow dike. Anyone approaching the fort that way would be easily gunned down, hemmed in by natural barriers.

So instead, Woodford prepared for a siege. He

ordered his men to cut logs and construct a barricade across the road, facing the bridge and the fort. Built in a sagging M shape, the breastwork was seven feet high and about one hundred and fifty feet in length. Off to the left, on a higher embankment, the Virginians piled dirt, mud, and logs as a battery for cannon—*if* the guns ever arrived with the North Carolina militiamen supposedly on their way to reinforce them.

The two armies settled into a stalemate of skirmishes. As the patriots worked, the British fired their cannon. Culpeper riflemen shot back, hiding behind the cluster of houses closest to the bridge.

As Nathaniel neared Basil, he could hear the old man moaning as he shivered, creating a kind of trembling hum. His breath made billows of smoky vapor in the frigid air, like a smoldering dragon. He heard Nathaniel coming and swung around, alarmed, dropping his musket with a clatter.

"Nathaniel! You frightened the life out of me."

"Forgive me, master." Nathaniel picked up the musket and handed it to Basil. He wondered what in the world the old schoolmaster would do if truly confronted by enemy soldiers. Perhaps Nathaniel should just sit Basil's watch with him.

"I've two more hours on my watch, lad. No need for you to stand out in the cold."

"It's all right," Nathaniel replied. "It's not as if it's warm in the tent. We've no straw. I was lying on mud. I might as well have been on a slab of ice. Besides, master, two pairs of eyes will keep a better watch."

It was a cloudy night, and the swamp coughed up a drifting fog. But in the splotches of moonlight, Nathaniel could see Basil's relief.

"I need to pace that way." Basil pointed toward the bridge. Nathaniel nodded and followed him, winding their way through the deserted houses.

He noted how stiffly Basil shuffled. His shoes worn thin, Basil had wrapped them in rags to protect his feet from the wet. But Nathaniel knew they were soaked. Just walking from the tent to the church had left his own toes damp, the wet from the grasses quickly saturating the thin leather of his shoes and seeping through his woolen stockings. Nathaniel was immensely grateful for the shoes Mistress Maguire had given him the previous year—tight and cracked as they were. Many of the men had none at all.

"Stop," Basil whispered. "There it is again. Listen, Nathaniel. What do you think that is?"

They stood rooted. In the cold night along the waters, sounds traveled far, couriers of nature's doings. Nathaniel could hear a slight breeze pushing bare branches about, rattling, the rhythmic lapping of the river along its banks as its tide meandered southward. He cupped his hand behind his ear and strained to capture more, but there was nothing. . . . Wait . . . that was odd . . . a *kerplunk,* as if a large fish had just jumped out of the water and splashed back in. But that was a sound of summer—no fish played about in frigid December waters.

Basil and Nathaniel eyed each other nervously.

"Back home in Scotland," Basil breathed, "there are many tales of monsters lurking in the lochs. In such an eerie place as this, it is easy to imagine such things."

Kerplunk. Kerplunk.

Clouds passed across the moon's face and blackened the earth. Basil disappeared from Nathaniel's view, even though he was mere steps away.

The world was silent again, nothing save the wind and water. Where had he heard something like that *kerplunk* before? Where? Nathaniel puzzled.

It came to him like a slap to the face—boats! That was an oar going into water.

Nathaniel gasped, turning into the night, trying to see Basil. "Master, we need to—"

But at that very moment, Nathaniel felt shadows brush past him. There was the muffled sound of something rushing through grasses.

Heart pounding, Nathaniel held his hands out and felt his way to the edge of a building. "Master?" he whispered, creeping along the wall. He sensed a body pressed up against the house just ahead of him and made his way toward it.

A flash of light. Nathaniel saw a ball of fire lurch up from the ground, somersaulting over and over itself until it crashed into the roof of a house. Immediately the thatching caught flame.

He heard more rustling. Another ball of flame jumped up. That roof flared. Torches. Someone was throwing torches onto the roofs to set the town ablaze!

He had to warn the camp! Hurry! Nathaniel reached into his pocket for his fife, desperately trying to remember the call to arms. Would his chilled fingers work the notes? Hands trembling he lifted the little wooden alarm to his lips. He blew, but his numb lips only spluttered. He tried again.

"No, you don't," hissed a deep voice in the darkness. Huge, strong hands grabbed Nathaniel's throat, knocking the breath out of him. The hands starting squeezing, shaking him. "No, you don't."

Choking, coughing, Nathaniel dropped his fife. He grabbed onto the hands, tore at the fingers locked around his throat. Tears of pain ran down his face. Needles of light pierced his vision as he fought passing out.

"No, you don't," the voice kept repeating.

Nathaniel felt his feet being lifted off the ground.

Kick! his mind screamed. *Kick, or you're going to die!*

Nathaniel flailed, feeling like his neck was about to snap. One of his kicks landed a blow. He felt himself topple over, the hands still wrapped around his throat like a hangman's noose. A knee was on his chest, pressing him to the ground.

Nathaniel gasped for air, but sucked in nothing. His chest felt like it was going to explode. He tried to scratch the hands around his throat, but he could no longer feel his own arms move. This was the end.

A ball of fire shot up over his head. Nathaniel felt the torch's burning brightness light up his face. But he could no longer see. He was dying.

Nathaniel!

He heard his name. Oh, so far away it sounded. Was his mother calling him? Suddenly the hands let go his throat. Nathaniel felt himself lifted and dragged.

He must be dead. These were either angels or devils carting him to heaven or hell. He tried to recite the Lord's Prayer. *Mother, speak for me,* he thought.

"Nathaniel!" The voice spoke again, but this time it sounded closer. He felt himself dropped and his shoulders being shaken. "Breathe, boy. Don't let me have killed you."

Nathaniel began to feel air coming . . . in . . . out . . .

in . . . out. He forced his eyes open. His eyelids felt as if they weighed a hundred pounds.

The clouds drifted away from the moon. Nathaniel could just barely see a face hovering over his.

"Thank God." The voice sighed. "Breathe, boy."

"Moses?"

The face smiled. "That's right. You be all right now. Lord, have mercy. I almost killed you, boy. I never would have forgiven myself. Never."

Nathaniel focused more clearly. Moses wore a simple, frocked uniform. On his shirt were painted the words "Liberty to Slaves."

"Moses?" Nathaniel was so confused.

"Ensign Moses! Look at me, Nathaniel, a soldier in the Royal Ethiopian. Now, rest a minute. I be back to take you."

"Where?"

"To liberty, boy. Across the river with the British. Ain't you heard? Lord Dunmore say indentured servants what fight for him go free, too. There's an indentured man run off from George Washington with us. He's good for information about that fellow. May lead us up the Chesapeake right to Washington's house to capture his wife as hostage. They be glad to hear what you know about the soldiers camped here." Moses stood up.

"But, Moses, I'm a fifer with Virginia's Second Regiment."

"That man you calling master sell you into his fight?"

"No, Moses. It's not like that. I'm free now. I chose to fight."

Moses crossed his arms in disgust. "You going to fight for people who whine for their own liberty and keep me in chains?"

"But . . . but," Nathaniel struggled. Moses was right. How could they justify that? "But Moses, Dunmore owns dozens of slaves. Has he freed them? Hasn't he sent back slaves who've run to him who belong to loyalists? Right back to God knows what punishment? Didn't he turn you away when you tried to help him at the palace? Don't trust him, Moses. He's deceitful. He set a trap in the magazine that near killed me. Don't fight for him."

"You want me to fight for slave masters?"

"Aw, Moses, it'll be different when we're done with this fight. How could it not be? You'll see. I'm sure that—"

A musket shot interrupted him. "To arms!" It was Basil's quavering, shrill voice. "To ar—"

There came an answering musket shot. Voices

began to shout around the tents. A fife began calling into the night.

"Moses!" Nathaniel struggled to his feet. "The camp is up."

Moses grabbed Nathaniel's arm. "Can you run, boy? Here. I'll carry you."

"No!" Nathaniel pushed him off. "I can't go with you. Join me, Moses. Join the patriots. Take off that British uniform before they see you." He held up his hands imploringly.

"No." Moses stepped back, shaking his head. "This shirt is my liberty. You come with me."

Stunned, baffled, the two friends stared at each other in bitter disappointment.

"There! Stop them!"

Nathaniel looked back and saw dozens of Virginians rushing to fight whatever was in the night. And there was Moses. All alone. None of his regiment in sight. No British grenadiers to stand for him.

Great God! He didn't want to think about what the regiment might do to him. Nathaniel shoved Moses. Shoved him into shadows. "Run, Moses. Run!"

His friend hesitated.

"Run!" Nathaniel pushed him again then turned and darted toward the oncoming Americans. "They went this way," he called, pointing in the opposite direction of Moses. "This way. Hurry! I saw more of them with torches! Dozens of them, I think!"

Believing, the men ran. Glancing over his shoulder as he followed, Nathaniel saw Moses had disappeared.

He slowed and stopped, winded, heartsick, wondering if he'd ever see his friend again. So many sudden, forced good-byes between them. And now their separate quests for liberty could make them enemies. How could that be?

Nathaniel covered his face. The world made no sense!

When he was indentured, he hadn't tried to understand anything, he just had to survive it. How was he going to be responsible for himself, how could he make the right choices, if he couldn't understand the workings of the world or the adults who ran it?

If ponies rode men and if grass ate the cows . . . then all of the world would be upside down. . . . Basil's song came to Nathaniel. Basil! Basil could explain it to him.

Then, like a kick to his stomach, Nathaniel remembered the sound of Basil's voice in the dark, cut short.

Where was Basil?

❧ Chapter Thirty-eight ❧

NATHANIEL FOUND BASIL sprawled on the ground, holding his head. Several men were huddled beside him.

"Lad! You're alive! Thank goodness! I was frantic with worry when I couldn't see you!" Basil's excited shouts completely echoed Nathaniel's thoughts. Basil tried to stand up, but toppled over, dazed. One of the men caught him. "Oh my," swooned Basil. It was then Nathaniel saw that blood flowed down his face.

"Master, are you hurt?" Nathaniel cried.

"A bit," Basil murmured. "Although I can't recall how exactly."

"Someone's cracked his skull open with the butt of a musket," the man holding him explained. "But your old friend is the hero of the night. Sounded the alarm, he did, and saved this town from burning—maybe even our camp from burning. I say three cheers for Mr. Wilkinson, eh, lads?" he sang out to the men who were beginning to gather around, back from their chase of redcoats, all of whom had disappeared back into the night.

"Huzzah!" the men crowed.

Looking completely perplexed, Basil modestly said, "Oh, it was nothing, my friends. Nothing at all. Nothing you wouldn't have done." He looked as if he would fall flat on his face.

Nathaniel rushed to help prop him up, and Basil grinned at him like a drunkard. "Me a hero. Imagine, lad! Oh, marvelous." His grin disappeared and he touched his fingertips to the steady trickle of blood coming down his face. "I say, though, Nathaniel, wicked headache. Do you suppose Mistress Maguire has something for this?" He fainted. Nathaniel buckled, trying to hold him aright.

"Here, lad." One of the burly frontiersmen scooped Basil up and carried him in his arms like a baby back to the camp hospital. Nathaniel skipped anxiously along behind. "Don't worry, lad," said the soldier. "He'll just have to sleep it off for a day or two."

While Basil recuperated, very proud of the twelve stitches in his head, the Americans and British continued to spar with one another.

Moses's raiding party had been small, sent by the

British to flatten the town's houses to provide their fort a clearer line of fire. They torched five buildings. But thanks to Basil, the rest remained standing. All the Ethiopians and loyalists had slipped back into the darkness without being caught. To retaliate, Colonel Woodford sent a scouting party across the river the next night. They burned a few buildings themselves and returned unharmed. Another evening, John Marshall led a quick hit-and-run raid across the causeway, returning safely fifteen minutes later.

During daylight hours, riflemen fired at any redcoated grenadier who appeared atop the fort's battlements. The British occasionally hurled a cannonball at the American breastworks. Neither side accomplished a thing in the standoff that seemed like it could go on forever.

It came to a point that a cannon being fired caused little reaction among the Virginians. One morning, at dawn, that became a mistake.

Nathaniel and the other musicians had just finished playing reveille.

KABOOM!

"There 'tis," muttered one of the drummers, "the redcoats' morning salute."

"Don't you think they could leave off and save it for

a proper battle?" complained another. Unimpressed, the musicians began to disperse.

Pop . . . pop . . . pop . . . pop.

Nathaniel paused. Another skirmish. Out of curiosity and nothing else to do, he trotted toward the bridge just to see what was up. Within ten steps, his mouth dropped in horror. Marching across it was an endless red surge of British grenadiers, six abreast, row after row of them, bayonets fixed and glinting in the dawning light.

BOOM!

A cannonball hit one of the houses near camp. Shingles and timbers flew. The house collapsed, exploding into a blaze.

How could it be? Somehow, in night's darkness, the British had pulled their four-pounder to the end of the bridge without being seen. Now everything in the camp—everybody—was in full range of its blast.

"Boys! Stand to your arms! To arms!"

Suddenly, the camp swarmed with men yanking on their breeches and scrambling to load their muskets as they ran to the barricades. Dodging, sprinting, knocked down by men hurrying, Nathaniel fought his way back to the musicians.

He careened to a halt beside the other fifers.

Fighting to keep the fife level against his shivering lips, Nathaniel played the oddly serene tune of eighth and quarter notes. Shouldn't he be blaring out a screaming run of sixteenth notes to reflect the terror, the urgency, the lunacy of facing down lifelong soldiers from the best-trained army in the world?

Pop-pop-pop-pop.

CRACK . . . crack, crack, crack.

BOOM!

The musicians played the music's repeat as billows of smoke began to collect along the bridge from the gunfire.

"All right, lads," shouted the drum major. "Find your company and stand your ground. Listen for my calls."

Nathaniel looked around, unsure of where to go. Everyone had scattered so quickly to take a position. He could see the tall figure of John Marshall and other Culpeper Minutemen dashing to the embankment to the left of the bridge. The 2nd Regiment must be at the breastwork facing the oncoming redcoats.

He joined the chaos of darting, shouting patriots. Grown men with long legs outran him. He slowed to give way. They were far more needed than he. And how much use would he be without Jeremiah? The drum and fife worked together in battle. And the drum was definitely more important if the troops needed to make a flanking movement. Like Basil, Jeremiah was in the camp's hospital, convalescing with the sick, his back still raw.

But when Nathaniel reached the breastwork and squeezed himself into the protection of its shadow, there was Jeremiah. His drum was in position, held with a strap across his back. He was obviously in pain. However, when he saw Nathaniel, he nodded in a kind of salute.

Startled, Nathaniel nodded back.

Peeping around the men and breastwork, Nathaniel saw that the situation was even worse than he had imagined. A vanguard of British was marching through the dense smoke from blazing buildings. Behind them came grenadiers, in perfect parade formation, marching to the cadence of two drums. Waiting on the far side of the bridge to follow were The Queen's Own loyalists.

Terrified, Nathaniel tried to steel himself by the shouts of the older men. But they were flustered, too.

"Why didn't we see them coming?"

"I can't believe they're coming straight across the causeway!"

"How did we miss their moving the cannon so close?"

"Can anyone tell their number?"

"Great God! There are hundreds of them. Could

they have marched here from Norfolk last night?"

The line began to waver. Some of the men lowered their muskets, gaping, terrified. Others began to instinctively inch backward, almost in a trance of fear. Nathaniel could feel the urge to flee tingling through them all.

"Steady, boys, steady." A calm voice broke the spell.

It was Basil, head bandaged, a tranquil smile on his face! He spoke in a soothing voice, much like the tone Nathaniel took with spooked horses: "They are hemmed in by the bridge and the swamp, poor fools. If we keep our heads, lads, we can knock them down like ninepins." There was something about his logic, something about an old man standing among them, wounded but confident, that reassured them.

The men took in deep breaths, swelling their chests, filling up the words embroidered on many of their shirts: *Liberty or Death.*

"Give me liberty or give me death." That was the stark choice Patrick Henry had laid before them, the stark reality of Dunmore pronouncing them traitors. It had to be their credo.

They held.

"Make ready!" a distant British voice shouted. The grenadiers stopped and aimed.

"Get down, boys! Get down!"

"FIRE!"

A hail of lead whistled toward them. Nathaniel crouched and gritted his teeth, hearing bark and wood fly as the balls met their shield of logs. He remembered too well what those little pieces of lead felt like when they hit.

The Virginians popped up, took aim, and fired back. *Crack, crack, crack, crack.*

Smoke and the stench of gunpowder choked them all.

"Reload!" shouted a regiment lieutenant. "Reload!"

In flurried unison, voices muttering curses and prayers, the line of Virginians reached into boxes at their waists. They pulled out cartridges, bit off the tops—spitting them out in a shower. Shaking hands poured powder into their muskets' pans.

Scraaaaaaaaape. Dozens of ramrods scratched along musket barrels, cramming cartridges down into the explosive powder.

Click, click, click, click. Flintlocks cocked.

Within twenty seconds, the men were reloaded and took aim. Waiting, the overwhelming sound was of the men panting.

"Hold your fire! Hold your fire until they are within fifty yards!"

On the British redcoats came, drums beating. Their faces were beginning to be visible—perfectly shaved, determined faces, no emotion on them. In front of them marched a tall, lanky captain, his face set, grim.

"Fire!"

CRRRRRRACK . . . *crack* . . . *crack* . . . *crack*.

A thunderous echo of shots rang out. Redcoat after redcoat fell, grasping at their sides, their legs, their heads. The front ranks flattened into piles of groaning men. The British captain crumpled too, holding his knee.

The Americans paused. Surely, so bloodied, they'd stop.

But the English captain was not about to give up.

Stunned, the Americans watched him pull out a white handkerchief and wrap it around his knee. Almost instantly, it soaked through with blood. He straightened up, took off his hat, and waved it. "Remember our ancient glory, men!" the captain shouted. "The day is our own!"

The British grenadiers climbed over their wounded and marched on.

"Reload! Reload now!" shouted the Americans.

"*Fire!*"

"Fire!"

The barrage was deafening. Nathaniel looked to Basil, who was shouting something he couldn't hear.

The British kept dropping, kept coming, following their captain.

"Good God! They're almost on us!"

Crack . . . crack . . . crack . . . crack.

Finally, a mere fifteen feet from the barricade, the British captain fell, riddled with bullets.

Without him, the grenadiers broke. They scrambled backward, crushing one another in their rush and the confines of the narrow bridge.

From the left came a whooping onslaught of Culpeper riflemen, clambering over their embankment to take cover farther down, nearer the bridge. They opened up on the British. The British returned fire.

It was a fifer's duty to drag the wounded out of battle. With the gunfire now off to the side of them, Nathaniel remembered that job. Looking about, he saw that all the patriots seemed fine. Only one was nursing a wound to his hand. Basil was helping him.

Several other Virginians crawled from behind the barricade to pull wounded British to safety. Nathaniel wriggled out to help. Coming around the edge of the logs, Nathaniel staggered to a halt. Blood was everywhere. Bodies were broken and writhing. He doubled over and retched.

"Here, boy. Pull yourself together. Help me!" One of his company was dragging a young redcoat.

Nathaniel hesitated, still sickened.

"Quickly, lad! Before the firing starts again!"

The thought of being completely exposed to musket

balls kicked Nathaniel into action. He grabbed the red-coat's collar and pulled.

"Don't scalp me! Please, don't scalp me!" the redcoat screamed.

Settling him behind the barricade, the patriot answered, "What, man? I am no savage. Who told you we would scalp you?"

"Lord Dunmore told us to fight to our death because if any of us were captured, you would scalp us out of spite, like Indians."

The patriot laughed. "Well, we are warlike, man. We will stand against you. But don't believe everything you are told. I'd heard that you lobsterbacks all had horns, flesh-and-blood devils. I see none on you."

Crack-crack-crack-crack.

Nathaniel flattened himself to the ground. The battle's smoke enveloped him. He waited for more death to rain. He waited . . . waited.

Through the gunpowder fog came a muffled shout—"Cease firing! Cease firing!"—and the sound of a lone fife, singing out peace.

Awash in relief, Nathaniel stood to take up the cease-fire song. Here, there, there again across the line of battle, the high-pitched song of the fife called an end.

It was the most beautiful music Nathaniel had ever played.

◎ Chapter Thirty-nine ◎

WHEN THE BATTLE'S smoke drifted away across the swamp, the patriots found seventeen British grenadiers dead, forty-nine wounded. Every American—save the one with the slight wound to his hand—was completely unharmed.

Dunmore had called for such a foolhardy head-on assault because he was confident that the Virginians would turn tail and run. Well, the twenty-minute battle had proved him wrong. The patriots could stand their ground and stand it well. It was an astounding victory for the untrained little army.

The British abandoned the fort that night. The patriots' way to Norfolk was now clear.

Among the captured were two dozen escaped slaves of the Royal Ethiopian Regiment. Trying to be inconspicuous, Nathaniel anxiously walked through them as they sat on the ground. Moses was not there. Nor was he among the dead. Nathaniel could hope he was still a free man.

With sorrow he watched the Ethiopian soldiers as they were handcuffed together in a long chain that bound them with the loyalist prisoners. Once again slaves, they were to be marched back to Williamsburg to be reclaimed by their owners or to be sold in the West Indies.

Moses's words haunted him: *You going to fight for people who whine for their own liberty and keep me in chains?*

Nathaniel tried to think instead about the heroics of an African who'd fought with the Americans. A freeman named Billy Flora had been one of four sentries keeping watch that morning. While the other three fired once into the thick rows of British and then retreated, Billy loaded and fired eight times before running across a plank to the breastwork in a barrage of bullets aimed specifically at him. He even stopped and pulled the board up behind him, preventing the redcoats from using it, before taking cover.

Moses was brave like Billy Flora. Oh, if only Moses could join them! How Nathaniel wished he could make it so he could. Surely men like Patrick Henry or Thomas Jefferson—men who spoke so eloquently and heatedly about human dignity and rights—would see the injustice of keeping other people in slavery. The only answer Nathaniel could see was to win their fight against the British first. And then, surely, surely, patriot leaders would right that wrong.

Nathaniel turned his eyes away from the prisoners and hurried away, needing to clean himself up as best he could. The whole regiment had been ordered out to give the fallen British captain—who had led the grenadiers so valiantly—a full-honors funeral to pay homage to his courage.

A few days later, sitting by their tent, Basil elbowed Nathaniel. "Look at all these boys, lad." They were watching three newly arrived companies of Patrick Henry's 1st Virginia Regiment and several hundred North Carolinians try to find dry space for their tents. With their number now swelled to over a thousand fighters, the patriot army would march on Norfolk soon.

"As the twig is bent, so is the tree inclined," Basil quoted one of his many proverbs. "Now that we've shown we can actually survive a fight with British regulars, more men will join our ranks. We might actually have a chance, Nathaniel. We might actually."

Basil pulled out his precious copy of *Robinson Crusoe*. "Do you remember when Robinson takes on twenty cannibals with only himself, his man Friday, and a few pistols and muskets? Oh, the courage of it. Not unlike untrained farmers or old schoolmasters taking on the world's best-trained army, eh, Nathaniel?"

Nathaniel smiled to himself. No matter how much he wanted to claim himself as a soldier, Basil would forever and always be first a dreamer, second a teacher. Himself, what was Nathaniel?

"Nathaniel Dunn?"

Nathaniel looked up to see the pock-scarred man who'd laid the salt in his wounds from the whipping. "Aye?"

"A word?"

Nathaniel stood. The man grunted and pointed, walking a little distance away from Basil, who was flipping pages and muttering happily to himself.

"Your regiment will be leaving soon."

Nathaniel nodded.

"Some of the Culpeper men, meself included, are to stay behind to secure the fort."

"Aye?" Nathaniel wondered what the man wanted.

The man hesitated and scowled. "Are you the same Nathaniel Dunn what come across the Atlantic on *The Planter* in the year 1772?"

"Aye." How would he know, thought Nathaniel.

"Know you what happened to your father?"

Nathaniel felt his breath quicken. "No. Do you?"

The man nodded. "He was taken to the frontier, beaten to clear acres of dense forest for fields."

"Did he die there?"

"No."

"Well, what happened?" Why was this man being so mysterious? Nathaniel wanted to shake him. "Do you know where he is?"

"Aye," the man growled.

"Where?" Nathaniel nearly shouted.

"Here."

Nathaniel grabbed the man's arm. "Show me!" He pulled on him. But the man stayed rooted, motionless.

Suddenly Nathaniel realized that this man, masked with those horrendous scars, was his father. He dropped the man's sleeve and stepped back.

In silence, they stared at each other. Finally, his father spoke, "I'd always thought those eyes of yours weak, boy. I see steel in them now."

Anger overwhelmed Nathaniel. "Where were you? Why didn't you come for me?"

His father seemed surprised. He answered matter-of-factly: "My heart was dead, boy. Died when they poured your sweet mother into the sea. I wanted to die myself. I almost did. The work about broke me. Then I caught the pox. I was lying from that when the Indians raided the frontier settlements. They killed everyone at our place and almost scalped me. I think the pox scared the savage off. Probably figured I was death itself."

"Why didn't you come for me then?"

"I didn't know where you were."

"Did you try to find out?"

"No."

"Why not?"

His father shrugged. "Was busy trying to survive. Set meself a cabin in the wilderness where no one could claim me. I only came out when I heard about the Culpeper Minutemen. Gave me the chance to kill Englishmen what done this to me."

Nathaniel reeled from the information. He didn't matter to his father at all then—certainly not enough to search for. His new, hard-won sense of self-worth wavered.

"Oh, oh, Nathaniel," Basil called out excitedly. "I've found it. Such a rousing passage! Come hear it, lad."

Nathaniel felt Basil's hand reach into the waters to pull him up, yet again. The moment of doubt passed. He mattered to Basil. Family didn't have to be blood relations, he reckoned.

Nathaniel called back over his shoulder to Basil: "In a moment, master."

"Does that old man own your time?"

"He did once. I am free of it now."

"So you can join the Culpeper. Then we can go back to the cabin. In the hills, it is, beautiful. I can use your help to clear it."

Nathaniel had oft imagined a reunion with his father. And this was about as good as he'd envisioned—an offer of a future together. And yet, now that it was here, it fell flat. He hardly remembered this man. And this man had left him adrift. It was only the war that had thrown them back together.

Nathaniel heard Basil, exclaiming behind him. "Yes, yes, oh, wonderful!" He was reading, as usual. "What a writer!"

Nathaniel smiled, listening to the old man's delight. Basil had found his courage, just as Nathaniel had. Still, he needed Nathaniel, if nothing else but to help him carry his books on the march.

Nathaniel glanced about at the men of the camp, shabby but determined. They needed him too. They needed his music. Their cause called him.

He looked at his father with renewed confidence. "I am sorry, Father. I cannot stay. I wish to go on with my regiment."

It was hard for Nathaniel to read any expression on his father's face; his scars were so deep and puckered. But it seemed that he respected the decision. "After this fight is over with, then."

"Aye, Father. Perhaps then we can meet."

His father grunted. "Where would you be?"

Nathaniel hesitated. Where would he be? He thought a moment, not having imagined any "after." He had never before planned for a future. But after a moment, he thought on Basil's courtly good-bye with Mistress Maguire, and on Maria's poem. "I think we will be visiting in Williamsburg."

His father nodded. He held out his hand.

Nathaniel took it, firm, and shook good-bye. "Till then, sir."

"Aye."

Nathaniel watched his father disappear among the soldiers. He took in a deep breath of clean, cold air. He felt it fill him up, brace him, strong and straight. He looked to the sky, to the wispy clouds veiling a pale blue. The color of sky and mist mixed together as the world awoke, just as his mother had described the color of his eyes. It was a beginning, a new day for him, for his country.

Nathaniel had made a choice, no longer afraid of its responsibility, knowing full well that there were no guarantees of happiness or success, just possibilities.

The line about hope his mother so loved came to

344

him, just as it had the day he was sold. The day he had wanted to die of sorrow. The day that Basil came into his life. The day he first heard of the cause of liberty.

Hopes all things? Aye, perhaps now he could.

© Author's Note ©

Mark Twain, that witty American author who wrote both "truthful" journalism and "made-up" fiction, said this about the two: "Truth is stranger than fiction, but that is because fiction is obliged to stick to possibilities. Truth isn't. Fiction," said Twain, "has to make sense."

And there's the challenge of creating a story, not simply reporting it. As we know, real life can make no sense whatsoever! Fiction, on the other hand, has to be believable. Characters must react in ways that are in keeping with their personalities and the circumstances in which they find themselves. This is especially true in historical fiction in which the plot and its moral challenges grow out of the times. The setting, dialogue, and day-to-day details must be accurate.

That being said, history can present a writer with a wonderful and frustrating paradox: it can send the imagination soaring at the same time it hobbles it.

That's because the trick, as Twain so adroitly pointed out, is finding and then sticking to possibilities.

Let me tell you some of how this affected *Give Me Liberty*.

My editor suggested I write about the Revolutionary War. There are many masterworks on that conflict set in Boston and Massachusetts where the physical battles—the shots heard round the world—began. So I aimed my setting instead for Williamsburg and Virginia, where so many of the impassioned and catalyzing words of the Revolution were penned.

One of the first things I discovered was a brief but pivotal battle in December 1775 at Great Bridge, just outside Norfolk where the Chesapeake Bay opens onto the Atlantic Ocean. Some historians equate the battle in importance to Concord. Untrained, ill-fed, ragtag volunteers not only stood up to well-equipped, professional British grenadiers, they completely dominated the skirmish, winning it in a mere twenty minutes. As a result, the Virginians reclaimed the strategically important port town of Norfolk. They broke the momentum of Royal Governor Lord Dunmore and his fleet of warships. Within a few months, Dunmore left Virginia waters altogether. Had Dunmore succeeded in holding Norfolk, he would have cut the colonies in half, bottled up Virginia, and denied General Washington and the Continental Army of the men and food Virginia would supply throughout the war.

It was a perfect climatic ending to a book.

In that battle was another gem of a detail that ignited my imagination. Many runaway slaves fought at the Battle of Great Bridge, not for the Americans, but for Dunmore, as part of his Royal Ethiopian Regiment. They mocked Patrick Henry's slogan, "Liberty or Death"—which the Virginia regiments emblazoned on their hunting shirts—by wearing a sash that read: "Liberty to Slaves." The terrible irony of that insisted I create a slave character with the Ethiopians who had to face off with a close friend fighting with the patriots. So, history quickly provided the inspiration for an ending, two characters, and a moral dilemma. It also presented a theme—how people had to seek liberty in many different ways. It is a perplexing and disappointing reality that white Americans fought for their own freedom while continuing to deny African Americans theirs.

Here's how history boxed me in. I wanted my main character to be young and an indentured servant. There were many indentured servants in America, especially during the early years of the Jamestown settlement, when as many as 40 percent of those colonists were bound property. Many indentured servants were literally worked to death during that time. Those who survived were owed freedom dues as lucrative as fifty acres of land. Such possibilities kept the practice going. Scholars estimate that between 1700 and 1775, half the white European emigrants were free, while 33 percent were indentured and 17 percent were bound-out convicts.

Hoping to start anew, indentured servants sold themselves and their labor for four years or more in exchange for the price of Atlantic passage. Some of them, young boys in particular, did not come willingly. The term "kid-nap" was coined during the mid 1700s. A bank failure sent hordes of people to London, looking for jobs. Many vagrant boys were simply rounded up and put onto boats heading to America. Scores of poor families embarked together, only to find they could be separated and sold apart in the land of opportunity. These boats were mostly cargo ships, so the hold in which they made the six-week passage was dank and disease ridden. If a family member died past the voyage's halfway mark, a child might be responsible for paying off the deceased's passage—his or her time—as well as his own.

However, by the 1770s, slave labor was steadily replacing that of indentured servants in Virginia. So, to stick to possibilities, I spent hours reading ads in the *Virginia Gazettes* announcing the arrival of ships bringing indentured servants to Leedstown. I was looking for tradesmen who truly purchased them.

There I found carriage maker Elkanah Deane. Deane advertised for apprentices and journeymen. He also ran notices about his indentured servant, John Hunter, who ran away three weeks before one of his journeymen, Obadjah Puryer, also disappeared. Sound familiar? Edan Maguire is based directly on Elkanah Deane, who had in fact followed Lord Dunmore from New York to Williamsburg, thinking the association would guarantee him a prosperous business.

Deane purchased a lavish house on Palace Green and announced that he had many fine riding chairs, phaetons, and carriages to sell. He also advertised rooms to rent, fine liquors for sale, and that his wife would take orders for stays. He did spar in the papers with a competitor, who dubbed him "the Palace Street Puffer." His ads requesting payment progressed from respectful to anxious to belligerent, threatening his customers with public exposure of their debt if they did not pay. He clearly was an ill-tempered taskmaster.

As I wrote, I decided to use a fictional name because, as often happens, the character took on a personality and an opinion of his own. As his actions came to parallel the king's oppression of the colonies, the character grew more sinister and paranoid than what I could absolutely verify by his ads.

Still, there is something tragic about Edan and the real-life Elkanah. His decline and bitter disappointment represent how the Revolutionary War destroyed the fortunes of countless merchants. Many did nothing worse than simply try to remain neutral. Others were falsely accused of loyalist activities by rivals or disgruntled servants. A few were tarred and feathered; several were dragged into the woods outside Williamsburg, given mock trials, and scared into running groveling apologies for their opinions in one of the *Gazette* papers; others left what they had spent a lifetime building and fled to England.

In many ways, our revolution against the British king and his Parliament was a civil war. Not everyone wanted a break with England. In fact, had you told leaders such as Thomas Jefferson or George Washington as late as 1770 that within five years they would be fighting for independence, they would have been shocked. Americans were proud to be part of the British Empire. They simply wanted their rights as Englishmen respected and their colonial legislatures to have the same authority as Parliament. Taxation without representation violated those fundamental rights. Had the British Parliament heeded their petitions and been a little less patronizing, less brutal in their response to American protests, we might still happily belong to the United Kingdom. Once the British blockaded Boston and put Massachusetts under military rule, however, there was no turning back.

Even so, it took fourteen months of fighting before colonial leaders could bring themselves to declare independence from their mother country. Throughout the long seven years of the Revolutionary War, a third of the populace was actively loyalist. Another third remained neutral, desperately hoping the conflict would end. Only one in three Americans was a true patriot. They were gentlemen and yeomen, educated and illiterate, hardy, determined, plucky, idealistic—a new breed of man.

Here are the other true facts and people in *Give Me Liberty*.

All protests and confrontations—from the silent march supporting Boston to the marines stealing gunpowder to the patriots burying the British captain with such homage—happened when and where I described. My imagination provided *probable* conversations and characters, based on newspaper accounts, memoirs, and letters of the day. Patrick Henry, Thomas Jefferson, George Washington were in and out of Williamsburg at the times depicted. Patrick Henry's spellbinding oratory did rouse the country to action. After the Revolution, he was distrustful of a strong central (or "Federal") government. Instead he pushed for the Bill of Rights as protection against it and served Virginia several times as governor. Jefferson's interaction with Nathaniel is make-believe, but the third president's musical talents and romancing of his wife were well known.

George Washington, although a strong advocate for the Non-importation Agreements, was not seen initially as the critically important leader he would become. Without his undaunted courage, his steady and steadying commitment, the country clearly would have failed miserably in its quest for liberty.

At that time, Peyton Randolph—a name few know today—was called the father of our country. Speaker of the House of Burgesses, the first president of the Continental Congress, Randolph was the man most trusted to design persuasive policies to prod the king and stabilize the fledgling association of thirteen colonies. Sadly, he died of a stroke in October 1775, shortly after his loyalist brother, John, fled Virginia for England. John left his violin behind for his cousin, Thomas Jefferson. After he died, per his request, John Randolph's body was carried back to Virginia, the land he loved. He is buried beside his brother Peyton in the chapel of the College of William and Mary.

The first Supreme Court Chief Justice of the United States of America—who molded the court into a truly powerful third branch of government—fought with the Culpeper Minutemen during the Battle of Great Bridge. He was a tall, commanding, well-read, enthusiastic nineteen-year-old. His name? John Marshall, the frontiersman I imagine befriending Nathaniel. He was indeed the eldest of fifteen children, known for his convivial nature, hearty laugh, and ability to negotiate squabbles. Alexander Pope was his favorite writer.

President James Monroe was a student at William and Mary in 1775. He was one of a handful of teenagers who stormed the governor's palace to make off with all Dunmore's guns and swords. Peter Pelham was both organist and jailer. Maria Rind; her mother, Clementina; and her cousin John Pinkney lived and championed liberty's cause in their paper. Maria's fate is not as happy as I would have wished. Her cousin died in 1776, and Maria was bound out as a servant to another family.

The character of Ben Blyth grew out of snippets of information about the patriot activities of Williamsburg youth. A number of them did break into the magazine in the early hours of Whitsunday, June 4, 1775. A spring-gun booby trap left by the British wounded two for sure. The only participant named in the newspapers was Beverly Dixon, and he may have been the mayor's son. In a deposition made in 1833, when he was seventy-three years old, Robert Greenhow, son of the Williamsburg merchant, told how he had been part of a company of boys led by a then fourteen-year-old Henry Nicholson. He said the boys raided the magazine and made off with blue-painted stock guns. I included the Guy Fawkes bonfire after seeing an ad run by "an association of protestant boys" stating their plans to host one. I had been looking for something else entirely. See what a surprising and pivotal treasure hunt research can be?

Basil is a mixture of influences, partially found in journals kept by two schoolmasters: John Harrower, an indentured Scotsman, and Philip Fithian, who left New Jersey to tutor Robert Carter's children in the Northern Neck of Virginia. Teachers and musicians were, indeed, jacks-of-all-trades. There was a "surgeon" in Williamsburg who also purchased teeth, taught swordplay, and repaired harpsichords! Basil evolved according to his own demands. He came to represent the palpable excitement of the Age of Enlightenment, the ideas that inspired men to dare all.

Much of Basil and Nathaniel's friendship blossomed from the mechanics of getting fourteen-year-old Nathaniel into the Virginia 2nd Regiment. To join, given his age, he would need to be a fifer. The importance of music within Nathaniel's odyssey, therefore, grew and prompted me to include the many songs patriots wrote to rally the country. Playing or singing in an ensemble can coax shy children like Nathaniel—too reticent to join playground games—into communicating and bonding with their peers. It's like magic. Music speeds Nathaniel's journey to spiritual liberty, much as fife "calls" bring men to duty.

I leave it to you to determine Moses's fate after Great Bridge. Here are the facts that can guide your imagination: five thousand African Americans fought in the colonial patriot forces, with the minutemen, militia, and the Continental Army. There were two famous black regiments: the 7th Massachusetts Regiment and the Rhode Island Regiment. But most African Americans, whether freemen or slaves purchased to be soldiers or substituting for their masters, fought side by side with whites, including forces from Virginia. Toward the end of the war, one fifth of our Northern regiments were African American, making the Continental Army the most racially integrated American force until the twentieth century.

Some of Dunmore's Royal Ethiopians lived to gain their freedom. Eventually five hundred more runaways joined the three hundred who belonged to Dunmore's forces at the time the Battle of Great Bridge took place. But many died of an epidemic of smallpox and fever.

Only three hundred were still alive when Dunmore left Virginia for New York in 1776. Once in New York, the regiment was dissolved.

Tragically, it would take another war to grant African Americans the freedom and equality proclaimed by the immortal words of the Declaration of Independence: "We hold these truths to be self-evident: that all men are created equal; that they are endowed by their Creator with certain inalienable rights; that among these are life, liberty, and the pursuit of happiness." (Despite Abigail Adams's plea to her husband, John, our second president, to "not forget the ladies," it would take even longer before women were considered equal and afforded the right to vote in 1920.)

How could men fight for their own liberty while holding others in chains? Moses raises this with heart-wrenching incomprehension. More specifically, how is it that Thomas Jefferson—the man who penned the eloquent, persuasive words that changed the world—and George Washington—the man who led a people through bloodbaths, starvation, and killing winters to forge a new nation—could be slave owners? It is a baffling and deeply distressing question.

Both Jefferson and Washington professed to abhor slavery. Washington called it "a wicked, cruel, and unnatural trade." He did help create legislation that banned the importation of new slaves and longed for a plan that would abolish slavery altogether "by slow, sure, and imperceptible degrees." In 1789, as president, he signed an ordinance prohibiting slavery in the new Northwest Territories, which eventually became Ohio, Indiana, Illinois, Michigan, Minnesota, and Wisconsin. Hampered by Virginia laws that made it extremely difficult for an owner to release his slaves while he was alive, Washington did free all his servants at his death.

Probably the most moving words Jefferson wrote in his Declaration of Independence condemned slavery. He railed against King George, saying he had "waged cruel war against human nature" by "captivating and carrying" a "distant people who had never offended him" into "slavery in another hemisphere, or to incur miserable death in their transportation thither."

The Continental Congress crossed out those words.

The paragraph was extremely controversial with Southern owners and New Englander shippers who profited from the trade. The delegates wanted a unanimous passage of the Declaration. South Carolina and Georgia refused to sign anything that stated slavery violated "the most sacred rights of life and liberty." So what could have been the beginning of the end for slavery during the Revolution was removed.

Although he never freed his own slaves, Jefferson tried to outlaw the horrific practice again in 1784. He introduced legislation to Congress that would abolish slavery in every state by the year 1800. The motion lost by a single vote.

Just months before his death, the eighty-two-year-old Jefferson acknowledged that he had left the task of freeing a race of people to the next generation. "The abolition of the evil is not impossible," he wrote a young friend. "It ought never therefore to be despaired of."

New ideas and the power of words to spread them spawned the Revolution and our country. It was truly a radical, remarkable notion that every person had the ability and the right to govern himself. It was a hope, a leap of faith in ordinary people that turned the world upside down.

This, of course, is a theme I hope resounds throughout *Give Me Liberty*. I had planned to strike it like a bell at the conclusion, by having Basil read Thomas Paine's *Common Sense*, a fifty-page pamphlet that was published shortly after the Battle of Great Bridge. It was an instant bestseller, read on the street, read to the troops, read to and by all who could get their hands on a copy. In direct, easy-to-understand language, at a time Americans were hesitating about what step to take next, *Common Sense* called for a declaration of independence.

Paine's words ennobled and spurred a nation of people.

But the facts of history stopped me. Given the time it took for news to travel in colonial America, copies of *Common Sense* didn't make it from Philadelphia to Virginia until early February, two months after Nathaniel's story, as I could best tell it, was done.

So instead I will conclude now with some of Paine's stirring words:

"Nothing will clear up our situation so quickly, so efficiently, than that of an open and determined declaration for independence. . . . the blood of those already killed cries out for it. It is time to part. . . .

"Remember that virtue and ability are not hereditary. . . . We have it in our power to begin the world anew. . . .

"Oh, ye that love mankind. Ye that dare oppose not only the tyranny but the tyrant, stand forth. America shall make a stand not for herself alone, but for the world."

❦ Prelude to Revolution ❧

1764–1773

1764   Parliament passes the Sugar Act to raise money to pay for the costs of the French and Indian War. It taxes sugar, textiles, coffee, wines, and indigo dye.

1765   The Stamp Act, the first direct tax of Americans in the 150-year history of the colonies, is passed. All printed goods— newspapers, legal documents, playing cards—must carry a fee-stamp. The Quartering Act requires Americans to house and feed British troops. Outraged, colonists ban together to defy the law. They boycott British goods. In Boston, a radical organization called the Sons of Liberty, is formed. Mobs intimidate stamp collectors.

1766   The Stamp Act is repealed. The Declaratory Acts state that Britain still has the right to pass any laws regarding the American colonies.

1767   The Townshend Revenue Acts impose taxes on paper, tea, lead, and paints.

1768   Massachusetts sends a "circular letter" to all colonies, urging them to boycott British goods. British troops occupy Boston.

1769   The Virginia House of Burgesses passes a resolution opposing "taxation without representation" and the British government's plans to put American protestors on trial in England. The resolution also bans further slave importation.

MARCH 5, 1770   The Boston Massacre. A mob harasses British soldiers with snowballs. The soldiers fire into the crowd, killing five and injuring six.

APRIL 1770   The Townshend Acts are repealed except for duties on tea. The Quartering Act is not renewed.

NOVEMBER 1772   A Boston town meeting sets up a committee of correspondence to communicate with other nearby towns and endorses the concept of self-rule.

MARCH 1773   The Virginia House of Burgesses appoints a
committee of correspondence to communi-
cate with other colonies regarding British
actions. New Hampshire, Rhode Island,
Connecticut, and South Carolina follow suit.

MAY 1773   The threepenny-per-pound tea tax takes
affect. Colonists must buy their tea from the
British East India Company, cutting out
American merchants.

DECEMBER 16, 1773   The Boston Tea Party. Colonists disguised
as Mohawk Indians dump 342 chests of tea
into the Boston Harbor.

1774

SPRING   Parliament closes the port of Boston until
the tea is paid for. It passes the Coercive
Acts, ending self-rule in Massachusetts. It
occupies Boston with troops.

JUNE 1   Williamsburg observes a day of fasting,
humiliation, and prayer in support of
Boston. Royal Governor Dunmore dis-
solves the House of Burgesses.

OCTOBER 26   The First Continental Congress meets in Philadelphia with delegates from every colony except Georgia. Congress passes the Non-importation Agreement to boycott British imports and discontinue the importation of slaves. It promotes the formation of local militia groups.

1775

MARCH 23   Patrick Henry pushes Virginia to create an army, delivering his rousing "Give me liberty, or give me death" speech.

APRIL 18–19   Lexington and Concord. Ordered to suppress rebellion in Massachusetts, General Gage marches seven hundred redcoats to Concord to destroy the colonists' weapons depot. Warned by Paul Revere and other riders, seventy Massachusetts militiamen face them. A "shot heard round the world" begins a skirmish. Eight Americans are killed and ten wounded. Colonists attack the redcoats at Concord and harass them all the way back to Boston, killing or wounding 250.

APRIL 21 In the pre-dawn hours, British marines—acting on the orders of Virginia's Royal Governor, Lord Dunmore—empty Williamsburg's magazine of most of its gunpowder.

APRIL 23 Massachusetts Provincial Congress calls 13,600 American soldiers to surround Boston, beginning a year-long siege of the British-held port.

MAY 10 American volunteers led by Ethan Allen and Benedict Arnold capture Fort Ticonderoga in New York. The Second Continental Congress convenes in Philadelphia. In June, it unanimously appoints George Washington commander in chief of the Continental Army.

JUNE 17 The Battle of Bunker Hill. In the first major battle of the war, two thousand redcoats storm a Boston hill held by Americans, ordered to not fire until they see "the whites of their eyes." By the third assault, Americans run out of ammunition and flee. The British lose half their number, the Americans four hundred, including an important leader, Dr. Joseph Warren.

JULY 5   The Continental Congress sends "the Olive Branch Petition," once more expressing loyalty to the king and the hope for reconciliation. The next day, Congress also adopts a declaration on the causes and necessity of taking up arms against the British. King George refuses to read the petition and instead declares the Americans to be in a state of open rebellion.

DECEMBER 9   The Battle of Great Bridge. British and Virginia troops clash near Norfolk. The British suffer 40 percent casualties while no American is harmed. The twenty-minute battle prevents the British from controlling the Chesapeake Bay.

1776

JANUARY 5   New Hampshire adopts the first American state constitution.

JANUARY 9   *Common Sense* by Thomas Paine is published in Philadelphia.

MARCH 4–17   American troops capture Dorchester Heights

overlooking Boston. The British evacuate to invade New York.

JUNE 28 South Carolinians deflect a British naval attack at Charleston.

JUNE-JULY New York harbor is occupied by thirty British warships with twelve hundred cannon, thirty thousand soldiers, ten thousand sailors, and three hundred supply ships.

JULY 4 A new United States of America boldly declares its independence through the stirring words: "We hold these Truths to be self-evident, that all Men are created equal, that they are endowed by their Creator with certain inalienable Rights, that among these are Life, Liberty, and the Pursuit of Happiness."

It will be another seven long years before the British give up their fight to rule America and the peace treaty ending the Revolutionary War is signed on September 3, 1783.

ꝰ Bibliography ꝰ

Histories and Biographies

—Boorstin, Daniel J. *The Americans: The Colonial Experience.* New York: Random House, 1958.

—Coffman, Suzanne E. *Official Guide to Colonial Williamsburg.* Williamsburg, Va: Colonial Williamsburg Foundation, 1998.

—Holbrook, Jay Mack. "Virginia's Colonial Schoolmasters, 1660–1776." Ph.D. diss. Georgetown University, 1966.

—Holton, Woody. *Forced Founders: Indians, Debtors, Slaves & the Making of the American Revolution in Virginia.* Chapel Hill: University of North Carolina Press, 1999.

—Hume, Ivor Noel. *1775: Another Part of the Field.* New York: Alfred A. Knopf, 1966.

—Malone, Dumas. *Jefferson the Virginian.* Boston: Little, Brown, 1948.

—Mayer, Henry. *A Son of Thunder: Patrick Henry and the American Republic*. New York: Grove Press, 1991.

—McCullough, David. *1776*. New York: Simon & Schuster, 2005.

—Morgan, Kenneth. *Slavery and Servitude in Colonial North America*. New York: New York University Press, 2001.

—Selby, John E. *The Revolution in Virginia, 1775–1783*. Williamsburg, Va.: Colonial Williamsburg Foundation, 1988.

—Smith, Jean Edward. *John Marshall: Definer of a Nation*. New York: Henry Holt, 1996.

—Van Der Zee, John. *Bound Over: Indentured Servitude & American Conscience*. New York: Simon & Schuster, 1985.

18th-century Journals

—Dewees, Samuel. *A History of the Life and Services of Captain Samuel Dewees, a Native of Pennsylvania, and Soldier of the Revolutionary and Last Wars*. Baltimore: Robert Neilson, 1844.

—Farish, Hunter Dickinson, ed. *The Journal and Letters of Philip Vickers Fithian, a Plantation Tutor of the Old Dominion, 1773–1774.* Charlottesville: University Press of Virginia, 1957.

—Mays, David John, ed. *The Letters and Papers of Edmund Pendleton, 1734–1803.* Charlottesville: University Press of Virginia, 1967.

—Riley, Edward Miles, ed. *The Journal of John Harrower: An Indentured Servant in the Colony of Virginia, 1773–1776.* Williamsburg, Va: Colonial Williamsburg Foundation, 1963.

—Tarter, Brent, ed. *The Orderly Book of the Second Virginia Regiment,* September 27, 1775–April 15,1776.

Music

—Camus, Raoul F. *Military Music of the American Revolution.* Westerville, Ohio: Integrity Press, 1975.

—Keller, Kate Van Winkle. *Fife Tunes from the American Revolution.* Sandy Hook, Conn.: Hendrickson Group, 1997.

—————. *George Washington: Music for the First President*, a companion music book to the recording by David and Ginger Hildebrand. Sandy Hook, Conn.: Hendrickson Group, 1999.

—Keller, Kate Van Winkle, Mary Jane Corry, and Robert M. Keller. *The Performing Arts in Colonial American Newspapers, 1690–1783 Text Database and Index*. New York: University Music Editions, 1997, CD-ROM.

—Maurer, Maurer. "The Library of a Colonial Musician, 1755." *William and Mary Quarterly* 3 (October 1950): 39–52.

—————. "The Professor of Musick in Colonial America." *Musical Quarterly* 36 (1950) 511.

—McNeil, Keith and Rusty. *Colonial and Revolution Songbook*. Riverside, Calif.: WEM Records, 1996.

Everyday Colonial Life

—Bullock, Helen. *The Williamsburg Art of Cookery or, Accomplish'd Gentlewoman's Companion*. Richmond, Va: Dietz Press, 1938.

—Cotner, Sharon; Kris Drippe, Robin Kipps, Susan Pryor. *Physick: the Professional Practice of Medicine in Williamsburg, Virginia, 1740–1775*. Williamsburg, Va.: Colonial Williamsburg Foundation, 2003.

—Gilgun, Beth. *Tidings from the 18th Century: Colonial American How-to and Living History*. Texarkana, Texas: Scurlock Publishing, 1993.

—Flynn, Norma Twilley. *Puttin' on the Dog: A Potpourri of Colonial Sayings and Customs*. Sold in Colonial Williamsburg stores.

Specifically for Young Readers

—Brenner, Barbara. *If You Were There in 1776*. New York: Simon & Schuster, 1994.

————. *If You Lived in Williamsburg in Colonial Days*. New York: Scholastic, 2000.

—Cox, Clinton. *Come All You Brave Soldiers: Blacks in the Revolutionary War*. New York: Scholastic, 1999.

—Egger-Bovet, Howard, and Marlene Smith-Baranzini. *Brown Paper School: U.S. Kids History; Book of the American Revolution.* New York: Little, Brown, 1994.

—Moore, Kay. *If You Lived at the Time of the American Revolution.* New York: Scholastic, 1997.

—Nixon, Joan Lowery. *Maria's Story: 1773.* New York: Delacorte Press, 2001.

—Taylor, Theodore. *Rebellion Town: Williamsburg, 1776.* New York: Thomas Y. Crowell, 1973.

—Wilbur, C. Keith. *The Revolutionary Soldier, 1775–1783.* Guilford, Conn.: Globe Pequot Press, 1969.

❧ Acknowledgments ❧

I AM GREATLY indebted to the many historians who have written such thorough, painstakingly researched accounts of the American Revolution and the thoughts, doubts, hopes, and people who built it. Their books taught me and fueled my imagination.

Re-enactors are "amateur" historians who bring distant times vividly to life. I owe a large thanks to several who spent hours answering my questions, demonstrating their crafts, or guiding me to other sources. Fife major John Glover, of the 1st Virginia Regiment, repeatedly played duty calls and explained the daily life of a Revolutionary camp musician. Todd Post, founder and president of the 2nd Virginia Regiment, generously guided me at the beginning of my research, pointing me to several important primary documents, such as the *Orderly Book of the 2d Virginia Regiment*, kept during the Battle of Great Bridge. The details I gained from them so enlivened Nathaniel's story. Dr. David Hildebrand, of the Colonial Music Institute, also offered advice about sources and the reality of musicians' lives.

There were many with the Colonial Williamsburg Foundation who graciously shared their knowledge: Tim Sutphin, manager of the Williamsburg Fifes and Drums, explained the teaching and customs of fife players and drummers, verified historical elements, and provided costuming for reference. Others who provided valuable information include historians Linda Rowe and Kevin Kelly; Dale Smoot of the gunpowder magazine; wheelwright Chris Wright; and Pete Wrike, an expert on the Ethiopian Regiment who shared information from his pending book, *Slave Soldiers, Gentleman Officers*. My deepest gratitude goes to Juleigh Clark, public service librarian at the John D. Rockefeller Library who patiently and thoroughly answered countless e-mail inquiries from me, helped me negotiate the foundation's astounding digital archive of the *Virginia Gazette* (www.pastportal.com), and located wonderfully rich articles or long-ago testimonials.

As always, my editor, Katherine Tegen pushed me to ask better questions of my characters. If you find value in these pages, thank her.

My children, Peter and Megan, and my husband,

John, are my muses, my devoted and diplomatic fans, my first editors. This book started percolating during our many family trips to Williamsburg as I witnessed my children's delight in the governor's maze, in listening to Patrick Henry and Thomas Jefferson interpreters, and in trying to play instruments and games of the period. Their constant wonderment about the human race and how we have become who we are inspires me to try to understand it myself through writing.